# Tarot

## B. D. Edkins

SPINNAKER BOOKS

Spinnaker Books

Texas

ISBN: 978-0-578-60793-1

Library of Congress Control Number:  2019919407

This is a work of fiction, and all the names, places, incidents, and characters portrayed in this novel are the product of the author's imagination or are either fictitious or are used fictitiously.

Addition Novels available by B. D. Edkins

Hollow Wings

Waltzing with the Dark Angel

Sapphire

The Mark – Jack Kohl Detective Novels Book 1

## DEDICATION

To my wife and best friend, Sherry

A special note of Thanks

To my editor and friend, Verna Carter

# Table of Contents

# Chapter One

New Orleans – May 1971

Kohl knew that the Bourbon Orleans Hotel was one of New Orleans' most haunted sites. At a very young age, he learned that the building was home to as many as 18, maybe 20 spirits, some dating back to the Civil War.

Constructed in the early 1800s by the entrepreneur, John Davis, the building was the site of the luxurious Orleans Ballroom. So great was its success that Davis soon constructed the adjacent building, the Théâtre d'Orléans or, The Orleans Theater, where he established the French Opera in America. By the early 1880s, the buildings had fallen into disrepair and in 1881 were sold to the Sisters of the Holy Family, who converted the site into a convent, orphan asylum, and public chapel. It was during this period that the Yellow Fever of 1905 drastically increased the ranks of the phantoms. As the nuns cared for the sick orphans, many of the children and caregivers would succumb to the disease. In 1964 the building was sold again and converted into the French Quarter hotel, The Bourbon Orleans.

Even today, Kohl thought as he entered the hotel elevator, hotel guests report sounds of children's spirits playing in the hallways.

Kohl pressed the button for the sixth-floor, wondering if the spirits of the two victims in Room 644 would be checking out or signing the poltergeist register for a much longer stay.

With a slight shudder, the elevator came to an uneasy stop, and the doors opened. Kohl stepped out into the narrow hallway and followed the signs to room 644. There was only one uniformed police officer standing next to the door of the room. Ghost or not, the decorum of the hotel calls for a low profile in this matter. Well, Kohl thought as the corners of his mouth curved into an unconscious smile, decorum, and the fact that the hotel manager was a close friend of the mayor.

"Hi Sal," Kohl said as he placed his hand on the officer's shoulder before passing through the open doorway.

"Hey, Jack," the officer replied. "Matty is already inside."

He instantly spotted his partner, Matty, standing next to Dr. Meeker from the city coroner's office. Meeker was kneeling next to the bed studying one of the victims. Matty was also facing toward the bed, preoccupied with the two bodies, and didn't notice him enter the room. He stopped and observed the two women.

The doctor's hair was rolled tightly into a bun and perched at the back of her head. Jack had come to know that this hairdo was part of Meeker's standard dress code while working a murder. Most of the time, her thick, jet-black hair hung in long, graceful curves over her shoulder; the available light reflecting in such a manner that the curvatures looked like highly polished glass.

In contrast, Matty's hair was a light acorn color reminding him of elflocks, tangled, or tossed by the wind. Often during a raid, her hair was pulled back into a solitary ponytail held together by a single rubber band. Although she was volatile by nature, she carried herself confidently with a cat-like demeanor. Jack trusted no one more than Matty.

"Ladies," he said as he approached the two.

Meeker stood up slowly, her body tall and trim. "Hello, Detective," she said, the warmth of her smile echoing in her voice.

Matty's mouth tightened when she looked over to see Jack's familiar face. "Hey, Jack," she said, an easy smile played at the corners of her mouth.

Jack looked over at the two naked bodies lying on the bed. He surmised that the couple was in their late thirties. He would call neither of them athletic, but both seemed lean and fit. Both wore a wedding ring on their left hands.

"Married?" he asked.

"Yes," Matty volunteered, "but not to each other."

"Okay," he sighed, "mister and misses adultery."

Jack's face took on an unpleasant twist as he studied their bloody faces. In both cases, blood had seeped from their eye sockets and both nostrils. Both victims had the same pinkish secretion around the mouths. As if this wasn't bad enough, the bed and wall behind it had droplets of the blood flung in wild arching patterns covering a large portion of the area. There were no signs of a bullet or knife wounds visible.

"Damn," he said through clenched teeth, "these two really humped the bunk."

"Yep," Matty answered as she knelt to get a closer look, "they were obviously humping each other until someone stepped in and did this."

"What do you think, Doctor?" he asked.

"Well," she said, her mouth thinning with disgust, "I almost peed myself when I first walked in."

Uncontrolled laughter came simultaneously from the two detectives. "I'm not familiar with that medical term, Doctor," Jack grinned, "Can you explain that statement in layman's terms for us?"

"Well," she said, flushing miserably, "what I meant to say was when I first saw the two victims, I thought we were dealing with a case of hemorrhagic fever, but…"

"Hemorrhagic fever," Matty snorted. "That's a bit rare in these parts, isn't it?"

"Extremely," she agreed, "but New Orleans is a port city with ships coming here from every filth-encrusted port in the world. You both know what ship born influenza did to this city back in the early 1900s."

"Yeah," Kohl said, shaking his head, "pretty bad. What made you consider hemorrhagic fever?"

Meeker cleared her throat, "The signs and symptoms were indicative of the virus, but then I quickly ruled it out."

"How come?" Matty asked.

"The virus has a two to three-week incubation period." Meeker explained, "These," she said, pointing to the two bodies, would be late symptoms of the virus. I don't think the two of them would have been screwing like a couple of rabbits in heat if they were in the late stages of hemorrhagic fever."

4

"Good point," Kohl added as he walked around to the other side of the bed.

"They died sometime between 8:15 pm last night when they checked in, and 8:50 am this morning when discovered by the maid," she confirmed.

Jack continued looking around the bed and floor. "8:50 am. That's a little early for maid service, isn't it?"

"Yeah, I thought so too." Matty added, "So I checked with the maid. She said that there was a "Make up Room" sign hanging on the door. So she figured the guest was an early checkout, and she entered the room when no one answered her knock."

"I bet this made her day," he said, grinning. "Any idea what did happen here?"

Meeker crossed her arms over her chest, "Some type of poison I'm beating. Of course, we won't know until the autopsy, when I can run a toxicology test."

"How was it administered?" Jack asked.

"Excuse me?"

Jack scanned the room. "How did they get poisoned? Did they take it themselves? Was it given to them by someone else?"

"Maybe they took it before they came into the room. You know, thinking it was a sexual performance enhancer," Matty offered.

"Not likely," Meeker countered, "From the looks of things whatever it was, it acted very quickly. I'm no toxicologist, but I'm willing to bet that whatever it was, it's toxicity rating is a five or six."

"Five being bad," Jack frowned, "and six being the walking dead?"

"Correct," Meeker confirmed. If they would have taken the drug while let's say, downstairs in the bar, there is a good chance they would have never made it up to the sixth floor."

"So," Jack offered, "how did it get in their systems? Look around the room," he said, pointing to several areas in the room, "none of the hotel glasses have been used, and I don't see any cups or bottles that they would have brought themselves. No food or food containers. Not even a gum wrapper."

Matty walked away from the bed and into the bathroom, "Nothing in here, Jack. The trash can is also empty."

Jack moved around the bed and stood next to Meeker. "maybe a poison dart?" he asked in jest.

Matty walked out of the bathroom and joined the two at the bedside. "Who in their right mind is going to stand by a let someone shoot, not one but two of them with a poison dart?"

"All good questions." Meeker stated, blinking with bafflement, "Let's hope the autopsy will answer some of these questions." Meeker motioned for the techs to prepare to remove the bodies. "I would like to check the contents of her purse and anything the man had on him," she added as she removed her latex gloves, "One of their possessions might be tainted with the poison."

Matty started to remove her gloves, "Oh shit, Jack," she hissed. "I almost forgot this," she said, snatching a large manilla envelope off the desk in the corner of the room. She offered the envelope to him. "This was lying on top of the bodies when we first came in the room."

He retained his affability, but there was a distinct narrowing of his eyes as he accepted the package. "What's this," he asked as he opened the envelope and looked inside.

"A card," Matty offered as she picked up her belonging and slowly made her way to the door. Doctor Meeker was right behind her.

Jack recognized the plastic evidence pouch inside the larger package but couldn't make out what was inside. He tilted the envelope and allowed the evidence bag to slid out into his open hand.

No sooner had the pouch hit the palm of his hand when the room began to change. He instantly felt the familiar knots tighten within his stomach, and as before, an uncontrollable wave of acid welled up from his belly. The color of the room transitioned into sepia tones looking like an old silent movie. The movie began to play.

Jack looked toward the bed. It was obvious that the couple had just finished having sex and were now lying intertangled on the bed. Suddenly, both sat up and looked at him. He instinctively stared catatonically at the two fearing, as always, that they could see him. He finally relaxed, convincing himself that this was not the case. The two were looking toward the door.

It was the woman who jumped out of bed, quickly grabbing the bathrobe draped across the back of the chair and headed for the door. She fastened the robe around her as she looked through the peephole. After only a few seconds, she unbolted the door and swung it open. There, standing in the hall, was a charcoal colored figure holding an unopened bottle of wine.

The small hairs on the back of Jack's neck stiffened at the sight of the charcoal figure. It took him less than a second to figure out that the apparition was not that of Daniel Jorgensen, the serial killer he had stopped three years ago. This specter was not as tall or bulky as that of Daniel.

The figure followed the young woman into the room and went through the normal fanfare involved with opening a bottle of wine. The waiter then filled the two wine glasses that had accompanied the bottle. Jack noticed that the man who was now sitting up in the bed was giving directions to the woman. She obediently went to the man's pants and fished out several bills and handed them to the waiter. She then escorted the figure back to the door and re-secured it once he had left. Jack hated the fact that he could never hear what was transpiring. *It would make things much easier,* he thought as he watched her return. In a single fluid motion, she allowed the bathrobe to fall to the floor and picked up both wine glasses. As everything was transpiring in the sepia tone, it was difficult to say for sure, but Jack was almost positive that it was a red wine they were about to drink.

She carefully sat on the bed, handing her lover one of the glasses, and after an affectionate toast and kiss, the two drank from their respective glasses. Every muscle in Jack's body tightened in anticipation of what was to happen next, but things seem to remain normal as the two sipped the wine and were obviously involved in some light conversation.

Both seem to have finished about half of the amount in their glasses when things became more amorous. They momentarily stopped as each took the time to place their wine glasses on their respective nightstands. After several long passionate kisses, the woman pulled the sheet away from the man and straddled his naked torso. She leaned forward, placing her lips on his.

*Christ,* Jack moaned inwardly, *am I going to have to stand here and watch this shit?* But then his eyes widened with alarm as the woman sat up and began coughing. Not once or twice but a consecutive string of gagging and coughing until she spat blood with such violence that a good portion splattered against the wall over the man's head.

Her lover moved out from under her and laid her on the bed, clearly deeply concerned. But, before he could figure out what was happening to his partner, he too began to cough violently. Soon the two of them were fully in the grip of the poison. Blood was now seeping from their eyes and nostrils. Jack flinched as their bodies began to dance in a massive fit of convulsions. Both were frothing at the mouth its color white at first until it mixed with the blood from their lungs or esophagus. Just as fast as it started, it stopped, and the two came to rest in the final position he had witnessed upon first entering the room. Slowly the sepia tones faded.

"Jack, you coming?" Matty asked as she peeked around the wall leading into the bedroom.

"Yeah, sure," Jack faintly answered as he turned to follow his partner.

Matty's face tightened as Jack faced her. "You alright, Jack?"

"Yes," he answered lightly, rubbing his stomach, "I can't remember the last time I've eaten."

"I was just thinking about eating myself," She said, slowly walking down the hall. "I crave some meat."

"Wait," Jack said, stopping in mid-stride, " I left the envelope in the room. Be right back."

He trotted back down the hall and turned into the room. The room had turned back to the sepia color of his visions, and there at the bedside was the sketchy charcoal figure of the waiter. Jack slowed, and finally stopped as he watched the image collect the wine glasses off each nightstand and deposit them into a heavy plastic bag. He then methodically whipped down the tops of the nightstands and added the quarter-full bottle of wine into the bag and twisted it closed. From inside his jacket, the man pulled out a card and gently laid it on top of the bodies.

Jack looked down at the plastic evidence pouch in his hand. Inside was a single Tarot card; the card was mostly a picture of two naked people, a man, and a woman. The only words printed on the card were across the bottom. The words were, The Lovers. He slid the evidence pouch back into the larger manila envelope and exited the room.

# Chapter Two

Jack shot up on the bed, his breath catching in the back of his throat. The early morning air felt cool against his bare skin. It was that mystical time of morning that lies between the serenity of the moon and the pulsing heart of the rising sun. A smaller figure joined his silhouette; her jutting breasts and narrow waist a stark contrast to the strong and powerful contours of his outline.

Her fingers slid tenderly over his bare arm. "Troubled dreams," she asked, her tone was compassionate yet assessing.

"Yes," Jack answered, his voice no more than a whisper, "always troubled."

Clarice gently kissed him on the shoulder, her lips softer than a feather's touch. Tenderly she led him back toward his pillow until his head relaxed. Jack swung her head into the cradle of his arm. Molding the soft curves of her naked body into the contours of his, Clarice exhaled slowly, "Jack, you need to find a balance in all of this."

"I thought I was through with this," he said tersely. "For two years now, I've been free of the visions. I was so sure that they had died with Daniel Jorgensen at the bottom of that damned elevator shaft."

"Something like this just doesn't die," she said, "it is more like a wellspring, you draw from it when you need it. Just because you don't drink doesn't mean it's not available."

Jack squeezed her gently, his hand resting on her buttocks. "I'd take a beer over your wellspring any day."

"You can get a beer anytime," she said with a twinge of disappointment. "Your gift is one in a million."

"Yeah," Jack countered, "tell me what store this gift came from, and I'll take it back today and exchange it for a nice rod and reel." He thought about what he had just said, "I like fishing," he said, thinking out loud.

The events of the day circled back through for the hundredth time. Visualizing the two people choking to death never got easier. With his free hand, he pushed his hair away from his eyes. "Tell me again about the tarot card."

Clarice pushed herself up onto her elbow, allowing her to look into Jack's eyes. "As I told you before," she said with a faint hint of irritation in her voice, "I don't know much about them."

"But a lot of the voodoo shops in the quarter offer card readings."

Clarice sat up next to him. "For the love of everything Holy, Jack," she retorted, "those places would sell snake-piss in a squirt gun if they thought the tourists would buy it."

Jack couldn't control the burst of laughter that shot from his mouth, "that's for damn sure," he said, continuing to show amusement.

His infectious laughter brought a wide smile to her face. She was pleased that she could break the dark spell that had come over him. When he laughed, he seemed to be a young boy again. It was one of the many things she loved about him.

Jack took a deep breath and released it, slowly trying to suppress his laughter. "So Voodoo Queens don't use tarot cards then."

Clarice shook her head, "no, no tarot cards."

Jack locked his fingers behind his head, "so who does use tarot cards?"

Clarice's eyes flared at the question. "Damn it, Jack, now you're trying to interrogate me," she said, pointing her index finger at his face, "keep it up, and I'll stitch your lips closed."

Jack raised his hands in mock surrender. "Whoa, no need to go there," he reassured her. "I was just curious, I mean, they're all over the French Quarter. Between the card readers around Jackson square and the various shops, there must be two or three dozen of them performing readings on any given day."

Clarice thought about his statement and finally relaxed. "I would guess most of them are just charlatans trying to make a few bucks," she said as she thought deeper about his question. "The rest, I don't know, gypsies, shaman, witches, just about anyone who truly practices the art of divination and healing in one way or another."

Jack shot up on the bed. "Witches, did you say witches?"

"Yes, of course, witches."

Jack shook his head as if trying to clear his thought process. "Witches, real witches," he said in disbelief, "broom flying, crooked nose, wart-faced, ugly witches? Are you telling me that there are real witches out there?"

"Oh, first of all," she said in a jovial tone, "I wouldn't go around calling them crooked nose, wart-faced, or ugly, Jack. That could land you in a lot of trouble. Besides, most of the ones I know are quite beautiful. And, to answer your question, there are witches out there."

"No way," Jack said in total disbelief, "they're supposed to be old hags or crones, things of fairy tales."

Clarice eased off the bed and headed toward the bathroom. The outline of her naked body in the morning light made Jack forget about witches. He watched her as she moved into the bathroom. Within seconds she turned around and stuck her head out from the doorway.

"By the way, Jack," she smiled deviously, "I'm considered to be a witch, now answer your phone and go to work."

He flinched at the first ring of the phone. "I hate when she does that," he said, fumbling with the receiver. He was finally able to put it to his ear, "Kohl," he said as he stretched his neck to get another look at Clarice.

"Jack, it's Matty, are you okay?"

He watched Clarice test the temperature of the shower with her hand. Bent over as she was, he could not help but marvel at the tightness of her muscles and her overwhelming beauty.

"You okay, Jack," Matty said for the second time.

He continued to watch Clarice as she slipped into the bathtub behind the shower curtain. "Yeah, fine," he sighed, "I was still asleep. What's up?"

"The Lieutenant has moved up our meeting this morning," she said, "you'll have to take a quick run through the shower and get dressed. He wants to talk to us as soon as we both get in."

It was obvious to Jack that she was probably in a half-dressed state herself, trying to talk to him on the phone as she fumbled with her clothing. "Not a problem," he said, pushing himself off the bed, "I'll meet you there." He dropped the receiver back into the cradle without waiting for a reply, as he knew Matty had also done. He moved toward the open door of the bathroom. He stopped and stared at the silhouette of Clarice behind the shower curtain.

"Oh Christ," he sighed at seeing the outline of her nubile curves, "running through the shower is not going to be easy."

\*\*\*\*

Jack thumbed through his notes as he waited for Matty and the Lieutenant to show up. For some reason, Lieutenant Steel had decided to move the meeting from his office to one of the smaller meeting rooms. It was fine with him as it would allow him and Matty to spread out all of their notes. It was amazing how much they had collected in a single day, and balancing all of this crap on their knees was always a pain in the ass.

"Jack," Steel said in the way of a greeting as he entered the room.

Jack started to rise but was waved down.

"Where's your partner?"

"Right here, Sir," Matty said, depositing her pile of paperwork on the desk.

"Let's cut to the chase on this one, shall we," Steel said, adjusting his chair. "What have you found out so far?"

Matty cleared her throat, "Well, the two victims are Brandon Willow, age thirty-eight, and Kristine Trisser age thirty-two."

"Mr. Willow was a senior partner in his family's company, Willow Financial Investments," Jack added. "It's a close-knit family business run by his father and, up until yesterday, three brothers."

"Total assets," Matty interjected, "are about 636 million."

Jack flipped through the paperwork in front of him. "A large portion of their investments are in real estate."

"And," Matty continued, "a lot of that real estate has natural gas and oil under it."

"You've spoken with the widow?" Steel asked.

"Yes, Sir," Matty answered, "We visited her home just after noon yesterday."

"How did she handle the news?"

"She was hard to read," Matty said thoughtfully, "She was grief-stricken but pissed at the same time."

"We're not sure," Jack added, "if she wasn't a little more pissed that her husband was caught screwing Mrs. Trisser, than his dying on her."

"That's right," Matty said, "It seems that the Willows' are among the Who's Who of New Orleans, belonging to all the right social groups. We think she's afraid the affair will end up in the gossip column of the paper."

"One thing of interest," Jack added, "while we were at the house, Mrs. Willow met with us in her husband's private study. There were several pictures of him in Mardi Gras costumes. From what we could gather, he might have been a member of the Krew of Comus."

"Comus?" Steel said, his brow rising slightly, "how is that significant?"

"Well," Jack continued, "ever since their conception in 1856, The Mistick Krew of Comus has guarded the identities of its membership and the privacy of its activities with an aggressive fervor."

"So?" Steel prompted.

"So," Matty picked up, "this is an ultra-secret group with major ties in Banking and Government. Supposedly they are also part of the Death Skulls and Bones society."

"Also," Jack added, "there are rumors that over the years, several high-level people have died at the hands of these people."

"All by poisoning," Matty added.

"Is there any proof of any of this bullshit?" Steel asked.

"Not a single drop," Matty said flatly.

"Fine," Steel said, anger starting to show in his voice, "let's get back to police work. Is the wife a suspect?"

"No, sir," Matty answered, "while her husband was supposedly in Baton Rouge for two days on business, Mrs. Willow was at her sister's house for her niece's eighth birthday. The niece had nine girls stay over for a birthday sleep-in."

"The sister," Jack volunteered, "and Mrs. Willow were the two chaperones.

"Sounds like a solid alibi," Steel said, "what about Mrs. Trisser."

Jack flipped through his notes until he found the information on the women. "Mrs. Trisser was an Officer of the Bentwood Title and Trust Company. She has a degree from the Emory University of Law in Atlanta. The title company's main office is in the National American Bank building. Which is the same building as Willow Financial Investments."

Matty leaned forward, setting her elbows on the conference table, "Bentwood has done a lot of title work for the Willow's firm, so we believe that the two of them first met through their business relationship."

"And they, at some time or another, took it private." Steel smiled.

"Yes, sir," Matty said, matching his smile, "very private."

"What's Mr. Trisser's alibi?"

"He has the best one of all," Matty answered, "He's an Electrical Engineer. Works for one of the oil drilling companies and has been on an offshore rig for almost three weeks. When he got the word of his wife's death, the company flew him back just three days ahead of his normal rotation."

"What about the perpetrator," Steel prompted, "anything yet?"

"Nothing, sir," Matty sighed. "The only solid piece of evidence was the tarot card left at the scene."

"You said there were some good prints on it."

"That's correct," Jack said, sliding a report toward Steel. "This was waiting for us this morning. As an officer of the title company, Mrs. Trisser was required to carry a bond. The thumbprint on the card matches the one on her bond paper-work."

"What about the other print?" Steel asked, looking up from the paper-work Jack had given him.

"We believe it belongs to Mr. Willow," Matty answered, "but we're waiting for confirmation from the Feds."

"Willow was in the Army," Jack added. "It will take a while to get a report back."

"Any other reason this tarot card was at the scene?" Steel asked.

"We're not sure, sir," Matty sighed, "it could be a sick joke, we're still digging into that."

"And the poison, if it was poisoning?"

"We spoke with Dr. Meeker right before the meeting," Jack volunteered, "she completed the autopsy on Mrs. Trisser last night. They are running toxicology panels later today. We should know more by tomorrow. Mr. Willow's autopsy is later today."

Lieutenant Steel thumbed through the documents in front of him. He finally sighed, clasped his hands together, and stared at the two of them. It was with an odd stitch of disappointment that he began to speak, "Let me summarize this investigation so far."

"Sir, we've only been working on this for less than thirty-six hours," Matty said in a preemptive strike to what was coming next.

"Don't interrupt, Detective," he quickly shot back. Steel hesitated as he rethought what he was about to say. "The two of you have only been working this case for a little more than twenty-four hours, and already I am getting enough pressure from above to turn coal into a diamond. So far, the only thing we have to show for your work is one scrap of evidence, a tarot card with the victim's fingerprint on it."

Jack found it very interesting that Lieutenant Steel included himself in the, 'we.'

"You have no suspects," Steel continued, "no witnesses, and maybe a flimsy motive for murder, seeing that both of the spouses have damn good alibis." Steel shook his head, "you're not even sure how they were poisoned, let alone what type of poison was used."

A swift and alarming thought entered Jack's head as he listened to the Lieutenant. *He's going to pull Matty and me off this case*, he thought, *he might be getting pressure from above to give it to someone more seasoned. Shit, he might drop it in Beachmen's lap!*

He tried to devise a way to stop Steel's current thought process. He couldn't let this case be pulled out from under their feet, but the only option he could come up with involved throwing Matty a huge curveball. It was the one thing he hadn't even mentioned to her, let alone discuss it in any manner. He searched anxiously for any other way out but came up empty. If she didn't play along, it would look like they were two of the most inept detectives in the precinct, and they would certainly lose control of the case. He swallowed with difficulty before finding his voice.

"Lieutenant," he said, interrupting, "Matty and I have a theory that the killer gained access to the room by impersonating a hotel room service waiter."

"A waiter?"

"Yes, sir," Jack continued, "It's the only feasible answer. There was no sign of forced entry or a struggle in the room. Also, it seems that both victims took the poison unknowingly."

"Go on." Steel prompted.

"Now we figure that the only way this could have happened was for someone to be invited into the room, someone they would not suspect."

"Like a waiter or bellman," Matty added.

"It's simple," Jack continued, "offer the couple a complimentary bottle of very expensive wine. Say, with the compliments of the hotel."

"We did find out that Willow was a wealthy, aristocratic type of asshole," Matty added, giving Jack a forced smile and a tense nod of consent. "Having the hotel management acknowledge his importance with a very expensive gift of wine would seem normal."

"That's right," Jack continued, "so they pour the wine, have a drink, and the rest is history."

"One thing," Steel said, "there were no wine glasses or wine bottles in the room. You two didn't even find a single drop of wine anywhere in the room."

"Exactly," Jack exclaimed as a new sense of confidence brightened his face, "but remember, the killer knew exactly what type of poison was in that bottle, and because of that he or she would have known how long it would take for the poison to take effect."

Matty nodded her head in agreement, "Then all the killer had to do was return to the room after their deaths and tidy up the place by removing all of the evidence."

"And," Jack said, adding the pièce de résistance, "place the tarot card on their bodies as he or she left the room. Then, they took the time to hang the "Makeup Room" card on the door, ensuring the maid would enter later."

The three sat in silence as the Lieutenant absorbed the information. Jack glanced over at Matty as they waited for a response from the Lieutenant. He noticed that she was biting down hard on her lower lip, the look in her eyes was sharp and assessing. He had come to know that look by heart. He would have a lot of explaining to do after the meeting.

"It seems to fit," Steel finally admitted. "Have you spoken with the hotel management about this?"

"That's our first stop after this meeting," Matty assured him. "We're betting that there was no room service or waiter sent to the victim's room that night but, if there was, so much the better."

Steel slowly gathered up his notes, taking the time to process the information from their meeting. He finally closed his notebook with a definitive slap. "Okay, you two, as I said before, I'm getting a lot of heat on this case, and yes, I believe it's coming from the political friends of Brandon Willows family. They want answers, and of course, they want them now. So let me spell it out for you." Steel leaned in closer, "I will run interference for you for as long as I can, but that won't be too long, understand?"

"Yes, sir," Jack and Matty answered in unison.

Steel's brows drew together in an excruciating expression, "The moment these people start using my shirt collar as their private crapper, you're finished."

"We understand, Lieutenant," Matty assured him.

Steel stood, signaling the end of the meeting. "Matty, I need to see you for a few minutes."

The two quickly gathered up their notes in silence. Jack wasn't sure he wanted to meet Matty's eyes until they were out of shouting distance from the precinct.

"Jack, I'll meet you out front," Matty said as she followed the Lieutenant out of the room.

"Fine," Jack answered as if everything was right with the world, "I'll check messages and see you there."

# Chapter Three

Mama Billy's Restaurant was a small family eatery located on the outskirts of the French Quarter. It catered to, what they like to call, the local folk. It wasn't that they didn't like the tourists or their money, it was just that they didn't have the name or advertising of the well-known spots. Even so, they never wanted for more customers as by noon on most days, there was a line to get in.

Jack and Matty sat at a four-top along the wall, both sipping on a tall glass of unsweetened iced tea. Jack would always add a slice of lime and sugar to the drink, making it to his personal preference. Both he and Matty thought the sweetened tea had way too much cane sugar in it and could never figure out how people came to like it so sweet. After becoming Matty's partner just over two years ago, Jack soon learned her personal preferences for many things. He thought her taste in iced tea was a bit weird for anyone as she only took her tea with honey. *People would drink hot tea with honey*; she would say, *why not iced tea then*. He also found out that she detested refined sugar, which she considered poison.

"Meeker's late," Matty said for the second time in the last ten minutes.

23

"Yep," Jack answered, knowing the statement didn't require a response at all, but it was the only thing that passed as a conversation between them since they left the Bourbon Orleans. "I thought you weren't mad at me."

"I'm not," she said, her right eyebrow rising a fraction. "I told you I thought that you were truly thinking on your feet this morning. It bought us some time anyway."

Jack's mouth twisted wryly, "Well, I know your cat didn't die because you don't have one. So why the glum mood?"

"I guess it's the Lieutenant's fault," she answered, her jaw betraying her deep frustration.

"He gave us some time to get ahead of this case, so I don't see your beef," he said, hoping to get a reaction out of her.

She offered a curt smile, "That's true, but there was a small caveat he gave me after the meeting."

"Okay," Jack sighed, "let's have it."

Jack watched as her eyes turned dark and insolent. "Baton Rouge wants to send down a 'special' investigator to help us."

"That's a crock of shit," he managed to say through clenched teeth.

"Now who's cat died?" she teased. "The Lieutenant agreed to hold them off as long as he could. Where in the hell is Meeker!" she spat, her tone irritable and restless.

Jack looked up just in time to see Dr. Meeker enter the café. Her walk was slow, her hips swaying from side to side as she made her way through the crowded tables. "Here she comes now."

"Hey, Matty," Meeker smiled as she sat next to Jack. "Jack, how are you?"

"Been better," he smiled, "but I can't remember when."

Matty shifted in her chair, "A little late, Doctor."

Meeker adjusted her chair and rearranged the silverware in front of her. "Sorry, the traffic light was out coming across Canal Street. There's never a cop when you need one."

Jack caught the waiter's eye and gave him a thumbs up. The man simply nodded and went into the kitchen. "So, what's the news from your side of the street, Doctor?"

Meeker looked around the table to assess just how close they were to the next table and adjusted her voice so as not to be overheard. "It was poison alright," she almost whispered, "and a very strange concoction at that."

"So, it was a poison cocktail?" Matty asked.

"Yes," she answered, her dark eyebrows arching mischievously, "the main ingredient was Cicuta, commonly know as water hemlock."

Jack placed his iced tea down in front of him. "Nasty stuff, I'm guessing."

"The worst," she offered, her faint smile held a touch of sadness. "This stuff can kill in minutes. It's the most toxic plant found in North America."

"The same stuff that put old Socrates down, right?" Jack asked.

Meeker nodded her head in agreement. "So," Matty said, chewing on her drink straw, "you said it was a cocktail?"

"That's correct," she answered, "there was a considerable amount of warfarin in the blood." Meeker studied the look on the faces of the two detectives. "Warfarin has two major uses," she continued to explain, "one is used in the medical field, and one is for commercial use. Both have the same result in the human body."

"And that is?" Matty asked impatiently.

Meeker ignored Matty's edginess and continued with her explanation. "Warfarin is an anticoagulant used to help prevent heart attacks and blood clots in human patients. It's a blood thinner. As a commercial product, it is the main active ingredient in rat poison."

The waiter moved up next to the table, carrying a large tray containing their lunches. The three waited as the young man skillfully moved the heavy plates on to the table. From memory, he was able to place the two plates of red beans and rice in front of Jack and Dr. Meeker. The blackened chicken Caesar salad was Matty's.

Seeing the dish in front of her, Meeker offered Jack a thoughtful smile of approval. He grinned back as her smile sent his pulse racing.

"Hemlock, rat poison," Matty said as she gracefully cut into the chicken, "sounds like either would have done the trick. Why use both?"

Meeker wiped the corner of her mouth with the paper napkin that had been wrapped around her silverware, "As close as I can figure the combination caused a quick but bloody mess."

"So," Jack asked, "their deaths were the killer's main goal, but not before he made a statement."

"That's true," Meeker agreed, "but there was something else, something that our toxicology group couldn't identify."

"What was that?" Matty asked.

Meeker leaned forward in her chair, and then, in a controlled voice whispered, "there were minute traces of an organic residue that still needs to be identified."

"How long will it take to identify it?" Jack asked with a mouth full of red beans.

Meeker wrinkled her nose as she shook her head from side to side, "my guys don't feel comfortable working with it, so they sent it to the Pharmacology Department at Columbia University in New York."

"So it could take a while," Matty said flatly.

The expression on Meeker's face was grim, "if they can identify it at all."

Jack continued to shovel his lunch into his mouth. "With or without the results from the University, we still don't know what type of statement the killer was trying to make."

"Or to whom," Matty reiterated.

"We figure that out," Jack sighed, "and we'll be rounding third and headed for home. By the way, Doctor, were there any liquids in the woman's stomach? Something that could have carried the poison?"

"There was," she said, clearly surprised that he had mentioned it, "there were about six ounces of red wine present in the stomach. More than enough to carry a lethal dose of the poison."

Jack shot Matty a conspiratorial wink at the confirmation of the wine then turned back to Meeker. "Were there any signs of blunt trauma or signs of either of them putting up a fight?"

"There was some bruising on both bodies, but likely it was caused by the massive convulsions they experienced," she affirmed.

"How about," Matty asked, "any signs of small puncture wounds or needle marks?"

"Meeker shook her head from side to side, "No, I was very careful in checking for those. I completely went through the hair and checked all of the usual places where a junkie might shoot up; you know, between the fingers and toes, armpits I even checked under their finger and toenails."

"Well," Jack said as he pushed his empty plate toward the center of the table, "we haven't found out anything more than we already knew."

"At least the kind doctor has confirmed several things that were questionable up until now," Matty added.

Meeker inclined her head in a small gesture of appreciation. Her eyes suddenly widened, "Oh, on another note, Jack. I got the invitation to your graduation. Thanks for inviting me."

"You're welcome," he smiled.

"Yes," Matty said, her smile widened in approval, "Masters in Physiology. He shouldn't have too much trouble finding a job when we get fired. Maybe he can get a job at Maison Blanche in their personnel department, you know, screening job applicants while I work as a security guard."

"Hey," Jack laughed in his usual halfhearted jovial manner, "I hear they give decent employee discount."

Meekers eyes darted from one detective to the other, "Seriously, are they going to fire you guys if you can't solve this case?"

Jack motioned to the waiter to bring their check. "It's not that bad. The Lieutenant is getting a lot of pressure on this one. And as the old saying goes…"

"Shit flows downhill," Matty finished for him.

Meeker relaxed a little as she dug through her purse for her wallet. "You two know that I'll do anything I can to help you."

"Got a spare bedroom?" Matty asked jokingly.

A young lady sped by the table, depositing the folder

containing their bill. Jack showed a tinge of annoyance that she placed it between the two women. He motioned for Meeker to pass the folder over to him.

Instead, Matty picked it up, "We're going Dutch on this, remember?"

"That's right, Jack," Meeker added as she fished several bills out of her wallet. She turned to Matty, "How much is it?"

Matty opened the folder and stared at the check inside. She immediately became wide awake as she scanned the crowd inside the café.

"It can't be that bad," Jack stated as he motioned for her to hand him the bill.

Matty looked intently at Jack for several seconds then shifted her attention back to the bill in front of her. "I think this one is for you, partner," she said coldly as she slid the folder to the center of the table.

She had purposely left the booklet open for all to see. There, inside the folder, was a single tarot card with Jack's name scribbled across it. The card depicted a single character about to carelessly walk off the edge of the cliff in front of him. At the bottom of the card was the title: 'The Fool.'

Meeker broke the silence between the three of them. "What does it mean, Jack?"

Jack swallowed hard, not being able to take his eyes away from the card. "Well, it's one of two things," he said slowly, "It's either a warning from the killer."

"Or?" Meeker pushed.

Jack's eyes traveled from one woman to the other and back again. Finally, he looked down at his empty plate, "Or, I am just minutes away from dying a horrible death by poisoning."

****

Louis Joseph Dufilho, Jr. of New Orleans became one of America's first licensed pharmacists in the early 1800s and opened his shop in New Orleans in 1823. A competitor to Dufilho's pharmacy was the Haitian owned, French Quarter Apothecary. This particular pharmacy didn't open its doors until 1834 and wasn't purchased by Clarice Justine's family until 1879. Clarice, the current owner, came from a long line of family licensed pharmacists who had proudly served the people of New Orleans with care and compassion. A lesser-known fact about Clarice Justine was that she also came from a long line of Voodoo Queens dating all the way back to 1804 in Haiti.

Jack pushed open the heavy front door. As it had for over one hundred years, the old Victorian shop bell above his head danced at the end of its brass spring with a slight jingle, alerting the shop clerk of a customer's arrival. He had visited the shop numerous times over the two years that he had known Clarice, but the sight of the shop interior never ceased to amaze him. As you entered, the first thing to catch your eye was always the massive wooden cabinets and shelving that lined both the left and right walls. The cabinets were solid oak with elegantly carved wood trim covering each section. The enormous cabinets were divided into three distinct sections.

The bottom section was designed for the storage of dry bulk goods and split into three rows of drawers. The bottom row consisted of eighteen-inch by six-inch drawers for storage of larger items. The two rows above this were made up of nine-inch by four-inch smaller drawers. Each drawer had a brass cup pull with a small paper label designed right into the brass plate. During an earlier visit, Jack counted the number of drawers across the wall one day while waiting for Clarice. There were twenty rows of the smaller drawers and ten rows of the larger bottom drawers closest to the floor.

"Hi, Jack," one of the clerks said as she passed by, "I'll tell her you're here."

"Thank you," he replied as he continued to study the cabinets.

The next section of the wall unit was cabinets enclosed behind double glass doors. There were three sets of double door glass cabinets. The trim of each glass door again showed the craftsmanship of intricately carved wooden frames. These doors protected three shelves stocked with every known shape and size of glass jars and bottles. Jack couldn't even begin to describe the jars individually, but the blue colored, hexagon-shaped vessels were his favorite. Something Jack had never known but was enlightened by Clarice was the image that adorned each of the glass panels. On each of the glass panels was a hand-painted image of a single snake wrapped around what had looked to him like a chalice. He knew the symbol of the caduceus with the two opposing snakes and wings representing the medical profession, but he had never understood the single snake and chalice. Clarice took the time to inform him that it represented the Bowl of Hygieia, the Greek Goddess of Hygiene, with a snake, the symbol of rejuvenation and renewal of youth as it casts off its skin, twined around the stem with its head poised above the bowl. It was, therefore, at one time, the medical symbol of the Pharmacy. Of course, today, it has been replaced by the symbol of the mortar and pestle and the ℞ character.

"Still mesmerized by the cabinets I see," Clarice said as she walked up to Jack.

His facial expression was that of a young child staring into a candy store window. "It's just I can't believe that this entire cabinet was made by hand," he said in awe, "I don't know if there are craftsmen today who could duplicate that."

"I doubt it," Clarice commented. "So, did you come here to look at my drawers, or is there something else on your mind?"

Jack looked at her, the double meaning of his gaze was obvious. "Your drawers are of great interest to me," he whispered as a vaguely sensuous light passed between them, "but sadly, I need your help on another issue."

Anxiety pulsed through her veins, "you haven't done something foolish, have you, Jack?"

"Funny you should say that," he said, vaguely gesturing to the rear of the shop, "could we talk in private?"

Without speaking, she motioned for him to follow her toward the back of the shop and her private office. Together, they walked around the front counter and continued deeper into the building. Finally, they arrived at the door of Clarice's office. Jack followed her through the entrance, closing the door behind him.

No sooner had the door closed than Clarice spun around and closed the distance between them. Their kiss was slow and unselfish. "What trouble do you bring to me in the middle of the day?" she asked, her eyes never leaving his.

Jack pushed back just far enough to allow him to slide his hand under his jacket. Momentarily he pulled out the tarot card from the pocket and held it up for her to examine.

Clarice took two steps backward, her eyes never leaving the card. "Where did you get it?" she asked flatly.

Jack turned the card towards himself so that he could view it for the hundredth time. "It came with my lunch today."

"Maybe you should take the restaurant off your list of places to eat," she offered as she took the card from his hand. "Was Matty with you? Did she get one?"

"I had lunch with Matty and Doctor Meeker," he said, sitting in the only chair in front of Clarice's desk.

Clarice moved around the desk, still studying the card. "And neither of them received a card?" she asked as she sat down in her chair. "Did you speak to the person who gave it to you?"

"No," Jack sighed, "too many people in the restaurant, a waitress dropped the check folder on our table and then disappeared. We couldn't find her, and the manager told us that no one matching her description worked there."

Clarice held the card up, "The Fool," she read aloud, "the woman obviously knows you."

"You're just as funny as Matty and Dr. Meeker," he smirked. "I don't guess you have any idea what it means?"

Clarice handed him back the card and leaned back in her chair. "I told you this morning I don't do Tarot card readings."

"Come on, Clarice," he whined, "you must know someone that can shed some light on these damn cards. This morning you said you were a witch. There's got to be a witch or two that goes to the same meetings as you do. Can't you ask one of them?"

"Jack Kohl," Clarice said with brutal detachment, "I am not a witch."

"But you said…," he protested.

"I said," she answered, her voice rising a full octave, "People say that I am a witch because I practice Voodoo. "People out there," she stated, making a theatrical gesture toward the French Quarter, "think that every Shaman, Oracle, fortune teller, clairvoyant and voodoo priestess is a witch! It's not true!"

"Clarice, please," he winced, "I was just going by what you said this morning. I didn't mean anything by it. When it comes to these things, I'm a babe in the woods."

Clarice eyed him suspiciously with contempt for several seconds before her demeanor softened. "I'm sorry, Jack," she finally said, her voice softening, "it's just, some times, it gets too much for me."

Jack leaned forward in his chair, "I understand," he said, "this place on a good day can get to the best of us."

Clarice held up the Tarot card and studied it again. "I know someone that might be able to help, someone I trust."

Jack's shoulders slumped as he relaxed, "thank you."

"Where is Matty?" Clarice asked, gathering her things.

"She has gone to speak with Mr. Willow and his two remaining sons while," he said, as he removed the card from Clarice's hand, "I'll discover what I can about this."

Clarice moved toward the door, "Where is your car?"

# Chapter Four

Gramercy was only forty-five minutes west of New Orleans and was originally an Indian/French settlement and trading post founded in the early 1700s. Jack also found out that the city was not incorporated until 1947 and had less than 2,600 residents.

"You didn't know someone in New Orleans that could have helped us?" he asked Clarice.

Clarice had taken off her shoes and now had her feet up on the dashboard of Jack's car. "There are plenty of people in New Orleans that could help," she stated, "but none that I trust as much as Aisling."

"An old friend?"

Clarice thought about her answer before speaking, "She is one of my oldest and most trusted friends. A lot more so than any of the witches in New Orleans."

Jack glanced over at her and then turned his attention back to the road, "so she is a witch then?"

Clarice smiled at the question, "she is a natural witch, ninth generation. Her family came from England and relocated to the New England area.

"Ninth generation," Jack mumbled as he did the calculation, "that means that her ancestors settled in this country sometime in the sixteen hundreds?"

"1645," Clarice confirmed.

"Wow, that is a long time ago. And Aisling's family were witches even before they came to America?"

"That's the way I understand it," Clarice stated, "she's an eclectic witch."

"You'd have to be a little strange to be a witch in the first place," Jack offered.

A slight chirp of a giggle slipped past her lips, "Not eclectic as in being strange. The first thing you need to understand is that Aisling is a hereditary witch; her magical gifts were passed down through her ancestors. Eclectic as just a form of practice. Aisling's family were mostly solitary witches, ones that prefer to practice a blend of several traditional forms to meet their taste." Clarice removed her feet from the dash and turned slightly to look at Jack. "Her family practice is a blend mostly of the traces of a Green Witch and a Hedgewitch."

"A green witch," Jack smiled, "I didn't know they came in different colors."

"Jack, dammit," Clarice said with an edge of impatience creeping into her voice, "you promised me that you wouldn't embarrass me in front of Aisling."

Jack shrugged his shoulders innocently, "I'm not trying

to embarrass you at all. I just didn't know witches came in colors."

"A green witch practices a nature-based or earthly orientated style. They work with herbs and medicines. I buy a lot of my herbs and some remedies from her for my shop."

"Then what's a Hedgewitch?"

"A Hedge Witch is more like a shaman dealing with the spirituality of the Earth. They are known to invoke the spirits. Aisling is one of the best witches I know when it comes to phantasmal interpretation."

"Phantasmal," Jack asked, scrunching his nose, "I have no idea what that means."

"And," Clarice said, ignoring his comment, "she knows more than most anyone I know when it comes to Tarot cards."

"So," Jack said thoughtfully, "she deals with Mother Nature a lot."

"Exactly," Clarice nodded, "now turn right at the next set of mailboxes."

Jack made the turn and followed the gravel road for better than a mile. The gravel soon gave way to dirt and, after a few hundred yards, gave way to more grass than dirt. When Clarice instructed him to turn left, he quickly found himself in the front yard of a small home that he assumed belonged to Aisling.

The first thing to catch his eye, even before the house, was the 1939 Ford F100 Truck. While the vehicle wasn't in show condition, it was still in great shape for its age. Its green paint worn by the sun showed no signs of rust or corrosion. The black metal front bumper was also in excellent condition. The license plate had golden yellow letters on a black background. A yellow pelican was stamped in the middle of the plate, separating the license number into two groups of three numbers also in yellow. At the bottom was the stamping "Louisiana 1939". Jack had to assume that it was the truck's original license plate.

The next thing about the truck to catch his eye was the large white goose perched on top of the roof over the cab. He knew it wasn't standard equipment on the truck that year, but the bird seemed to claim the spot as his own.

Jack exited the car and walked to the front of the vehicle. Instantly the goose rose up and began squawking in his direction. Jack was sure that the bird didn't like the intrusion.

"That's Abigail," Clarice said as she walked up next to Jack, "she's a Snow Goose. I don't see the others though." She said, scanning the area.

"There's more?"

"Oh, yes," Clarice stated, "there are at least two more that I know of."

No sooner had Clarice mentioned the other two geese when the two of them came waddling around the corner of the house. "The gray one with the white head is Albert," she informed him, "he's an Emperor Goose. The one with the black head and tan body is Spencer, a Canadian. You should keep your eye on him. He can be very unpleasant when he wants to be."

"Then they should know," Jack said jokingly, "that I'm carrying a gun and that I have a fondness for goose liver pate."

They had no sooner headed toward the front door when Aisling came around the same corner of the house where Albert and Spencer had appeared. Jack was shocked at the sight of the woman approaching them. Aisling was nothing like he was expecting. She was close in age to Clarice. Her hair was a lush, glowing auburn color, neatly pulled back and woven into a French braid. Closer to her face, several of the copper-colored ringlets had escaped the braids and fell loosely over her forehead. Her eyes, apple green in color, showed a depth of intellect and independence of spirit that he had only seen in one other person; Clarice. She wore a simple cotton sundress that, in the current light, betrayed her slim waist that flared into lithely curved hips.

Aisling approached Clarice first, offering her a gentle kiss, "Sister," she said, greeting her.

"Sister," Clarice answered, taking her arm in hers. Together they turned to Jack. "Aisling," she offered, "this is Detective Jack Kohl from the New Orleans PD. Jack, Aisling Dutetre."

Jack matched her smile and took the hand she offered. "Nice to meet you," he said warmly, noticing that her hands were rough, her grip, very strong. He also noticed that her fingernails were cut short and neatly trimmed. Her nails were buffed to a high sheen but not polished. *This woman*, he thought to himself, *works with her hands. She tends this farm herself.*

"Please call me, Jack," he insisted.

"Alright, Jack," she smiled, "I'd like that." Aisling motioned for them to follow her. "I've set up some refreshment out under the gazebo," she offered. "We can talk there."

The three geese followed behind squawking as they went. Aisling stopped and turned her attention to the birds. "You three must be quiet," she chastised, "these are our guests. Now stay out here in the front of the house." Jack was amazed; the three geese immediately stopped screaming, turned around and headed back to the pickup truck.

Jack had only seen pictures of English gardens, but what he saw now rivaled anything he could have pictured. The gazebo, built in a hexagon shape, was at least ten feet across at its center. Six white colonial columns supported the roof structure as well as braced the latticework enclosing two sides — the most beautiful flower beds he had ever seen surrounded the entire structure. The different colors of the flowers were too many to count. It seemed that everything was in full bloom. Spring, he thought, had certainly come to Gramercy. Behind the gazebo, two rows of hedges lined a walking path that made its way down to a small lake.

"Think there's fish in there?" Clarice whispered into his ear.

"I don't know," he whispered back, "but I'd like to find out."

"Please," Aisling invited, "have a seat. I have lemonade

or freshly squeezed apple cider."

Clarice turned to Jack as they made their way to their seats, "Aisling's lemonade is to die for; she has several trees on the property."

"What about the apple cider?" he asked. "I'll try that."

"Of course, I make the cider as well as the apple butter," she answered as she poured Jack a tall glass of cider.

Two smells instantly captured his senses; the sweet scent of apples and the unmistakable fragrance of cocoa butter. He knew that the fragrance of the apples came from the cider, and he guessed that the clean smell of the cocoa butter came from the soap Aisling must use for bathing.

"So, Detective Jack Kohl," Aisling said after pouring herself a glass of lemonade, "Clarice has told me that you have a few questions for me."

"Yes," he answered, placing his glass on the table in front of him, "if you don't mind."

"I don't mind at all," she answered, her eyes had a sheen of purpose, "if you are willing to pay the price I ask for the information."

"Price?" he asked as he looked to Clarice for guidance, "how much?"

Clarice's face glowed with a look of faint amusement, but she remained silent.

"You were right," Aisling said, giving Clarice a conspiratorial wink, "he is entrenched in the world of material things." She turned back to Jack, "I do not need your money, Jack. What I seek is an exchange of information."

"Information," he asked half in anticipation, half in dread, "what type of information would you like?"

Her smile masked her thought process, "Personal information about yourself, of course."

Jack leaned back in his chair rubbing the palms of his hands on his kneecaps, "Why would you want personal information about me?"

"Well, let's just say," she started, "from what Clarice has told me, you are somewhat of an enigma. It's not every day that you run across a person like you."

Once again, he looked to Clarice for guidance. This time her face was kinder, more understanding of his predicament. An expression of approval showed in her eyes. "Alright," he sighed, "how should we proceed?"

"Ask your question, Detective," Aisling said, leaning back in her chair.

Jack organized his thoughts, "I'm going to assume that Clarice has already filled you in on the murder case."

"Of course."

"And you know about the Tarot card we found at the scene."

"Yes, the card is the sixth card of the Major Arcana, The Lovers."

"I'm not sure what the Major Arcana is, but the card was The Lovers."

"I will explain the Arcana a little later. Where was the card found in relationship to the bodies?"

"On the male victim's chest."

"Was the top of the card facing toward him or away," she asked?

Jack pictured the crime scene photos in his head, "It was facing away from him, the top of the card was facing in the direction of his head."

"So," Aisling said slowly, "if he were to pick up the card, it would have been upside down to him, correct?"

"Yes…" Jack thought out loud.

Aisling shook her head as she pondered the information. "The Lovers card usually represents sexuality or romance. When the card is facing the person or upright, as we say, it usually predicts some elements of love, relationships, or unions. When presented upside down or reversed, it means just the opposite as in a break-up or end of a relationship."

"Well, their relationship was unquestionably ended that night," Jack smirked.

"And the card you received," she prompted.

Jack reached into his pocket, "This one," he answered, handing her the card, "The Fool."

Aisling studied the card, "Was it presented upright or

reversed?"

Again, Jack had to think about how he had received the card, "It was in the check folder instead of our bill so, if I were to open it in front of me, it would have been upside down."

"Alright then, Jack," she said, "Here is what I can gather from what you have told me. The Killer used The Lovers card as an expression of hate. As you said, their relationship was unquestionably ended by the killer's hand." Aisling held up the card she was holding, "this card is the first of the Major Arcana or the zero card because it is the zero point from which the journey, your journey, begins. Taking the first step, so to say."

Jack eyed her suspiciously, "And when it's reversed?"

"In your case," she said sternly, "it's telling you that if you proceed with your investigation, it will be a thoughtless move. You will be taking a major risk. Or maybe you will be foolish to pursue the endeavor."

"So," Jack slowly asked, "It's a warning?"

"Yes," she answered flatly, "you are being told to stay away, or if you are foolish enough to proceed with your investigation, you should do so with an open-minded caution because nothing good will come of it."

"Wow, all that from a little card," he stated.

"It's up to you to see how the card's meaning fits in your future. I can only tell you what I think with such limited information."

Clarice leaned forward, "Tell her about the poison, Jack."

"Right," he said, "the Coroner has told me that the poison used to kill these two people was a skillful blend of water hemlock, warfarin, and to date, an unknown substance, making for a horrible death."

Aisling's eyes became haunted by some inner anxiety, "the combination, mixed in the right proportions, would be very deadly."

"So, are you suggesting that whoever did this knows poisons?"

"Not at all, Detective," she stated, "The killer could have had another person concoct the mixture, but it does seem that they knew what results they were looking for."

Jack nodded as he thought about her answer, "There is a lot of research to show that women are six times more likely to use poisons than men. And the more disturbing statistic is that in cases involving poisoning, a clear twenty percent are never solved. Some other clues we have to the profile of a person that uses poisons is that they are methodical, clever, sneaky, and often emotionally unbalanced."

"Well," Aisling smiled, "that should narrow it down to a few hundred thousand people in and around New Orleans."

"Aisling," Clarice chuckled, "you should try living in the French Quarter."

"It does afford me with a high degree of job security," Jack stated as his smile broadened.

"That's one of the many reasons I live where I do," Aisling assured them. "Around here it's a major event if someone's cow breaks loose and makes it out on to the highway. Do you have any further questions for me, Detective?"

Jack's brows came together in an agonizing expression as he thought about her question.

"Come now, Detective," Aisling pried, "certainly, there's at least one question that you haven't asked."

"I don't think so," Jack answered, shaking his head from side to side.

Aisling sat motionless, giving Jack more time to consider her question. When Jack did not answer, her expression stilled and grew serious, "Jack, you disappoint me."

"How so?" he asked, projecting a naive innocence.

Aisling's eyes became compelling, magnetic, pulling Jack in. "Why don't you ask me if I think your killer is a Witch?"

"Well, as long as we've recognized the Elephant in the room," he said, "do you think the killer is a Witch?"

Her eyebrows shot up, her eyes lighting up with approval. "Nothing you have told me points to a witch's involvement," she answered sincerely, "sounds like a jealous wife or mistress."

"You forget," Jack pointed out, "the mistress died with him, and the wife has a solid alibi. At least for now."

Aisling's face lit with amusement, "Is there a rule that states that a man can only have one lover at a time? I would think that a jilted second lover might be more scornful than even the wife."

Jack's mind exploded with new possibilities. *Certainly, a rich, self-important man like Willow, could and most likely did have, two maybe three women on the side. I'll have to check this out with Matty.*

"What day were the murders?" Aisling asked.

Jack blinked several times as her question broke his line of thought, "sometime between Friday night on the 16th and early Saturday morning the 17th. Why?"

Aisling sat back in her chair and crossed her legs, "The 16th was the dark of the moon; that's all."

"The dark of the moon," Jack huffed, "if you are thinking mystical, witchy types of things, wouldn't the full moon be a more likely time for a witch to kill?"

The question amused Aisling, "You are partially correct. For a Witch, when the moon is full, it is in its most powerful phase and the best time to cast a spell."

"There you have it then," Jack said smugly, "a witch would have killed them during the full moon."

Aisling shook her head in disagreement, "A smart witch would never cast a dark spell on their victim no matter what phase the moon was in."

"Why not," Jack protested?

"Have you ever heard of the Witches Rule of Three?"

"No, what is it?"

Aisling sat up in her chair. It goes like this:

"Ever mind the Rule of Three, three times what thou

givest returns to thee, this lesson well, thou must learn,

Thee only gets what thou dost earn."

Jack noticed that Clarice was nodding in full agreement. He turned back to Aisling, "I come from a Catholic household. We learned that the Bible says a person shall reap what they sow."

"Exactly," Aisling confirmed, "it's a universal law of nature. You will find it in every corner of the world and all types of religion. It's a law that no one should break."

"Then," he said, shaking his head, "I don't know where you're going with this."

"There are two things to consider," she stated. "The first is if it were a Witch, he or she would want to avoid casting a dark spell that would invoke the Rule of Three. So no spell was cast, and they turned to poison to do their dirty work."

"And the second thing?"

"The Dark of the Moon is the best time for discarding things in one's life."

"Like discarding an unfaithful lover?" Jack asked.

"Sounds reasonable to me," Aisling confirmed.

Jack considered everything Aisling had shared with him and knew his line of questioning was coming to an end. The tensing of his jaw betrayed his growing frustration. It was now time for him to answer whatever question Aisling had in store for him.

As if she sensed his thoughts, she leaned toward him, her eyes taking on an ethereal appearance that seemingly was able to penetrate any defensive guard he might be attempting to mount. "Relax, Jack," she said softly, "I am only going to ask you a few questions that I'm sure you've asked yourself a thousand times."

He immediately noticed that she no longer addressed him as Detective but now was using his first name.

"How long have you had your gift of sight?" she asked.

He found her voice to be serenely compelling. "For several years now," he answered without a moment's trepidation, "but I have no control over it," he added, anticipating her next question.

She nodded her understanding. "When was the last time it happened?"

His right eyebrow rose a fraction, "You mean before the other night?"

"Yes."

His face suddenly went morbidly grim, "Two years ago," he answered, his mouth twisting at the memory, "the Daniel Jorgensen case."

"Yes," Aisling frowned, "so much death. And that was two years ago?"

"Yes," Jack confirmed.

Aisling leaned back in her chair, never breaking eye contact with him. "Have you had any murder cases between the Jorgensen case and the other night?"

A flash of humor crossed his face as his gentle laugh rippled through the air, "I work in the French Quarter," was his answer.

"So two years and, I'm guessing, several murders between the Jorgensen case and now and not a single vision. How do you account for the lack of apparitions?"

"I never said that I hadn't had any visions over the last two years," he answered tersely.

"No," she answered as if in deep thought, "but then you didn't need to. Why with Jorgensen, Jack? Why now?"

Jack turned to Clarice, his gaze anything but kind.

Clarice's hurt lay naked in her eyes, but she didn't speak. Jack turned his attention back to Aisling. *She is right*, he thought, *these are questions I've asked myself to no avail.*

"I don't have an answer for you," he said. "As I told Clarice, I thought that maybe the "gift" thing had just faded away; run its course." His mood veered sharply to anger and regret, "And to be perfectly honest, I couldn't have been happier when I thought it was all behind me."

"And now," she said, offering a slight shrug, "here it is,

once again confronting you." Aisling leaned back in her chair, closed her eyes, and seemed to relax. To a casual observer, she might have given the appearance of someone just soaking up the sun, but Jack knew this was not the case.

Suddenly Aisling opened her eyes and leaned forward in her chair. "Jack," she asked, "do you believe in the thing we call 'life force'?

"Life force?"

"Yes," she continued in a calm, controlled voice, "esotericism as some call it. Many believe in a mystical concept where there is a psycho-spiritual body overlaying our physical body."

Jack shrugged his shoulders. "Honestly, I haven't given it much thought, but I can certainly see where it might be possible," he admitted.

"That's good," she said, continuing. "If such a thing exists, then when a person dies, this energy dissipates until there is no trace of it."

"Okay," Jack said slowly, not understanding where she was headed with this line of questioning.

"I and others like me, believe that if the death is catastrophic enough, the energy almost bursts aggressively."

"Like an overcharged battery?" Jack offered.

"That's not a bad analogy," Clarice offered.

"Yes," Aisling agreed, "and you, Jack, are one of the very few people who can channel that energy to view their dying moments."

Jack shook his head from side to side as he processed her explanation, "I don't know," he said, "why don't I see this type of thing on all of the murders I handle?"

"The key is that the deaths are so horrific, so appalling that the energy is discharged in some different manner. Something that can be picked up by you."

Again Jack shook his head, "I still don't know. Energy is energy."

Aisling leaned in closer to Jack and held out her open hand. "I understand that if you detonate a small firecracker in your open hand, nothing much happens. But, she continued as she closed her fist into a tight ball, " take that same firecracker and hold it in a tightly closed fist," she said as she quickly opened her closed fist, simulating an explosion.

"And you can lose several fingers in the process," Jack finished for her.

"Yes, and that might be the difference we are discussing here. The tightly closed fist cases, like Jorgensen and Willow, and then the run of the mill bar shooting. By the way, have you ever returned to any of the murder scenes in the Jorgensen case or the hotel room where Willow was murdered?"

Jack quickly shook his head, "I've gone back to the D & K Warehouse where several of the murders took place. Why?"

Aisling interlaced her fingers and rested her hands in her lap, "Did you have any reoccurrence of the visions?"

Jack didn't need to waste time thinking about an answer, "No, never. Not even an inkling of one."

Aisling's face glowed with satisfaction at his response, "No, I would have been surprised if you had. I suspect that the energy dissipates very quickly."

The three sat in silence for several minutes until Aisling spoke again, "Jack, I want to thank you for your honesty, and unless you have anything further to ask me, we can relax for a while, enjoy the sun and finish our drinks."

After a long sip from his glass of cider, Jack found himself becoming more uncomfortable by the minute until a faint nagging voice whispered in his head, forcing him to speak up. "I have a general question for the two of you if you don't mind."

Clarice and Aisling exchanged a glance before Aisling spoke up, "What is it, Jack?"

"Well," he said, shrugging in mock resignation, if what you believe is, in fact, the truth, then the catastrophic events of the Jorgensen murders were exacerbated by the fact that Daniel used Voodoo rituals to perform the killings."

"It's possible," Aisling agreed, "so what is your point?"

"Well then," Jack said, an expression of satisfaction growing across his face, "if I call on some of my early high school algebra and set this up as a mathematical equation, then you have the following. In the Jorgensen case, a catastrophic event causes my visions. The catastrophic event is broken down into the horrific murder performed with the aid of magic. Therefore, if you use the same equation in Willow's murders, you have my vision caused by a catastrophic event. And again, the catastrophic event is triggered by a set of horrific murders plus an unknown catalytic agent; let's call it X."

"X?" Aisling asked.

"Correct," he answered with smug delight. "So if you solve for "X" in Willow's case, you will conclude that the only piece missing is some form of magic."

"So," Clarice said, following his train of thought, "you are saying that, in this case, X must equal witchcraft?"

Jack held up the tarot card, "Unless you can give me another direction to go in."

Clarice shook her head, sternly, "Voodoo is not some magical trick."

"Nor is witchcraft," added Aisling.

"Ladies, isn't the very definition of magic the use of any means that uses supernatural forces over natural forces?"

Clarice continued to stare at Jack, her brows drawing together in an agonized expression. "Sometimes, I think you read too much."

A momentary look of discomfort crossed Jack's face, "I'm sorry, Clarice, Aisling, I didn't mean that in a harmful way," he said as his expressive face changed and became almost somber. "It's just that it seems to me, the only time

I have the visions is when the case involves a supernatural force."

Aisling moved forward in her chair, looking at Jack intently, "you made your point, Jack, for now."

"For now?"

Aisling slid gracefully from her wicker back chair, "yes, Jack, there are still too many possibilities yet undiscovered." She regarded him with somber curiosity, "here's something for you to ponder. What if what you call supernatural forces is nothing more than a seldom-used natural force?"

Jack quickly stood, knowing that their meeting had come to an end. He put his hand out toward Clarice, but she stood without his assistance. "Sister," Clarice smiled, "let's get my supplies while Jack returns to the car."

"I can help carry them for you, Clarice."

Aisling extended her hand toward Jack, "it was a pleasure to meet you, Detective."

His dismissal was clear. "I'll be waiting in the car," he smiled, pointing toward the front of the house, "you ladies take your time. I'm in no hurry."

****

The ride back toward New Orleans was uneventful. That is if you consider Clarice's silence as ordinary. Several times Jack had glanced toward her only to find her staring out the window. He finally got up the courage to turn his head to the right and focus both of his eyes on her.

57

It was to no avail. Jack could not break the trance she had given herself to. With a sigh, he turned his attention back to the road ahead of him. It was in that split second that he saw the cloaked figure walk directly into the path of his speeding car.

Time came to a standstill as Jack reacted to the situation. With a lightning response, his foot moved from the gas pedal to the brake while his hands turned the wheel away from the figure. The whole time his brain blazed through the calculations ascertaining whether his reactions would be quick enough for him to miss the person in front of the car. It was in that split second that he realized it was not to be. He braced for the impact tightening his left hand on the steering wheel while throwing his right arm across Clarice's chest, pinning her to the back of the seat. The car veered over to the right side of the road throwing dust and gravel into the air.

The vehicle had barely come to a stop when Jack, gun in hand, exited the car, moving cautiously back to the point of impact. The fact that Clarice had exited the car and was now demanding an explanation for what had just happened was pushed to the back of his mind as he focused on the area in front of him. He quickly approached the area where the skid marks from his car marked the point of impact.

He was amazed to see that there were no visible signs of the accident other than the skid marks where he first attempted to veer away from the person. As he looked around, he performed a mental checklist of items denoting an accident. Of course, the first thing was that there was no sign of a body either in the middle of the road or lying along the roadside. There was no debris expected from such an accident. There was no blood, clothing, or broken glass or pieces of the grill of the car — nothing to mark the point of impact.

"Jack, what happened?" Clarice asked, blinking in amazement.

Jack turned around to face her as he slowly replaced his gun in its holster. He noticed that the intensity of the event had siphoned the blood from her face. "It's all right," he said as he reached out to comfort her. He instantly recalled the vision of the cloaked individual crossing in front of the car. His jaw clenched, his eyes slightly narrowing as he recalled the face buried within the recesses of the cloak's hood. It was the charcoal face of the unknown.

"Some small animal," he lied. "It shot across the road right in front of me." He took one more look around the area, "I must've barely missed it," he offered Clarice, finishing his lie.

Clarice's dark eyebrows arched wickedly, "and for that, you needed your gun?"

A thin smile made its way across his lips as he continued his lie, "I was afraid that I may have only injured the animal and would have to end its suffering."

"Well," Clarice said, looking around the area, "it looks like you are lucky. I don't see an animal anywhere."

"Yeah," he said as he gently led her back to the car, "some people get all the luck."

# Chapter Five

Justin Willow placed the glass under the small water spigot and pressed firmly against the trigger mechanism. A stream of crystal-clear water flowed into the glass. He held the glass up in front of the light and peered through the vessel. He tilted the glass slightly to one side and then the other, smiling with satisfaction. He was the one who had spearheaded the move to invest in the tiny Minnesota company that, he believed, would soon be the leading company in reverse osmosis water filtration.

While the company believed their process of liquid filtration would soon be the method of choice for many large companies and hospitals, Justin believed that the home consumer market was grossly underestimated. The company had already proven that reverse osmosis water filters would reduce a wide range of contaminants such as Calcium, Iron, Lead, Mercury, and Asbestos. Now they were making great progress on filtering out some poison and pesticides

With his empty hand, Justin leaned over and opened the door to the cabinet under his kitchen sink. It was a prototype system that took up all the available space in the cabinet, but he knew the RO system with additional research and development would become a manageable unit suitable for home use. Closing the cabinet, he stood erect and smugly toasted to himself.

He saw the splash of blood squirt across the kitchen counter even before he knew he had been stabbed from behind. The blade stuck out of the right side of his chest as he, still clutching the glass, staggered back until his attacker's body stopped his backward momentum.

Justin jumped at the sound of the sinister voice hissing in his ear. "May your suffering last an eternity," the hot breath rasped. The room spun as the floor rose up to catch him. The glass hit the kitchen tiles shattering into dozens of small pieces; his body slammed the floor a few seconds later. He stared at the brittle pieces of glass amongst small pools of crystal-clear water. Soon, the blood dripping from his open wound snaked its way over to the water. Wherever the two liquids met, water would absorb the scarlet liquid forming pinkish clouds floating across an unseen current. His mouth dropped open, "Oh." He said in a hushed voice. "Oh," he repeated as if nothing more profound came to mind.

Unexpectedly a searing pain began to grow in the right side of his chest. He looked down at the blade protruding through his rib cage. His once crisp white shirt was now muddled with blood seeping from the area around the razor-sharp blade. A dreadful moan escaped his lips as his hand reached for the burning blade. A momentary look of confusion crossed his face as his hand failed to respond to his command. As the agonizing pain grew stronger, his cries grew louder and louder until, choking on his own blood, he could no longer protest the pain and fell silent.

His assailant's footsteps pounded on the stone floor as they moved from behind him up to his side. He felt the pressure of the boot as it shoved him over onto his back. The movement did nothing to reduce his pain, and once again, he cried out as the butt of the knife struck the floor, pushing the blade further through his chest. It was several seconds before he could focus on the figure towering over him. His eyes widened as crimson bubbles burst past his spittle cake lips, "You!" he spat as his life force gushed out of him.

*****

Jack could feel the heat of the midmorning sun penetrate the skin on the back of his neck. The wave of heat felt like the fingers of a masseuse, kneading the tense muscles on his shoulders.

He ignored the sounds of the tourist milling about the street as a city street sweeper toiled to remove the remnants of the revelry from the previous night. He mindlessly weaved his way through large plastic bags of trash as he continued to make his way to the police station. He was halfway up the steps when Matty pushed her way through the door, pointing off to the right.

"This way, Jack," Matty said, still pointing down the street.

Jack quickly fell in line and matched her pace. "Christ, Jack," she said, looking in his direction, "you look like shit. What's the matter," she continued, "no bed bunny last night?"

He was pretty sure that Matty had no idea of his relationship with Clarice, just as he was also sure that Matty was under the mistaken idea that he had an endless parade of women falling in and out of lust with him on a nightly basis. Of course, he had done nothing to persuade Matty otherwise. The Playboy persona proved to be an excellent cover for his relationship with Clarice.

"We headed anywhere in particular," he asked as they crossed Royal Street.

Matty began to fish the car keys out of her pocket. "Another of the Willow boys has bit the dust."

Jack came to an abrupt stop, his hand resting on her shoulder, "poison?"

Matty managed a humorless smile as she met his eyes, "a dagger through his chest," she said flatly, "we'll know more after the good doctor examines him."

Jack stared out the passenger window as Matty drove them to the private residence of Justin Willow. They had barely spoken during the short drive, which was perfectly alright with him.

The previous evening's conversation with Clarice still clouded his mind.

"You're breaking up with me," he said as Clarice continued to gather her things.

"It's not like that, Jack," she insisted, "there are things that I must do, and you cannot be a part of it."

"So you're breaking up with me," he repeated. "I've had women dump me before," he said, pointing at no particular place in the room, "and this is what being dumped looks like."

"Oh, Jack," she whispered sincerely. Unspoken pain filled her eyes until spilling into a single tear. "We both knew that this moment would come."

"I never knew," he sighed with an odd twinge of disappointment, "I never thought for one moment..." His voice trailed off into the lonely silence.

"Jack!" Matty's voice boomed in his ear, "I don't know where your head is at, but it is time to go to work."

Jack blinked several times, refocusing on his surroundings. Matty had pulled the car up to the curb in front of a large colonial mansion. He had seen this home before or one just like it. He had often kidded that the only difference from the wealthy and people like him, were the multimillion-dollar track homes they lived in. He opened the car door and began the process of unfolding his long legs. Even before he was fully erect, he began to survey the area around him. Several police cars sat along the street. None of them had their lights on, nor were any police officers in sight. *It had been the silent call;* he thought to himself — no *lights, no sirens, no scene that might disturb the wealthy neighbors.*

He looked toward the entrance of the house. The door was slightly open. As he and Matty moved toward the house, he was instantly amazed by the sheer size of the door. He surmised that the wood was solid mahogany due to the slightly reddish tinge of the grain. In the center was a 100% fully beveled hand-cut crystal insert measuring approximately three-foot-wide and six foot in length. He knew that the cut of the crystal allowed for a maximum amount of brilliance and sparkle. On either side of the door were matching sidelights built into the frame. He was sure that his salary for a month wouldn't cover the cost of the crystal insert.

The transparency of the crystal gave the uniformed officer standing just inside a strange, mosaic profile.

"Hi guys," the young officer said, greeting them. "First floor, all the way to the back," he directed.

Jack lightly touched the officer's upper arm as a sign of appreciation, "Thanks."

Together Matty and he entered the kitchen and stopped next to the two uniformed officers that had set up the perimeter around the body. Even from their current vantage point, Jack could tell that the body had been moved. Justin Willow lay partially on his back, the butt of the blade stopping him from lying in a flat, prone position. The position of his legs confirmed that he originally been lying face down and, sometime later, flipped onto his back. The pooling of the blood on the floor also confirmed Jack's assessment.

"Someone moved him," Matty said flatly.

"Yeah," Jack agreed, "maybe the killer wanted to gloat, so he flipped him over so that they could have eye contact."

"Or, Willow was still alive, and the killer wanted to make sure he knew exactly who had done him in."

"Possibly," Jack mused as he caught the eye of one of the patrol officers. "Coroner here yet?" The officer shook his head.

"I can't believe we beat her here," Matty offered.

"Not by much, "Doctor Meeker stated as she entered the kitchen.

The three exchanged silent nods before turning their attention back to the victim. Doctor Meeker then began the ritual of rolling her hair into a tight bun. An escaping curl fell over her forehead and dangled in front of her eyes. The errant lock of hair was quickly recaptured and secured within the bun. As she slipped on her latex gloves, she slowly moved toward the body, coming up behind the man. When she was sure that she would not contaminate the crime scene, she carefully bent down to examine the body.

The fluid manner in which she moved always seemed to arouse Jack. No matter how she dressed, there always seemed to be a suggestion of nubile curves just beneath the material. Moments like this always brought back the image of her naked body hanging over the deathtrap that Daniel Jorgensen had set for them. Her figure was curving and majestic and always seductive. Instantly a second vision entered his thoughts because tied up next to her had been his partner, Matty. In contrast to Cynthia, Matty could only be described as a slim, wild beauty. Her figure was more athletic with chiseled curves versus the sculptured toned body of the Doctor.

Doctor Meeker stood and began to retrace her steps back toward Jack and Matty. As she removed her latex gloves, she motioned for the two to follow her. The three walked in silence until they were standing in front of Meeker's staff. With a slight nod, she gave the team the go-ahead to get started. Within a few moments, the three were left standing alone in the hallway.

"Isn't this where you're supposed to tell us that he's dead," Matty said, breaking the silence.

"It would be the second coming of Christ if he got up and went to the refrigerator for a beer."

"And?" Jack asked.

"That's one nasty dagger," she sighed.

"A knife is a knife," Matty said, her mouth pulling into a sour grin.

"I'm not sure about that," Meeker sighed, "that's not your ordinary household kitchen knife stuck through his ribs. As a matter of fact, I don't think I've seen one like that in my entire career."

Jack nodded, "In my short career, I've seen all kinds of knives on the streets. Switchblades, stilettos, all types of military knives and daggers and more kitchen knives than you could shake a stick at but, I've never seen anything like the one in there."

"Okay then, what does it mean?" Matty asked incredulously.

"I don't have an answer for you," Meeker said, "that is I don't have one yet."

"Well," Jack sighed, "at least there's no poison or tarot card."

"I didn't see a tarot card," Meeker nodded, "but we can't rule out poisoning until after the autopsy."

A dark figure of a man approached them. Jack caught a slight limp in his stride. He was one of Doctor Meeker's team. As he approached, he addressed Doctor Meeker. "Doctor, there's something you're gonna want to see."

Without speaking, the three followed the young technician back to the kitchen. In the few minutes that they had removed themselves from the crime scene, so much had happened. Various measurements were being taken while another team was in the process of setting up their photography equipment. All were busy in various stages of preserving the evidence.

Jack noticed that one of the technicians was leaning over the body, carefully holding the lapel of Justin Wilson's sports jacket. As they approached, the young woman held the jacket open and pointed toward the inside pocket. There, neatly tucked in the pocket, was the top of a card.

The three exchanged glances before Meeker spoke. "Alright, Katie," Meeker said softly, "you have an evidence bag ready?"

"Yes, ma'am," she said as she produced the bag.

"All right then, gently remove it and placed it in the bag."

The technician did as instructed using a pair of forceps, then sealed the card in the plastic bag and handed it to Meeker. Both Matty and Jack looked over her shoulder at the card. From what Jack could fathom from the picture on the card, it was three swords piercing a single heart. It looked to him as if rain clouds surrounded the heart, *maybe*, he thought, *thunderstorms*.

"First impressions," Meeker asked.

"Well," Matty answered slowly, "looking at the body, he was stabbed just the once."

"And not through the heart, I don't think," Jack added. "Maybe it's a visual reference to the three Willow males."

"You're right on the position of the knife," Meeker agreed, "the blade is far to the right of the heart. I don't know about the card making a statement about the Willow men."

Matty took the envelope out of Doctor Meeker's hands and continued to study the card. "The perpetrator could have just missed in their excited state."

"I don't think so," Jack stated, "look at the position of the blade. It is flat, horizontal, cutting between two of his ribs." Jack held up his right hand with two fingers pressed together in a horizontal position. "That way," he said as he pushed the two fingers between the fingers on his left hand, representing the man's ribs, "the blade was unobstructed as it passed through Willow's rib cage." He adjusted his hands. This time he held the two fingers in a vertical position and again pushed them through the crack in his fingers of the left. "A vertical blade would have hit the upper and lower rib bone, making it much more difficult to pass through the cavity. Also, there is a greater chance that the blade, while passing through the body, could either chip or become lodged in one or both of the ribs preventing the blade from going straight through."

"Excellent diagnosis, Doctor," Meeker said, amazed at the correctness of his presentation. "Did you learn that at medical school?"

Jack locked eyes with her, "No," he said smoothly, with no expression on his face, "years of hand to hand combat training and personal experience."

The two held their stare for several seconds before Jack pointed down at the body, "Whoever did this," he said, "knew how to handle a blade."

"And," Matty interjected, "they were more than likely a professional."

"And how would you know that?" Meeker asked in a voice of authority.

"Because," Matty said with an air of indifference, "the killer didn't miss Willow's heart; they avoided it as if they wanted him to die slowly."

# Chapter Six

Jack's heart skipped a beat as he pulled up in front of his house and noticed that Clarice's car was parked there. He hadn't had much time to think about Clarice throughout the day, but the ride home had been filled with thoughts of her. The prospect of her waiting for him inside the house lifted his spirits.

Jack lightly bounced up the front stairs and pushed open the door. He was almost giddy at the thought of her canceling her trip to Haiti. Inside the foyer, Jack's light-headedness quickly turned into alarm as he reached for his gun. *Something was unmistakably wrong,* he thought. He continued into the living room with his pistol drawn. He wasn't sure if it was his sense of sight or the unmistakably clean scent of cocoa butter that first alerted him to Aisling's presence.

"Hello Jack," Aisling smiled fully aware of his current combat stance. "Clarice told me you might be a little ah… twitchy."

"So," Jack asked as he slid his gun back into its holster, "did you use some witchy enchantment to unlock the door, or was it a more mortal means of entry?"

Aisling held up a small metal ring containing keys, "Clarice gave me these when I dropped her off at the airport this morning."

The confirmation that Clarice was now out of the country did nothing for his mood. "Obviously, one of them is the front door key I gave to Clarice several months ago." Jack took a seat in the high back chair directly across from Aisling. "And the other keys?"

Aisling, a devilish look in her eyes, studied the key ring. "One is to the door of Clarice's home and, of course, the third is to her car parked out front."

The set of his chin betrayed the mean streak he held within him. "And I guess you bewitched her to give them to you?"

"Not at all," she shot back, enjoying the verbal sparring that was occurring, "it was more of a potion than a spell."

"You drugged her?" he asked, with an expression of mockery.

"Actually," Aisling answered, as her index finger moved around in a circle as if she were stirring a liquid, "I bought her a demitasse at the airport."

Jack's face was expressionless. "And why are you here?"

Her eyes sparkled with dangerous intent. "I'm here to try and answer as many of those unanswered questions you have churning around in your head," she shot back, "so stop the tough guy bantering and ask them."

"The tarot card, a single heart pierced by three daggers; a

storm in the background, what does it mean?"

"They're not daggers," she answered, without hesitation, "they are swords. The card is from the Minor Arcana and is known as the *Three of Swords*."

"What does…"

"It has to do with pain and suffering, sorrow," she said, anticipating his next question. "The card represents events, sorrow, or pain that has pierced someone to the core."

Jack tugged lightly at his right ear. "The victim was pierced through the chest with a very nasty looking dagger," he offered.

"At present, I see no connection between the card and the dagger," she responded. Aisling noticed Jack's set expression, his lips but a thin line, his eyes dark and piercing, and the unmistakable tightness of the muscles at his jaw. "The rain," she said in a gentle, soothing voice, "usually denotes some type of relief from a past transgression."

"Transgression?"

"Yes," Aisling nodded, "the victim could have deeply hurt your murderer, causing them insurmountable pain and suffering."

The shock of discovery hit Jack full force. "Like the pain of a jilted lover?"

"No one is angrier than a woman who has been rejected in love," Aisling whispered.

"And," Jack added, "Hell hath no fury like a woman scorned," William Congreve, poet."

"The line is from his play *The Morning Bride*, written in 1697," she affirmed, "so we both get an 'A' in ancient literature. What of it?"

Jack leaned forward in his chair. "Do you remember our earlier conversation about Brandon Willow."

"Yes."

"You mentioned the fact that Brandon Willow could have had a second lover."

"Yes, what does this card have to do with him?"

Jack leaned back in his chair, a smug smile covering his face. "Maybe we have two brothers who have jilted the same woman."

Aisling was too startled by his suggestion to offer any reasonable objection to his theory.

"A woman's scorn times two," Jack said flatly.

They both sat without speaking for several minutes as they processed their recent conversation. An ambient light filtering through the large windows was the only illumination in the room. The muffled whir of a passing streetcar added to the mellow sounds enveloping the room. Jack and Aisling both seemed to meld into the stillness of the early evening.

"Jack," there was a calm softness in her voice, "were you at the crime scene all day?"

"The better part of the day," he answered matter-of-factly.

"Did you see anything," she asked?

Jack stirred slightly in his chair. "If you're asking about me seeing some type of apparition, then the answer is no."

"Why do you think that was?" her soothing voice probed further.

"Because," he said with a slight trace of laughter, "I made sure that I didn't touch anything."

"So touch can bring on the visions?"

Jack lifted his arms above his head and stretched, "It's almost 100% guaranteed."

"Weren't you the least bit interested in seeing what happened?" Aisling asked.

"Of course I'm interested," a cold thread of craving in his voice. "I just came home to grab a bite to eat and let the crowd at the crime scene die down." Jack stood again, stretching his tired muscles. "The house should be empty now," he said, checking his watch. "If you'd like to go with me, we can grab something to eat and then head back over."

Aisling sprung from her chair. "That would be great," she said in an almost childish voice, "can we go to the Camellia Grill? I'm dying for one of their hamburgers."

"Hamburger," he laughed, "I didn't think you ate meat."

Aisling quickly caught up with him and looped her arm around his. "I'm a witch, Jack. Not a vegetarian."

****

The Camellia Grill first opened its doors in 1946 and was located on Carrollton Avenue, just steps away from St. Charles Avenue. As a matter-of-fact, one could almost stumble into the restaurant after exiting the St. Charles Avenue streetcar. The restaurant only offered counter service and was well known for its friendly waitstaff.

Jack and Aisling sat side-by-side at the counter, enjoying their meal. Their conversation was light and free-flowing. Jack and she exchanged stories of their childhoods and their early school days. No one overhearing them would've guessed that upon finishing their meal, the two would be driving to a murder scene. Oddly, to Jack, it felt more like a first date.

Soon after sharing a piece of the Camellia grill's famous Pecan pie, Jack once again pulled up in front of Justin Willow's home. As he predicted, everyone from the police department and coroner's office had left.

Jack walked up to the huge front door, followed quickly by Aisling. The only signs that this was a murder scene was the 8 x 10-inch piece of paper posted on the front door stating the house was indeed a murder scene, and trespassing was not allowed. Glue on the back of the paper firmly held the official notice in place. Half of it stuck on the door, the other half on the doorframe. Opening the door would cause the paper to rip almost in half.

Jack removed a switchblade from his pocket and neatly slid

the tip of the blade between the door and the frame.

"Do you always take women to a murder scene on your first date," Aisling asked him as he slid the key into the lock.

He noticed that she stood so close to him that he could feel her soft, warm breath on his neck. He quickly pushed the pursuing erotic thoughts out of his head. "Of course," he said nonchalantly as he pushed open the door, "it prevents a battery of embarrassing questions later on in our relationship."

Instead of turning on the lights in the foyer, he locked the front door and made his way to the kitchen using his flashlight. Once he was inside the door of the kitchen, he flipped on the overhead lights.

"Boy," Aisling exclaimed, her voice echoing off the granite, "I could do some serious cooking in this place."

Jack moved closer to the sink. "I have it from a reliable source that the home will soon be on the market."

"I could never afford it," she said, "besides, I love my place in Gramercy."

Jack pointed down to the large puddle of dried blood a few feet in front of him. "This was the final resting spot of Mr. Willow. Judging from the blood splatter on the countertop, we figure he was standing facing the counter and was attacked from behind."

Aisling took a few steps closer to Jack's side. "Why didn't someone clean this mess up?"

"This is still an active crime scene," he answered," a cleanup team won't be called in until after the home is released back to the family."

"You mean to tell me," she said, shaking her head in dismay, "that this stuff won't be cleaned up anytime soon?"

"Nope."

"And who pays for the cleanup?"

"The family of the deceased, of course," Jack answered, "you'd be hard-pressed to get the killer to fork over the money for the cleanup. You about ready to get started," he asked in a low, almost tormented voice."

"Yes." She nodded.

Jack moved closer to the countertop, Aisling right on his heels. He carefully reached down and touched a droplet of dried blood on the granite. Immediately he felt the nauseating sinking feeling of wretchedness begin to swell in the pit of his stomach. Almost instantly, the area turned to the now-familiar sepia tone, and the gray figure of Justin Willow began to move toward the countertop. "It's starting," Jack said, "Willow is moving toward the countertop." He was planning to give Aisling a blow by blow description of everything he saw.

At that moment, Aisling took Jack's left hand into hers. His breath caught in his lungs, his eyes widening in astonishment as wave after wave of electrical energy pulsed through his body. "Aisling," he managed to murmur as he half turned to face her.

"Easy, Jack," Aisling cooed, "By making physical contact

with you, I'm now able to see everything you see."

The bigger shock came when Jack turned to face her. She no longer appeared as the auburn-haired seductive young woman that he had come to know but instead had transformed into an apparition of glowing beauty. There was a soft ivory glow about her curving figure. Her stance was almost regal. She looked unreal in the glaring overhead light. If it was even possible, her beautiful green eyes blazed even brighter, projecting an unrestrained inner fire. "What the hell," Jack exclaimed, the words stumbling out of his mouth.

"It's all right, Jack," Aisling assured him, "what you are seeing is my projected image in the astral world. My being able to tap into your vision gives you the capability to see me as I am in this plane of existence."

Jack looked at her in utter disbelief, "how in the hell is that even possible?"

"A conversation for a later date," she said, her eyes motioning Jack to pay attention to Justin Willow.

After a few seconds, Jack was able to turn away from her and refocus on Willow. The man was standing, facing the counter. Jack watched as the man placed the glass under a small spout. Water quickly filled the glass. It was obvious to Jack that, for some reason, Justin Willow was quite pleased with himself and the glass of water. Willow held it up to the light and studied it for several seconds.

From his position, Jack was able to catch the approach of a shadowy figure just inside his peripheral vision. Suddenly, he got a full view of the charcoal figure approaching. Every muscle in Jack's body jerked involuntarily as he took a step backward.

"Jack, what is it?"

From the size and mass of the charcoal grey figure standing in front of him, Jack swore he knew the man. "Daniel Jorgensen, he said in a suffocated whisper. The serial killer I dispatched three years ago."

"Well, if you killed him three years ago," Aisling said, trying to assure him, "Then this man is not him. I have never heard of anyone coming back from the dead."

Jack couldn't remove his eyes from the figure. "Even in voodoo?"

"Never," she affirmed. "Are you sure he was dead?"

The vision of Daniel Jorgensen lying in the bottom of the elevator shaft with two large metal spikes piercing his chest and head came back with certainty. "He was very dead," he assured her.

"Look," Aisling exclaimed as she pointed to the figure, "his right hand, the dagger."

He had noticed the dagger when the figure had first approached. "Yes, as you'll see in a minute, the charcoal man will thrust the blade through Willows back until it protrudes out of the front of his chest."

As if on cue, the huge dark figure with a single mighty thrust, pushed the dagger into the back of Justin Willow. The force of the blow was so great that the blade didn't stop until it hit the guard just above the handle. Willow stood motionless for several seconds before he collapsed to the ground. The blood seeping from the wound began to cover the floor as if it were using the dried bloodstain of the crime scene as a template. Jack watched as the huge dark figure took several steps backward and stood motionless.

"The dagger, Jack," Aisling repeated.

"Yes," Jack confirmed, "we have it in the evidence locker if you'd like to get a look at it."

Jack watched as Aisling took a step closer, mindful of the fact that she must retain contact with him. He could tell by her facial expression that she was studying the knife closely. "Anything wrong?"

Aisling stepped back from Willow's body. "Yes, there are several things wrong," she said again, pointing to the body. "First of all," she continued, "you see how the blade shimmers?"

Jack studied the blade. "Isn't that odd. Any idea what's causing it?"

Aisling swallowed hard before she answered. "Yes, the blade is coated with a magical potion."

"A poison?"

"Probably a magical poison," she confirmed.

Jack tugged lightly at her hand, resting in his. It wasn't until then that he noticed how tightly she was gripping his fingers. "You said there were several things that caught your attention?"

"Yes," she nodded, pointing toward the blade. "Jack, that is an Athame Kris Knife. It is a ceremonial blade often used in witchcraft."

"Well, it's been ceremonially stuck through Mr. Willow's chest."

"Jack, you don't understand," Aisling almost pleaded, "to use an Athame dagger to murder someone would suggest that the perpetrator practices the darkest of magic."

Before Jack could answer a new figure approached, this time, the figure was much smaller than the brute that had killed Willow. Even from a distance, Jack knew clear as day that it was a woman. To his amazement, her projection was not the usual charcoal outline, but that of a normal person. That is if you considered her appearance normal. Her looks were in stark contrast to that of Aisling's projection. Instead of a soft ivory glow, cold darkness surrounded her body, warding off any chance of approachability. Her stance denoted the posture of someone with a very painful, very old arthritic condition. The only similarity this person had with Aisling was the dreamlike aura about her.

He stepped closer to Willow's body, Jack was able to study her facial features more thoroughly. He gawked in disbelief, a knot tightening in his throat. The whites of the figure's eyes were dark as coal; her irises were scarlet red. Where Aisling's skin was supple and healthy, this woman's skin seemed to be stretched over her face by an incompetent Tanner. One feature of the woman's face was unforgettable. A large, *bigger than a half-dollar, he thought*, crater-like scar protruded on an area of her left cheek. The skin inside of the crater was raised and covered in small holes that at one time could have been regular pores, but now they were raw and enlarged. Each hole seemed to be infected with what Jack thought might have been microscopic parasites. Jack was forced to look away as he involuntarily retched at the sight of them.

The woman moved next to the body of Justin Willow. She placed the right toe of her boot under his left shoulder and, in a single motion, flipped him onto his back.

Jack was astonished. "Did you see how easily she flipped him over?"

Aisling failed to answer as she was so engrossed in what was happening.

"He's still alive," Jack whispered as if he was afraid to be overheard.

Justin Willow's eyes fluttered for a few seconds and then opened. Confused, Willow's eyes wandered restlessly around the room until they focused on the dark figure standing over him. His confusion turned to surprise then quickly turned into utter disbelief. A large tear rolled down his cheek as he mouthed the word 'You.'

As if by magic, a large tarot card appeared in the dark woman's hand. She slowly bent over and picked up Willow's limp hand. After pressing his thumb to the card, she gently peeled back the lapel of his sport coat and slid the card into the now exposed pocket. Without any further hesitation, the dark figure started to walk out of the room, closely followed by her accomplice.

Jack noted that the two did not take the path that would have taken them out of the front door. Instead, they moved in the opposite direction toward the back door of the house. "Look there!" Jack stated as he noticed a third figure fall line with the other two. "A third person," he confirmed.

As quickly as it had started, the vision ended. Jack felt Aisling's hand drop from his as the full weight of her body pressed against him. Instantly he scooped up her limp body and carried her into the living room where he gently laid her across a large sofa. "Aisling," he said softly as he checked her pulse, "are you okay?"

Aisling took a deep, unsteady breath as she lifted herself on the couch. "I'm all right," she said confidently, "it's just that I have never spent that much time in a vision, especially one of such intensity."

"Well, welcome to my world," Jack laughed. "I think it's time for us to leave."

With the help of Jack's hand, Aisling steadied herself and stood. It was a few seconds before she could take a step. "Jack," she said, "I have never experienced such evil in all my life."

Thoughts of Daniel Jorgensen flashed through his mind. "I have," he said as he headed for the front door.

# Chapter Seven

Jack lay in his bed, his eyes, trying to follow a single blade of the ceiling fan until he could no longer keep up with it and was forced to look away. He glanced over at the clock on the nightstand. The radium numbers glowed brightly. 2:32 AM, only eleven minutes had elapsed since the last time he checked. The thought of getting up and taking another shower entered his mind, but he quickly dismissed it as a useless gesture. His entire body flinched when the phone rang.

"Kohl," he answered in his official police voice.

"Jack, is that you?"

It was Aisling on the other end of the line, her voice soft and inviting. "Aisling, what's up? Are you alright?"

"Yes," she sighed into the other end of the phone, "I couldn't sleep, and I figured neither could you, so I decided to call you."

"That's right," he said in a much warmer voice. "I don't think I've been asleep for more than ten minutes at a time."

"Jack, I've never seen anything like this evening. I still have an uneasy feeling about the entire event."

He picked up the faint tremor in her voice as though she had just recalled a portion of their visit to Justin

Willow's home. "Have you locked all the doors?" he asked, feeling a little stupid after the words had escaped his mouth.

"Yes," she giggled lightly, "the windows and doors are all locked, and there are enough voodoo charms around this place to ward off even Godzilla."

"Then, you should easily make it through the night."

"No doubt," she answered. "Jack," she said with a slight hesitation in her voice, "I'm going to be heading back to Gramercy sometime tomorrow afternoon. I was wondering if we could meet for lunch tomorrow before I go."

"I would love to," Jack said with a sigh, "but I'm sure tomorrow will be full of meetings and shit storms." He regretted having to tell her that, but it was the truth. Steel would want a full accounting of yesterday's murder and a follow-up on the Brandon Willow case. Then there was the issue of how he would address what he saw earlier in the evening. He needed to speak with Matty. She was the best partner he had never had, and he felt closer to no one else in the department, but she had a very low tolerance for voodoo, and he was sure witchcraft would be no different.

When a long silence followed his answer, he knew that Aisling had been disappointed. "I tell you what, though," he said with an upbeat tone, "Sundays are usually pretty quiet around the shop. Maybe I could take a drive out to Gramercy. I'm sure there's at least one restaurant in town, right?"

"There are several," she replied, "but if you're going to come all the way out to Gramercy, I think protocol would demand that I cooked you a nice meal at my place."

"Home-cooked?"

"I make a mean chicken fried steak," she assured him. "All the vegetables come from my garden."

"Well, that sounds hard to resist."

85

"Great," she answered, "I'll see you around eleven then. I left my number on the pad next to the big chair in your living room."

"Sunday then." He instantly regretted his decision to travel to Gramercy knowing full well that it may be an entire week of Sunday's before he could dig out from under this case.

"Okay, see you Sunday," she said before she hung up.

Jack hung up the receiver and lay back on the pillow. He winced when his neck hit the cold, damp pillowcase. Instinctively in a single motion, he lifted his head and flipped the pillow to the dry side and plopped his head back down. He then closed his eyes, trying to prepare himself for the morning meetings.

****

The morning shit storms came with the intensity of a category five hurricane. He was forced to go directly to the meeting room closest to Captain Steel's office. No coffee, no pre-meeting with Matty, and no time to prepare. The usual gaggle of people was waiting for him. Captain Steele had taken his normal position at the head of the table while Matty chose to sit closer to the other end. The two chairs between Matty and Steel were occupied by Doctor Meeker and what looked to be one of her assistants.

Jack lightly touched Matty on the shoulder instead of saying good morning. Once he was around the table, he sat directly across from her. He offered Doctor Meeker a quick nod as he took his seat. She offered a smile in return.

"So it seems the plot thickens," Steel said to the group in general. "Matty, do you have any new information for us?"

There was no hesitation in Matty's voice as she answered. "Yes, sir, our initial analysis of the two crime scenes gives us enough information to conclude that the same perpetrator committed both murders."

"There's no chance that a copycat committed the second murder?" Steel asked.

"Not at all, sir. Several aspects of the crime were only known to the personnel sitting in this room."

"And they are…" Steel prompted.

"First of all, the tarot cards left at the crime scenes were from the same style deck. With an infinite number of different styles out there, it would be a lucky guess for a copycat to pick the same deck. Secondly, each of the cards had the victim's fingerprints on them. Thirdly, after speaking with Doctor Meeker this morning, we've learned that poison was used on both of the victims."

"That is correct," Doctor Meeker said. "This is Doctor Orel, from the University's toxicology department," she said, introducing the man next to her. "Doctor Orel," she prompted.

"Morning everyone." he started, "I have had the opportunity to study both cases, and in each case, a powerful blend of natural ingredients was used to poison both victims."

"The second victim, Justin Willow," Jack said, already knowing the answer, "was stabbed through the chest with a dagger. Are you saying that there was also a poison in the water glass?"

"Not at all," Doctor Orel said, "We found no traces of poison on any of the pieces of the glass collected from the crime scene, but we did find a coat of poison on the dagger used to stab Mr. Willow."

"Isn't that a bit of overkill?" Steel asked, wincing at the thought.

"Probably not," Meeker interjected, "the dagger penetrated the right side of Mr. Willow's chest, missing all of the major arteries. While it did pierce his right lung, this would not have been enough to kill him instantly."

Jack adjusted his legs under the table. He hated playing cat and mouse with the information he had, but no one would have understood how he received it or believe it for that matter. "Are you saying that the killer was an amateur, knowing that someone skillful with a knife would have gone for the heart or slit his throat."

"After discussing this in some length," Meeker said, "Doctor Orel and I believe that the killer carefully chose where to stab Mr. Willow."

"That doesn't make sense," Matty interjected.

"Think about it," Meeker continued, "it's like Jack said, if the killer was a professional, he could end Mr. Willow's life between heartbeats. We believe the killer was proficient with knives and knew exactly where to stab him. The killer wanted Willow to suffer."

Doctor Orel opened the folder in front of him. "The two poisons used were of different compositions," he said, pointing to the page in front of him. The poison used on Brandon Willow's was a fast-acting concoction causing convulsions and extensive bleeding from the eyes, nose, and eventually the mouth. Death was almost instantaneous." He thumbed through several pages until he got to what he wanted. He looked up and removed his glasses to rub his eyes. "On the other hand," he continued, "the poison coating the blade was of such a consistency that death would've taken somewhere close to an hour, maybe longer. The victim would have suffered severe pains in several of his major internal organs before dying."

"I did some preliminary work on the tarot card," Jack interjected. "The card is known as the three of swords. It deals with pain-and-suffering, which would go hand-in-hand with what Doctor Orel just told us."

"There was only one set of fingerprints on the card," Matty stated, "we don't have a match on the prints yet, but we're pretty sure they belong to Justin Willow."

"What about the card Jack received?" Steel asked.

"That brings up an interesting subject," Meeker stated, "We now believe that the card was meant for the three of us sitting at the table, not Jack in particular."

"Why the change in theory?" Steel asked.

Jack was taken aback by this revelation. Neither Doctor Meeker or Matty had discussed it with him. Sometime between the murder scene last night and this morning, the two women had discussed the possibility.

"When the check was brought to the table," Matty stated, "it was placed in the center of the table where any of the three of us could have reached. We feel that it was a warning for us, the investigating team, to back off."

Steel pointed at Jack. "What's your take on that?"

"It makes perfect sense," Jack said. He was pissed that the two women had not brought him in on the theory, but it was nothing that he cared to share with Captain Steel. "Even if," he continued keeping his anger in check, "somehow I would have agreed to walk away from the case, Matty and Doctor Meeker would have continued. So it makes much more sense that it was a warning meant for the three of us."

Steel nodded in agreement. "Do we have a motive yet?"

Jack and Matty answered simultaneously.

"Yes"

"No."

"Well, that's a definitive answer," Steel sighed. He pointed to Jack, "let's start with the yes."

"Well," Jack said, clearing his throat, "in the case of Brandon Willow, he was killed in bed with a third-party, not his wife. Since his death, his wife has been cleared and is not on the possible suspect list."

"Which does not," Matty added, "mean that he didn't have a second lover on the side."

"I agree, Matty," Jack said, "but both of these crimes included a young man who may be more promiscuous than we know. We also know that poison seems to be the weapon of choice in crimes of revenge."

"Detective Kohl has a point." Doctor Orel interjected. "The majority of the time, poison is used by a woman, often to kill their lovers or the other woman."

Matty shook her head, "revenge, yes, but why not revenge for a bad business deal. This family is involved in real estate and investments. There are plenty of ways to screw over an investor, even a woman. These murders could be nothing more than revenge for a deal gone south."

A uniformed officer walked into the room and headed directly to Captain Steel. Jack watched as the officer bent down and whispered in Steel's ear. Steel checked his watch and nodded. The officer left without saying another word.

"Alright," Steel said as he gathered up his papers, "it seems like we have quite a bit of work left to do on the motive. "Matty, what's your next move?"

Taking her cue from Steel, she began to gather up her files. "I've secured a meeting," she answered, "with Derek Willow, the father of the family and senior partner of the company, this afternoon."

"Excellent," Steel said as he stood. He once again looked at his watch, "let's meet again this evening at 4 PM and remember people; we are on the clock."

Once Captain Steel had cleared the room, Jack stood and prepared to go back to his desk.

"Jack," Matty said, "let's just stay here for a few minutes."

Jack started to retake his seat when Doctor Orel reached over the table and offered his hand.

"Nice meeting you, Detective." He said, shaking Jack's hand. He then shook Matty's hand and left the room with Doctor Meeker.

Suddenly feeling exhausted, Jack flopped back down into his chair. It had been a long sleepless night, and it was beginning to take its toll. He reached into his vest pocket and removed a small tin container kept closed by a single worn rubber band. He skillfully removed the rubber band and retrieved three aspirin from inside. A quick gulp of water and the pills were gone.

"Is that all you've had for breakfast?" Meeker asked as she reentered the room and closed the door behind her.

"Breakfast of champions," he said, rubbing his stomach.

Meeker took her seat and reached down under the table. When she sat up, a large Shipley Donut bag was in her hand. She carefully removed three large cups of coffee and placed one in front of each of them. As if it were a magic hat, she reached back in and pulled out a handful of sugar, creamers, and wooden coffee stirrers.

"God," Matty said, scooping up three packets of sugar, "you're a lifesaver!"

Jack picked up his cup, removed the lid, and took a large sip. "Boy," he said with a trace of laughter in his voice, "a couple of donuts would go great with this."

Meeker's right eyebrow rose a fraction as she stared at him skeptically. Without taking her eyes off of Jack, she once again reached under the table this time her hand came up with a second bag. Jack and Matty watched as she placed the second bag in between them and slowly tore the bag from top to bottom. There, between them, lay six donuts.

Jack's eyes glowed as he picked up one of the donuts. "You don't have a third bag under the table, do you? One with a Corvette in it?"

"Dream on, Detective."

"You're not pissed about our theory involving the tarot card?" Matty asked with a mouthful of donut.

The lines of concentration deepening along Jack's brows and under his eyes as he took another large sip of coffee, "Yeah, I'm pissed," he said, placing his cup back on the table, "I'm pissed at myself for not even considering that option." *Obviously, the two of them,* Jack thought to himself, *had forgotten that his name was scribbled across the card, not theirs.*

"Well, if it makes you feel any better," Meeker said as she daintily pulled apart a doughnut, "it didn't cross our minds until we were leaving the crime scene last night."

"I figured that's what happened," he said, starting on a second doughnut. What do we know about Derek Willow?"

Matty flipped through several pages of her notes, "the few people I've spoken to all think he's a major asshole."

"Well, he's tall, good-looking, and his boys are definitely a chip off the old block," Meeker added right behind Matty's statement.

"So, you *know* him?" Jack asked his smile, revealed a spark of eroticism.

"I met him several months ago at a charity event," Meeker said, ignoring Jack's innuendo. "He's as narcissistic as they come," she added, "he openly hit on me several times during the night; he was very persistent."

Matty's mouth pulled into a very sour grin, "you didn't…"

"Oh, please!" Meeker huffed while rolling her eyes, "You forget I worked in Los Angeles where narcissism is an art form."

The three laughed like children in a schoolyard. It suddenly dawned on Jack how much the two women meant to him. Not only had the three of them developed a unique working atmosphere, but the trust level between them was above reproach. For a while, after the Daniel Jorgensen case, he tried to convince himself that the women liked him because he had literally saved their lives. *It's not often,* he thought, *that you are targeted for death by a serial killer and survive. Not only had they survived, but they had individually grown stronger from the event.* Separately both women were powerhouses in their own right, but when they worked as a team, they were unstoppable. Somehow Jack knew that he had become the glue in their relationship, and that was the major reason that both women liked him. But an area where both women sharply disagree with him was that of the occult.

During the Daniel Jorgensen case, both women were very skeptical that Jorgensen used real voodoo to murder his victims. They thought it was more of a publicity stunt concocted by a mentally imbalanced murderer. While there was nothing to prove or disprove their theories, it was voodoo that helped him dispatch Jorgensen in the end.

Now within the Willows cases, there was too much evidence to disprove the use of witchcraft in both murders. Jack knew that none of it would help him convince either woman that witchcraft even existed. *Hell,* he thought *I've never seen witchcraft used in this case. I've seen no spells or potions brewed to slay the living. At best, we have a jilted lover seeking revenge on a cheating partner.*

"Jack?"

He flinched as he focused on Meeker.

"I asked if you wanted this last doughnut," Meeker said with a smile.

Jack took the doughnut. "Thanks."

"You seem distracted, Jack," Matty stated. "Something on your mind other than Derek Willow?"

Jack thought hard before answering. "Last night," he started with a slight hesitation, "I did a little more investigation on the murder weapon."

"It's an Athame Kris knife," Doctor Meeker offered.

Jack smiled. "I see someone else's done their homework," he said.

"And?" Matty asked, her demeanor betraying her annoyance.

"And," Jack started slowly, "it is a ceremonial blade used in the occult." Jack's expression turned grim as he waited for Matty's response.

Matty took a deep breath losing her smile, "Jesus, Jack; we're not going to start talking voodoo again, are we?"

"No," Jack answered with a thin smile, "no voodoo here, but the term occult does cover a broad spectrum of possibilities."

"Jack's right," Meeker interjected, "so far, in this case, we have the use of tarot cards as a medium of communication. Now we see the use of an Athame ritual dagger."

"And we have the fact," Jack added, "that at least one of the victims, Brandon Willow, was a member of the Krew of Comus, a secret society."

"It's a carnival crew for Chris'st sakes," Matty said, "they're not the Ku Klux Klan."

"That's true," Jack agreed, "but you can't deny that they're one of the oldest and most secretive groups in New Orleans."

"Listen, you two," Matty said, rising from her seat as if propelled by some mystical force, "we are not going to turn this investigation into some type of bogeyman chase through the French quarter." Matty made eye contact with Jack then Doctor Meeker before continuing, "Now if you don't mind, we have an appointment with Derek Willow, one of the most prominent businessmen in New Orleans, so put away your juju beads and holy water and let's get back to reality."

# Chapter Eight

The National American Bank building, located at 200 Carondelet Street in the central business district of New Orleans, was only ten minutes from their office. The twenty-three-story building constructed in 1928 under the direction of Louisiana architect Moise Goldstein was the first public building in New Orleans to utilize indoor air-conditioning.

Seated in the outside waiting room, Jack quickly understood that the forty-five-minute wait to see Mr. Willow was nothing more than a power-play. He quickly discussed it with Matty and Doctor Meeker, who both agreed with his assessment. The three agreed to take a softer approach, not wanting to play the man's game.

Finally, they were escorted into Willow's office by a young woman who, as Matty put it, was 120 pounds of flesh stuffed into a 90-pound plastic bag. Jack wasn't sure but, he was almost certain that he had seen the young lady before working in one of the strip clubs on Bourbon Street.

The corner office was as opulent as they expected. The first thing a person would notice was that the twentieth story of the building offered a commanding view of the city. All the office furnishings were carved out of Cypress trees harvested from the swamps of Louisiana. Jack had read somewhere that Cypress grown in the swamps of

Southern Louisiana, tended to have a richer, redder color than other areas of the country. The rich color was a result of the salt content in the brackish water where the trees grew. Harvesting Cypress in the swamp was difficult at best, thus making the cutting and removal expensive.

Mr. Willow was nowhere to be seen, so the three took the opportunity to meander around the office and study the memorabilia placed strategically around the room. There were pictures of Willow taken with President John F. Kennedy and the current President, Richard M. Nixon. There were also photographs of him posing with Louisiana Congressman Edwin Edwards, Louisiana Governor John McKeithen, and last but not least, Prime Minister of the United Kingdom, Harold Wilson. There were also many recreational photos taken with friends and family. One photo, in particular, caught his eye. It was the photograph of Derek Willow and his three sons, all dressed in Mardi Gras regalia, most likely at the Krew of Comus Ball. A fifth figure stood in the center of the four men. The Mardi Gras costume did nothing to hide the fact that it was a seductive young woman, whose firm, smooth bosom, and shapely arms were mostly uncovered. The tightness of her costume accented her slim waist which flared into seductively round hips and long thighs. Jack understood that all of this was part of Mr. Willow's strategic game, known as *I'm important. You are not.*

Jack leaned over to Doctor Meeker as she passed close by, "This man has some serious issues."

Meeker continued to walk by but answered Jack in a sing-song voice, "I told you so."

"Ah, Doctor Meeker," Derek Willow blurted out as he appeared from a hidden door that led to a private bathroom, "I see you've come to take me up on my offer."

"If your offer was to discuss the death of your two sons, you're correct," she smiled graciously.

Jack noticed his movements were swift, and with a commanding air of self-confidence. He understood how women could find this man appealing.

"Derek," Meeker stated, presenting her colleagues, "this is Detective Matty Wilcox and Detective Jack Kohl. They are the two detectives handling the investigation of your son's deaths."

Jack moved forward to shake Willow's hand but stopped short when the man avoided him altogether by walking behind his desk. Jack had noticed earlier that the size of the desktop reminded him of an aircraft carrier deck.

"And not doing too well of a job of it," Willow chided as he pointed to the chairs on the other side of the desk. "Please, have a seat."

In preparation for the meeting, someone had arranged three chairs directly across from where Derek Willow would be seated. Two of the three were matching high backs while the third was nothing more than a small secretarial chair.

"Cynthia," Willow said, pointing to the centered chair, "please have a seat. Detective Wilcox, the one to her left and Detective…"

Jack was already seated on the secretarial chair; his legs crossed in a very feminine position.

"Thank you, Mr. Willow," Matty started, "I know how hard this must be for you."

"I must say, Detective Wilcox," Willow said, interrupting her, "I didn't know that the NOPD had such beautiful women on the force. A change in your apparel would be not only welcome but could get you a promotion to at least Captain."

"At least," Jack replied, trying to swallow his amusement.

"That's sweet of you to say so," she said, sharing a smile with him. Matty turned in her seat to face Jack, "Jack," she said, her mouth now pulled into a sour grin, "why don't you start?"

As Jack drew a breath to start, he was quickly waved off by Willow's right hand. "Listen, folks," Willow started, "the answer is no to all of the empty questions you are about to ask."

"No?" Matty asked.

"That's correct, no? I don't know of anyone who would have wanted to kill my two sons; I don't know what the killer's motivation may have been, and I don't know the answer to the other thousand useless questions you may have. My two sons were good, law-abiding citizens who were pillars of the community. Instead of wasting my time, you should be out hunting for their murderer."

Willow's prepared speech faded in Jack's ears as he took inventory of the items on the desk and top of the credenza. One of the things he noticed was a small collection of crystal figurines clustered close to the phone. There was quite the menagerie of figures not unlike the ones on Jack's own desk back at the precinct. Willow had a unicorn, a dog, a swan, and a clown amongst the group. The difference Jack thought was in the fact that these figurines were probably very expensive where Jack's collection was made mostly of paper origami crafted for him by Matty. As far back as he could remember, Matty had always had a fondness for creating Origami figures.

While he had never confronted her with the origin of her enthusiasm for the art, he had heard stories. The most believable was the story of her being laid up after a shooting accident that almost left her paralyzed. It is believed that she picked up the art while convalescing from her wounds. In any case, he had become the main benefactor of her work. On any day, he could walk up to his desk and find a new figure sitting there.

He was the proud owner of an elephant, giraffe, crane, and numerous flowers. She had even made an old-fashioned Sheriff's star. There were also numerous pieces scattered about his home. It was not uncommon for him to undress at night and, from time to time, find an origami piece in one of his pockets. He never could figure out how she was able to slip the piece in his pocket without his catching her. Jack never had the heart to throw one away; thus, his collection grew.

Jack looked up from the desktop to see that Derek Willow's mouth had stopped moving. The man instead stared at Jack as if waiting for an answer. Jack smiled and turned to Matty.

"Well," Matty said to him with a slight tinge of aggravation in her voice, "do you want to go look at the two victims' office with me or not?"

"Sorry," Jack apologized, "I was just gathering my thoughts. I would be happy to go with you."

No sooner had Jack answered when a young lady entered the office. "This way detectives," she said, beckoning the two to follow her.

Jack stood up from the small chair, stretching his limbs. "You coming with us, Doctor?"

"No, Detective Kohl," she said, remaining in her chair, "I'm going to stay here and catch up on old times with Derek."

Jack could tell by the look on her face that she would rather do anything than being alone with Derek Willow but, he figured she probably had a good reason to endure the man's company.

The young woman first led Jack and Matty to Justin Willow's office. As expected, it was a mini version of the father's workplace. While not a corner office, it still had two large windows looking out over the city. The furniture was made of Cyprus like his father's but proportionately smaller in size. *No carrier deck for a desktop here*, Jack thought.

The desktop was void of everything except for a desk phone. It had obviously, been cleared of all personal and work items and given a good coat of polish.

"No, fingerprints here," Jack whispered to Matty.

"Was Justin always this neat?" Matty asked as she picked up the receiver from the phone and studied it.

"God no," the young girl giggled, "I think it was a competition between him and Brandon to see who could have the most clutter on their desk. Sometimes it would take me days to find a letter or a note buried in the pile."

Matty bent down and studied the file drawers of the desk. She then opened the large bottom drawer. "Empty," she said, looking up at Jack.

"Mr. Willow's only been dead for less than two days," Jack said in a soft, modest voice, "what happened to his stuff?"

"Senior had us categorize and place all of his paperwork in file boxes, then had them removed to our file room. All of the man's personal effects have been boxed up and moved there also."

"Senior," Matty asked, "you call Derek Willow, Senior?"

"Yes, ma'am," the young woman answered, "Mr. Willow is the president and senior member of the corporation. He likes for us to address him as Senior."

Jack walked away from the desk and began to study the photographs that were still on the walls.

"Senior would not allow us to remove the photographs," the young woman answered in anticipation of Jack's question, "he was afraid that we would do damage to the wall while removing them. We have a decorator coming in this evening to remove the pictures and repair any damage."

Jack continued to study the photographs over the credenza. "Wow, Matty," Jack exclaimed while motioning her to come closer. The photograph was of Justin Willow standing next to what Jack imagined to be a trophy size sailfish hanging from a rope on a dock, "look at the size of this fish."

When Matty was standing next to him, Jack moved slightly to his right, making contact with Matty's left side. The move effectively blocked the young lady from seeing what was going on in front of the two detectives. Jack then pointed to the area where the credenza came close to the wall.

"Damn," Matty said, noticing the tiny blood splatter behind the credenza. "I've never seen a fish that big," she said, continuing the charade.

Maintaining their position, Jack pointed to three of the frames, all of which showed signs of damage. He noticed that the frames had been repaired, and more than likely, the broken glass replaced, but what they had failed to repair was several slight scratches made on the photographs where the glass splintered. He looked over his right shoulder toward the young woman, "was this taken in the Bahamas?"

"I'm not sure," she replied, "the family often spent time down in the Caribbean."

"Together?" Matty asked.

"Sometimes," she replied, "but not always. Often one of them would go on vacation while the others stayed here to cover the office."

Once again Jack pointed to the photograph, this time he singled out a woman scantily clad in a two-piece bathing suit. She stood just inside the frame and was not clearly in focus. He nudged Matty ever so slightly as he continued to study the photograph.

"Does this office have a private bathroom like Mr. Willow's," she asked, turning to the woman.

"Of course."

"May I see it?" Matty asked.

Jack waited until the two women had entered the bathroom and out of sight before he attempted to move the credenza away from the wall. As luck would have it, the credenza had been emptied along with the desk, so moving it was a lot easier. He quickly removed the sheet of paper from his notebook and pushed the button on his switchblade knife. With the credenza moved, he was able to see that the blood drip was about 4 inches long, with a fair amount of blood dried at the bottom. Carefully he scraped the blood from the wall onto the notebook page. Carefully, he folded the page and slid it into his pocket. He had just replaced the credenza when the two women exited the bathroom.

Jack turned and faced the two women. "I'm going to assume that Brandon Willow's office has been cleaned out like this one."

"Even more so," the young woman nodded, "all of the pictures on the walls were removed some time ago by the decorators. As I said earlier, they are scheduled to come in this evening and remove the remaining pictures in this office. At the same time, another crew will be replacing the old wallpaper in Brandon's office as part of the preparation for the new tenant on Monday.

"New tenant?" Jack asked.

"Yes," she said, "our senior legal counsel will be moving into the office on Monday."

"I see," Jack said as he lightly pulled at his right earlobe, "then, Matty, I don't think there would be any purpose for us to have a look at his office."

"Probably not," Matty agreed, "I think we've wasted enough of this young lady's time."

"Don't be silly," the young woman smiled, "it was my pleasure." The woman pointed toward the door, "I'll escort you back to seniors office."

As they turned the corner, they saw Doctor Meeker standing with Derek Willow just outside his office. Even though Meeker was showing great restraint, Jack could tell that she was more than a little ticked off. "Ready to roll, Doctor?"

"Whenever you guys are." Though she hid it well, the tensing of her jaw betrayed her deep anger.

"Thank you again, Mr. Willow," Matty said, none of them offered their hands.

The three headed to the door in silence.

"Remember Cynthia," Willow said in a loud voice, "we still have to firm up that dinner date."

A muscle flicked angrily at Meeker's jaw, "I'll check my schedule and get back with you," she promised.

They were almost to the door when Jack suddenly turned around and took a few steps back toward Willow. "Mr. Willow," Jack asked politely, "I almost forgot to ask. Where is your third son, Matthew? Is he in the building?" "I'd like to talk to him."

Derek Willow slowly closed the gap between them. Although he was smiling, his brows drew together in an agonizing expression. "My son Matthew is no concern of yours," Willow grunted. He has been removed to a safe location until this madness is over."

"We could give him police protection," Matty offered sincerely.

"Police protection?" Willows lips twisted into a cynical smile, "I've already taken care of his protection. I've hired a private security firm to be with him twenty-four seven. I'm the only one who knows where he's at, and it's going to stay that way until this murderer is captured or killed."

"You and the security firm, right?" Jack asked.

"What?" Willow scowled.

"You said that you were the only one that knew where he was at," Jack said, "but it's you and his security team that knows where he's hidden, correct?"

A long, uncomfortable silence filled the void between the two men. Derek Willow finally broke the standoff, "good day detective," he said before turning and walking away.

Once again, the three did not speak until they were inside the elevator. No sooner had the doors closed, then Meeker blurted out, "please tell me there's a fucking firehose somewhere in this building!"

Jack and Matty stared at each other, their mouths open wide. Words failed the two tongue-tied detectives.

Meeker physically shivered. "If that slimeball would've touched me one more time, I think I would have actually thrown up on him."

"Firehose?" Jack mumbled.

"Yes, firehose," she hissed, "it's the only way I can be sure to get his particular stink off of me."

"So, I guess," Jack asked, "a long-term relationship with him is out of the question?"

Meeker responded by clutching her arms close to her chest and rolling her eyes.

"Well, we might have something to take your mind off of him," Jack said while patting his shirt pocket, "we were able to retrieve a blood sample from Justin Willow's office."

"Can you have one of your technicians run down here and pick it up?" Matty asked. "They'll have to be very careful. There's not much of a sample."

Meeker opened her purse and started searching through the items inside. Within a second, she produced a clear plastic sample pouch. "Put it in here," she said, handing the bag to Jack, "when we get to the first floor, the bank is sure to have a payphone. I'll tell the technician to meet us at the front door."

Jack carefully removed the folded piece of paper from his pocket and slid it into the plastic bag before sealing it. "Do you always carry an evidence bag in your purse," he asked?

"Of course," she quickly replied, "you guys carry guns; I carry evidence bags."

# Chapter Nine

Jack entered the small conference room and sat at the opposite side of the table from Matty and Doctor Meeker. A glance at his watch confirmed that they were twenty minutes early for their 4 PM meeting with Captain Steel.

Jack exchanged glances with both women, "I have checked my sources at the two largest private security firms here in New Orleans. Neither group has any knowledge of a security detail contracted by Derek Willow."

"It could be hush-hush even in the security firms," Matty offered, "your contacts may not be aware."

"It's possible," Jack admitted, "but these two guys reside on the executive floor. If Derek Willow contracted for twenty-four seven security service, I don't think you can keep something like that quiet amongst the executives."

"Okay," Matty offered as she worked on her latest Origami piece, "let's say Willow is lying, where does that put us? He could have hidden his son with some of his friends."

"Or," Meeker added, "considering he might not have many friends, he could have contracted with an out-of-state firm."

A momentary look of uneasiness crossed Jack's face. "Well, for now, the whereabouts of Matthew Willow is at a dead end." He glanced at Meeker, "Anything on the blood sample?"

"Yes," she nodded, "the blood sample you gave me is B-positive, and I checked both Brandon and Justin Willow. Both men were A-positive."

"So, you think we have a third player," Matty asked.

"It's possible," Jack confirmed, "the blood came from someone."

Just then, the uniformed police officer stuck his head into the room. "Hey, guys, Captain Steele wanted me to tell you that the meeting was moved to the large conference room."

The three gathered their paperwork and headed down the hall. Matty was the first one through the door and abruptly stopped just past the door frame. Jack, close behind her, stopped quickly in order not to run into the back of her. The procession then slowly entered the room, and Jack, for the first time, could see why Matty had hesitated.

The large conference room had seating for ten people. Six of those chairs were already occupied. Captain Steele had taken his customary seat at the head of the table. To his right, to Jack's dismay, sat Detective Beachmen, his doughy midsection lapping over the edge of the conference table. Next to him sat Beachmen's partner, Detective Petersen, his tall, lanky frame affording him no chance of buying an off the rack suit that would fit him, but he bought them anyway. Both men offered him a conspiratorial smile reminding him of a pair of Cheshire cats.

Matty made her way to the other end of the table and sat at its end. Jack and Meeker then took seats to her left and right.

Jack immediately began evaluating the woman sitting next to Captain Steele. He guessed her age to be somewhere in her early forties, medium build and carrying a few extra pounds. Her face was framed in a pageboy style showing signs of premature gray. The high cheekbones of her face were accented by bullish icy blue eyes, keen and assessing. Even now, they were working overtime on summing him up.

Captain Steele coughed lightly, bringing the room to silence. "Everyone's here now, so let's get started. Those of you under my command already know each other, so I will dispense with the introductions and go right to introducing our guests."

*This woman has never been a wanted guest in anyone's home,* Jack thought.

"This is Emma Salton, State Special Investigator for the Governor's office. Seated next to her is Teresa Mallard and Kathy Witton, her assistants.

"Thank you, Captain Steele," she said, smiling without humor. "I have read the reports on this case and let me say right up front that I feel the progress of this case is lackluster at best. It is my duty to keep this group focused and to bring this case to a swift conclusion."

Jack half raised his hand, "excuse me, do you think you'll have this wrapped up by Friday," Jack asked Salton with a fixed level stare.

Emma Salton was obviously caught off guard. "What," she asked, a spasm crossing her face, "what do you mean by Friday?"

Jack quickly took the opening. "Well, with this investigation now headed by three state special investigators and the fact that you have specified that you're looking for a swift conclusion, I was hoping you would be finished by Friday."

"Why Friday?" Doctor Meeker asked innocently.

"Well," Jack said, leaning back in his chair, "I have a lunch on Sunday, and if Ms. Salton can get this wrapped up by Friday, I won't have to cancel my date."

"See what I told you," Beachmen belched out, "he is nothing but an insolent pup."

"Okay, knock it off," Steele sighed.

Jack smiled inwardly. Five years ago, he had worked on his first high profile case when he was a key member of a task force investigating the Trotter twins kidnapping case. New Orleans, oil millionaire, Justin Trotter, awoke one morning to find that his twin twelve-year-old girls had been abducted right out from under his nose. Trotter was a multi-millionaire with as many political connections in the state capital as he had oil wells. Some say that his influence went as far as Pennsylvania Avenue in Washington, DC.

After three weeks, the feds, state, and locals were at a dead end. The abductors were uncanny. A plan for the payment was given to Trotter and the police. A trap was set up to catch them when they attempted to grab the money. Jack remembered that they even had a backup plan to follow the perpetrators if the trap failed.

He painfully recalled that all hell broke loose when they lost the money and the kidnappers. Everyone began pointing fingers, blaming anyone who had even heard of the case.

A few of them believed the girls would never be returned, at least not alive. He recalled the immense pressure everyone was feeling. He remembered how the team began to splinter, the terrible infighting between its members; several times, they had almost come to blows.

It was then that he and his then partner, Jim went off on a wild tangent, following a line of thinking that had been dismissed by their superiors several times. Within ten hours, the girls were released unharmed, but the group was never able to mend their differences. Jack painfully remembered that two police officers lost their lives that day; one was his partner Jim, the other was Detective Beachmen's younger brother.

Jack had learned a lot about handling high profile cases back then, and the painful experience was going to help him now.

"Mr. Kohl," Salton answered, giving Jack a dark smoldering look, "first of all, I am not taking over your investigation. I am here to assist you in this matter."

Jack smiled to himself; he had gotten her to admit that her group was not taking over the case. He knew that would be the way it would start. By reconfirming that she was not in charge of the case, no blame would fall on her. She was free to meddle and obstruct without fear of reprisal but, it meant that the case, for now, was still in Matty and his hands. "So," Jack said loudly, startling most of the group, "who would like an update,"

"Continue," Steele sighed.

"We've just come back from speaking with Derek Willow," Matty said, taking the opportunity to allow Jack to cool down, "and I'm afraid he wasn't much help in the matter."

"How so?" Steele prodded.

"He was a bit angry that we have not been able to move further on this case, but on the same hand, he was unwilling to offer any assistance in identifying the killer."

"We were allowed to inspect," Jack interjected, "both Brandon and Justin's offices, but both of them were in an almost sterile condition."

"What do you mean, sterile?" Beachmen asked.

"The offices of both had been emptied of all personal and business-related items," Matty answered. "In fact, they were getting ready to wallpaper and repaint Brandon Willows office."

"I believe there were still a few photographs on the wall of Justin Willow's office," Kathy Witton interjected.

Doctor Meeker's eyebrow shot up in surprise, "How did…"

"That's correct," Jack answered in a voice loud enough to override Meeker's question, "there were a few personal photographs still remaining on the wall, but they are due to be removed this evening." Jack noticed that Salton's clamped mouth and fixed eyes were directed toward her assistant Kathy Witton, but she checked her emotion, and the matter went no further.

"We did obtain a small…" Meeker started to say but was again overshadowed by Jack.

"A small bit of information," Jack continued, "that Derek Willow had his youngest son, Matthew, hidden away somewhere. He then contracted with a security firm for twenty-four-seven security protection." Jack glanced over at Doctor Meeker and made sure they made eye contact. "Other than that, there's not much to tell you about the meeting."

"We'll continue to try and find out where Matthew Willow is hiding," Matty said, "it shouldn't take that long to shake him out of the tree he's hiding in."

Jack was surprised to see the nonverbal communication pass between Captain Steele and Salton. Instantly Captain Steele spoke up. "I want you two to stay on the two murders," Steele commanded. "I've already assigned Beachmen and Pettersen to follow up on Matthew Willow."

"Fair enough," Jack nodded.

"Ms. Salton and her group," Steel continued, "will be setting up shop in the small conference room."

\*\*\*\*

Tommie's was one of the few refuges in the French Quarter where a person could get a drink and not be overwhelmed by the nightly gaiety that was the trademark of Bourbon Street. It was an old establishment. Its tables and chairs, a mismatched collection of bargain-basement furniture resting on a floor that had been scuffed down to the bare wood, but it was quiet enough to carry on a private conversation. After their eyes adjusted to the dim light of the bar, Jack led the small group to their favorite table, which was farthest from the front door and on the opposite side of the bar away from the restroom traffic. It also offered a strategic advantage for Jack. It allowed him and Matty to have their backs to the wall and still have a commanding view of the rest of the room. Meeker had named the strange phenomena as the Detective Pacifier. The two detectives were never happy unless their backs were to the wall, and they could see whatever was coming their way.

The only illumination in the corner came from a neon Dixie® Beer sign, which, when reflected in the droplets of liquid scattered across the tabletop, shimmered like a handful of precious stones. Jack motioned to Tommy, standing behind the bar. The man nodded and immediately tossed a dry bar towel to Jack. Matty and Doctor Meeker waited patiently as Jack cleaned and dried the tabletop. Matty pulled up a third chair, and the three took a seat at the table.

Maggie, Tommy's live-in, and only barmaid, approached the table. "Wow," she smiled, "I don't think I've seen the three of you here at one time ever."

"Special occasion," Jack said, "the ship is going down, and we wanted a few more drinks before we're completely in over our heads."

"Okay then," Maggie smiled, "you want the usual then?"

Matty held up two fingers, "times two, Maggie."

Maggie had no sooner left the table than Meeker turned to the two detectives. "You two guys knew that Salton and her cronies had been to Derek Willow's office before us, right?"

"Of course," Matty said.

"Then," Meeker said with a slight smile of defiance, "why didn't you challenge her?"

"To what end?" Jack asked.

"To what end," she answered skeptically, "Maybe to confront Salton for her underhanded bitch of a move."

Jack very seldom called Doctor Meeker by her first name even though she had requested it back during the Jorgensen case. But when alone, both Matty and he addressed her as a friend and colleague.

"Cindy," Jack said, "the girl made a mistake by letting it slip. We now know that Ms. Salton is not going to be a team player."

"The young girl slipped up," Matty stated, "Salton's going to ream her ass for it. There's no reason for us to make a federal case out of something that we got for free."

"Got for free," Meeker asked skeptically, "what did we get for free?"

Four bottles of beer and two glasses of white wine appeared on the table. "I'll keep an eye on you guys," Maggie said as she shuffled off to help another customer.

Jack took a long pull on one of the beers, "well, for one thing; it only took us a couple of hours to find out that Ms. Salton is working with Derek Willow and not us."

"And what else?" Meeker prompted.

"We also found out," Matty said, starting her own beer, "that Derek Willow and Ms. Salton don't have a fucking clue where Matthew Willow is."

# Chapter Ten

The first thing that Matthew noticed when he came to was that he was lying on the floor, in the dark, spittle was running freely from his mouth. He managed to push himself up into a sitting position, wiping his mouth on his sleeve in the process.

The room was musty and smelled like a load of wet laundry left to sour and mildew. Matthew thought about calling out for help but then feared that if he did, someone might *actually* come.

The ground was damp and dirty, and when he slapped the ground next to him, it vibrated with a muffled thud. To his right, he spotted what might have been the only door to the room. Long shadows like dirty claws reached out for him from under the door. Using that dim light, he was able to judge that the opening was no more than two or three feet across. He crawled to the door and began studying its features. He traced the outline with his hand and confirmed that the door was no more than three feet across and approximately four feet high. Directly above the door was the ceiling constructed of heavy wood planks. He pushed against the door several times then, trying to remain quiet, he put his shoulder to the door and began to push with his feet. The door did not budge. He once again traced the frame of the door with his fingers. To his dismay, he was unable to find any latch or handle. Eventually, he turned and slid into a sitting position, his back against the door.

Suddenly remembering, his hand dropped into his pants pocket and dug inside. Carefully he withdrew a stainless-steel Zippo® lighter and, in a single motion, flipped the lid back, striking the flint wheel, causing the wick to ignite. The room was immediately filled with a dirty yellow light coming from the wick.

Matthew was correct on the rough dimensions of the room. The ceiling was not much more than four-foot-high, the width approximately ten feet while the depth looked to be twice the width. Because of the mud floor, he would've called it a root cellar except for the presence of rusty manacles attached to the stone walls by large rings. He breathed a sigh of relief when he had finally convinced himself that the chains had not been used in over 100 years. With the lighter heating up in his hand, he closed the lid extinguishing the flame. Unconsciously he held the closed lighter between both hands pressing it against his chest for warmth.

He recalled that at a young age, his father had insisted that he and his brothers attend urban escape and evasion classes. All three of the boys thought the classes were a waste of time, but his father continually reminded them that their wealth and status in life would make them targets for kidnapping and ransom. He closed his eyes, trying to recall the information and wishing he had paid closer attention to the instructor.

\*\*\*\*

Jack turned the car off the main highway onto the road that would eventually lead to Aisling's home. It had been a fruitless week of chasing down flimsy leads, dead-end theories, and terrible hunches. He and Matty had split up in order to cover more ground. They talked to the two men's friends and acquaintances. They covered current and past clients and re-interviewed family members. They even went as far as to contact Justin's ex-wife, who had returned to France after their divorce two years ago. Without mentioning it to Matty, Jack spoke with several people he now knew who dealt in the spiritual world. He had even talked with at least a dozen tarot card readers in and around the French Quarter, including having his fortune told three times.

It was Matty who suggested that the two take Sunday off to try and clear their heads and get a fresh start on Monday. Jack was appreciative that Matty remembered his comment about having a date on Sunday and knew the only reason she had declared Sunday a day of rest was because of him.

Jack turned the car into the entrance of Aisling's home. It was obviously Albert's turn to be on guard duty as the large Empress goose now occupied the lookout position on top of the 39' Ford. Jack exited the car and headed toward the front door. As before, the geese sounded the alarm, and the other two geese, Abigail and Spencer came around the right side of the house honking. As happened the last time, Aisling quickly followed behind the two geese.

She wore a terra cotta colored jumpsuit with a white body shirt. Her hair was not braided today but pulled back and held in place with a large, handcrafted metal barrette.

As always, her affectedly modest smile put everything into place. He immediately felt a slight tinge of remorse for all the 'ugly witch' comments he had made previously.

Aisling stepped forward, offering Jack her hands. When he took them, she bent in close and lightly kissed him on the cheek. "Bonjour, Jack," she said in flawless French, "Un bon voyage j'espère."

"Yes," Jack responded in French, "the trip was very relaxing."

Aisling locked arms with him as they walked around the house. "Your French is excellent," Jack commented as they cornered the house and headed toward the gazebo. "I thought your family was from England."

"We came to the Americas from England," she corrected, "but half of my family is French. My family lineage can be traced all the way back to my relatives, Vaden and Ophelia Audigert, in the 12th century. They were both accused of bewitching the local magistrate and convicted of witchcraft. They were put to the stake and burned just one day apart. Their daughter, Charlotte, was smuggled out of France to England. She grew up there and married an Englishman named Lach Coxson." Aisling pointed to one of the two chairs arranged on the gazebo. She had arranged a small table with refreshments between the two chairs.

"Thank you," Jack said as he took his seat, "but I'm sure the story doesn't end there."

"Oh no," Aisling said as she took the remaining chair, "it is said that Lach and Charlotte were disciples of Merlin and learned their magic from the master himself."

"Merlin," he said, surprised again by this unpredictable woman, "the real Merlin?"

Aisling laughing out loud, offered Jack a conspiratorial wink, "well, that part of our family lineage is a bit foggy but, I do know that my family practiced witchcraft until the sixteen hundreds when witch persecution in England became intolerable. It was so bad that my family changed their name and fled England to the Americas."

Jack watched as Aisling poured him a drink from the tall pitcher, "is that some type of witches brew?" he asked jokingly.

"Actually," she said, handing him the glass, "it's an old Southern potion known as a Mint Julep."

Jack took the drink in both hands and slowly raised it to his lips, "wow, that is very tasty." Jack removed a piece of mint from the glass and held it out, "I bet this came from your garden."

"Of course," she said as a satisfying light filled her eyes, "and everything is grown organically."

"Organically? Are you telling me that no pesticides, herbicides, growth stimulants, antibiotics, or chemically formulated fertilizers are allowed in the Aisling garden?"

"Not a single one," Aisling smiled.

"What about magically assisted?" Jack asked, his eyes glowing with enjoyment.

Aisling took a deep breath and adjusted her smile, "well, maybe just a little."

They both laughed and continued to enjoy their drinks while soaking up the midmorning sun. It was Aisling that broke the silence. "Jack," she started slowly, "does it bother you that I am an avowed witch?"

Jack thought about the question for several seconds. He considered everything he knew about the woman up until now then carefully phrased his response. "Aisling first let me confess that up until a week ago, I didn't know that witches actually existed. Two weeks ago, if you had asked me what a witch looked like, I would have referred you to the movie, 'The Wizard of Oz' or to one of the carnies down around Jackson square."

"But now," she prompted.

"Now," he answered, frowning into his glass, "being with you and seeing firsthand what gifts you have, it would be foolish of me to deny their existence."

Aisling put down her glass and took Jack by the hand. "Thank you for saying that, Jack," she said as several tears slowly found their way down her cheeks.

Jack was confused by her response, "you're welcome. I guess you don't run into many people who acknowledge your existence."

Aisling slowly dabbed the tears from her eyes. "It's not your acknowledgment of my being a witch that has moved me. It is the fact that you see them as a gift rather than a curse."

Jack shook his head, laughing.

"What's wrong?" she asked.

He leaned back, continuing to sip his drink contently. "It's just I find it strange that in your case, I truly consider them gifts, but when it comes to my own predicament, I only see it as a curse."

Aisling leaned back in her chair, studying Jack's face. "It's only natural that I consider them gifts because I was raised with them. In your case, it was thrust upon you after you had spent the last twenty-five years of your life without knowing."

"And, in my personal opinion, I could've gone another twenty-five years without having known."

Aisling stood and offered Jack her hand, "let's head inside; we can finish this conversation over dinner."

****

Jack turned the car onto the road heading back to New Orleans. He checked the seat next to him to make sure that the leftovers Aisling had given to him were secure then he settled in for the drive back.

They had not returned to their conversation about witchcraft during dinner. Aisling had given Jack a quick tour of the house before sitting down to eat. Much of the furnishings were magnificent antiques handed down to her over the years, and again, much of their conversation was centered around her family.

After dinner, she and Jack walked down to the lake. He had not noticed on his last visit, but there was a walking path completely around the edge of the lake. The walk had taken them the better part of an hour. It was then that he had learned that Aisling property was just over twenty-eight acres and, at one time, was part of a three-thousand-acre plantation built in the mid-eighteen hundred.

Jack slammed on the brakes and turned the wheel sharply to the left in an attempt to miss the figure standing in the middle of the road. The car spun out and ended up off the side of the road. No sooner had the car stopped than Jack exited the vehicle, his weapon in his hand. He quickly searched the area and found no trace of the figure that had so predominantly occupied the center of the highway. He started the car and headed back to Aisling's home.

The clouds above him started to darken, and by the time he had turned off the road, large raindrops had begun to fall. As he stopped his vehicle in front of Aisling's house, he was surprised to see Aisling and the three geese standing in the front yard waiting for him. He stepped out of the car and walked quickly toward her.

Aisling rapidly covered the distance between them. "Jack," she said hesitating, blinking with bafflement, "what happened, what's wrong? I felt something…"

He put his arms around her and pulled her tightly to his chest. He felt her stiff resistance quickly melt as she buried her head under his chin. The rain began to come down harder, neither of them released the other.

"We better get inside," she said as she pushed him back slightly.

They entered the front door, both shivering from the cold

rain. Aisling ushered him to a place in front of the hearth. She then raised her right hand and gently wiggled her fingers. "*Calore Ignis*," she said toward the large opening. Flames quickly leaped up around the logs within.

*Warmth of fire,* Jack thought, translating Latin to English or was the proper phrase *Fire of warmth*, he couldn't remember.

Aisling began stripping off her jumpsuit, "Take off those clothes, Jack," she said as her jumpsuit hit the floor, "I'll get you something warm to put on."

Jack's breath caught in his throat at the sight of Aisling standing in front of the fire. The skintight body shirt had gone down to just below her waistline, where the heavier material gave way to a lacy pair of attached underwear. He quickly noticed that her firm high-perched breasts were accentuated by her hard nipples caused by the cold, wet blouse. As she turned and walked toward the bedroom, he couldn't help but notice the wholesomeness of her seductive young body. He turned back toward the fire and shivered.

Aisling quickly returned, carrying a large comforter. She had discarded the body shirt and had slipped into a full-length terrycloth bathrobe, a towel wrapped around her head, and a pair of fuzzy slippers. "Get out of that wet underwear, Jack," she commanded as she held up the comforter. As his underwear hit the floor, she wrapped him in the warmth of the blanket. "Sit here," she said, pointing to the British two-seater."

Jack noticed that her voice had softened.

"I'll get us something warm to drink," she said as she picked up his wet things.

Jack pulled the blanket tighter around him and leaned toward the fire. He replayed the incident in his head over and over, trying to understand the phenomena.

"Here, Jack," Aisling said, offering him a large steaming mug, "careful, it's hot."

Jack took the mug and held it under his nose breathing in the minty aroma. "I guess you don't grow coffee beans," he said, taking a small sip from the mug.

Aisling sat next to him and took a drink out of her mug. "No coffee beans, sorry."

"Want to hear what happened," Jack asked, taking a bigger sip from the cup.

"I was hoping you'd offer," she replied, managing a tremulous smile.

"Well," Jack sighed, "it's happened twice now. Once when Clarice and I returned to New Orleans and then again tonight as I left your house." Jack again visualized the incident. "While driving back to New Orleans, a vision appeared in front of my car. No," he said, correcting himself, "a person, a full-bodied person, stepped in front of my car."

"Did you recognize this person?" Aisling asked.

Jack stared into the flames. "Actually, the first time it happened; all I was able to recognize was a charcoal colored figure."

"And tonight?"

"Tonight, I got a good look at the figure," Jack said as he turned to face Aisling, "it was our friend from Justin Willow's home."

# Chapter Eleven

Jack sat at his desk, going over the evidence for the thousandth time. He had spent the night on Aisling's overstuffed couch. Even though the couch was very comfortable, Jack managed to twist and turn most of the night. A lot of the time was devoted to trying to untangle the mystery shrouding his case but, he had to admit that a portion of his discomfort was because he knew that Aisling was sleeping in the next room. No matter how hard he had tried, the image of Aisling standing in front of him in the wet body shirt seemed to overcome his thoughts. When the minute hand on his watch noted that it was five AM, he decided it was time to head back to New Orleans.

Even with all of the information that he and Matty had gathered, it seemed somehow to defy their efforts to solidify it into something substantial. *I have to find this woman*, he said to himself.

"Couldn't sleep, either?" Matty asked as she slid up onto the corner of his desk.

"Not even close," Jack admitted as an image of Aisling

flashed through his head.

Matty picked up one of the photos of Justin Willow, studied it for a few seconds, and tossed it back on the pile. "I know it's right in front of our face, Jack."

"You get anything out of Beachmen?" he asked, already knowing the answer.

Matty squirmed on the desk, "He told me to fuck off."

"Well, at least he'll talk to you."

"I did get one thing out of the Petersen, though," she sighed, "Matthew Willow is definitely missing, and because of that, Beachmen and Petersen are taking the brunt of the heat."

"It's the woman," he said, his dark face setting into a rancorous expression.

"What? What, woman?" Matty sneered.

Jack's face hardened, "it's the woman who killed Brandon and Justin Willow. The same woman who was probably in those photographs on Derek Willow's credenza and Justin Willow's wall. The woman who is holding Matthew Willow even now. She's the woman that has a tremendous hard-on for the Willows' and is killing them one by one."

Matty chewed on her lower lip before looking at Jack, "All right then," she said, trying to disguise her annoyance, "let's say it's a woman. How do we go about finding her before she kills anyone else?"

A satanic smile quickly spread across his thin lips, "I have an idea."

\*\*\*\*

Jack waited in his car on the third floor of the parking garage across from the National Bank building. He looked up every time he heard the tattletale squealing of car tires either going up or down the ramp. With a little help from Aisling, he was able to convince the young lady working in Derek Willow's office to let him borrow several boxes of the photographs belonging to the dead Willow brothers.

While she was agreeable to bring him two boxes of the photographs, one of Brandon's and one of Jason's, she refused to take the one that Derek Willow had on his desk. In a compromising move, she agreed to Xerox a copy of the photograph he wanted so badly.

After about fifteen minutes, a navy blue fifty-seven Chevy Bel Air pulled into the parking spot next to his. He and the young lady got out of their respective automobiles, and they met at her trunk. Within seconds the exchange of the two boxes was made from trunk to trunk.

"Thanks so much, Sheila," Jack said, offering her a warm smile.

The young woman returned the smile without speaking and headed back to the front of her car. Jack had already decided that he would wait until the young lady had left before he would exit the parking lot. He looked in his rearview mirror as she backed out into the exit lane. Suddenly she stopped directly behind him, set the car parking brake, and jumped out.

Jack quickly slipped his hands into his jacket, his fingers resting lightly on his weapon. He continued to watch as Sheila moved to his side of the car. He noticed that she was carrying a large Manila envelope. He rolled down his window and waited.

"Here Detective Kohl," I almost forgot to give you the copies of the pictures on Senior's desk.

"Thanks again, Sheila. Are you going to be alright?"

The young lady offered him a weak smile, her face paling, "Yes, I think so," she answered as she ran back to her car and left.

After fifteen minutes, Jack started his car and put it in reverse. As he had previously agreed with Matty, she would be waiting for him at his home. They both had agreed that the original photographs would never be taken to the precinct for obvious reasons.

The other thing that they had agreed to years ago was that in a case like this where they would be working in a charcoal gray area, only one of them would take on the task. And of course, the person tramping through the gray area would be Jack. That way, Matty would always be in the position of plausible denial. If and when the heat came down on Jack, Matty could always step forward and promise Captain Steel that she, as senior partner, would keep Jack on the straight and narrow. Of course, they had never done anything quite this severe before and had no intention of getting caught.

Jack passed the usual parking spot in front of the house and pulled around on the side street to the back of his home. To the right, facing the street was the entrance to his garage. He turned the car so that he could back in. Before he had completed the maneuver, the two large garage doors were swung open. Jack backed in neatly, and within a minute, the doors were quickly closed.

"Everything go as planned?" Matty asked.

"Like clockwork," he said. Jack had arranged for two members of the photographic crime lab to help Matty and him remove each photograph from the frame, copy it, and then replace them. The two men now waited at Jack's trunk. "You two guys ready to go to work, Bobby?" Jack asked as he popped the lock on the trunk.

The two men had set up a portable photo lab in the back of Jack's garage. Based on the number of photographs that Jack had told them about, the technicians believe the operation would take no more than three hours.

They placed the two boxes of photos on a card table at the front of the assembly line. Their system was quite simple. Each of the photographs was laid on a horizontal plate. They were then checked for any dust or debris. Several lightboxes had been set up in such a manner as to supply ample light without putting a glare on the photograph. A 35mm camera was then set on a tripod and positioned directly over the original photograph. The camera was set to the micro setting, and the technician adjusted the focus until the entire photograph was in the frame. They allowed for a slight margin around the picture to ensure that the entire photograph was recorded. Jack and the technician had agreed to take three photographs of each print and would later pick out the best of each. The photograph was then replaced in the proper frame and placed back in the box.

Jack and Matty took on the task of removing photographs from their frames. The second one Jack picked up was the photograph of Justin Willow and his trophy sailfish. Jack was a bit worried that since the frame had been damaged and glued back together, it may cause a problem with removing the photograph. Jack flipped the frame over to study it more closely. It was then that he noticed the small splatter of blood on the felt backing.

He lightly touched the dried blood and instantly found himself standing in the sepia tone world of Justin Willow's office. It was the black witch and Justin Willow standing in the center of the room. Her image was not nearly as grotesque as she was when he had seen her standing over Willow's body. Jack surmised that the woman, not having committed two murders as of yet, had not suffered from what Aisling called the Rule of Threes. She was still quite attractive and, Jack looked closer, unexpectedly much older than he had first thought. After a second look, he assumed that she might be at least twenty years older than Justin.

Jack continued to watch the scene unfold. They seem to be talking, maybe flirting he surmised when suddenly Willow pulled her roughly almost violently toward him. Willow moved to kiss her on the lips. The witch responded; her lips parted as she raised herself to meet his mouth. He released her lips and stared into her eyes. Their breathing was becoming more rapid. He roughly pulled her blouse over her head, exposing her bare breast. The shirt was then callously tossed to the floor.

Then unexpectedly, a second kiss, much more punishing

and angry than the first. Standing on her tiptoes, the witch responded with equal force pulling his face to hers with both hands. Her stance was faulty and offered little resistance to Willow's advances. Slowly at first, their momentum pushed them toward the credenza until, in a sexual frenzy, the witch slammed into the photographs mounted on the wall breaking several of the frames. The collision did not phase either of them as Willow's hand moved up her thigh and under her miniskirt while she fumbled with his belt and zipper.

"Come on, Jack," Matty said, lightly punching him on the arm, "you're falling behind here."

"Sorry," Jack said as he opened the back of the frame, "I must've dozed off."

As the technicians had promised at the end of three hours, all of the photographs had been copied, reassembled, and placed back in the proper box.

"There," Matty said, placing the lid on the last box, "that wasn't so bad." Matty turned to the head technician, "When will we get the results, Bobby?"

The man was busy breaking down his equipment, "How's tomorrow evening sound?"

Matty turned to Jack. Jack simply shook his shoulders and nodded.

"I'll go inside," Jack said to Matty, pointing his thumb over his shoulder, "and arrange for pickup with Sheila." Without waiting for an answer, Jack left the garage and entered the back door of his house. As he reached for the kitchen phone, it began to ring.

"Detective Kohl," Jack said in his normal professional voice.

"Hello, Captain…"Yes, sir, she's here with me."

"Yes sir, I see," he sighed into the phone, "we'll be right there." Jack took a deep breath and let it out slowly, hanging up the receiver.

"You set up the meeting?" Matty asked, making her way into the house.

"No," Jack said, shaking his head regretfully, "that was Captain Steele on the phone."

"And?" Matty prompted.

"The night janitor at Willow's office," Jack said slowly, guilt buried somewhere deep in his chest, "found Sheila's body. She's dead; stabbed multiple times."

# Chapter Twelve

Jack and Matty waited patiently for the doors of the elevator to open. Amazingly, they had only seen two police officers on their way up. The first was the officer who unlocked the first-floor entrance to the Bank building; the second stood quietly at his post by the elevator door. The officer smiled and nodded his recognition of the two detectives. "They're waiting for you upstairs," he said as he pushed the button to retrieve the elevator.

The two elevator doors slid open, allowing all of the clamor of an active crime scene to spill into the car. Jack allowed Matty to exit the car before he followed. Neither of them stopped until one of Doctor Meeker's technicians approached them.

"Hello, Megan," Jack said to the middle-aged woman, "Where is your boss?"

"Detective Kohl, Wilcox," she said, pointing toward Derek Willow's office, "she's inside the big office."

They stepped just inside Willow's office and stopped,

taking in the scene. Someone had strewn all of the items on Derek Willow's aircraft carrier size desk onto the floor. Jack noticed several of the crystal figurines that he had seen earlier were now scattered about the floor. A-frame evidence marking tents were already next to each item.

The only item now occupying the top of Derek Willow's desk was Sheila's naked body. She lay in a prone position, both of her arms hanging over the two short sides of the desk. Her legs were straight, in line with the rest of her body. Even from where he was standing, Jack could see each of the knife wounds along her back. He noticed that while the wounds started at her neck and went down to her waist, they were not in a perfectly straight line. He also noticed that the blood streaks from the wounds had not puddled or followed the contours of her back as dictated by gravity but instead followed no sensible pattern, streaking in several different directions.

Jack leaned in close to Matty, "This is not the original murder scene."

"No, it's not," Matty agreed, "the blood streaks suggest she was killed somewhere else, then carried her and dumped her on the desk."

"Is this a private conversation," Doctor Meeker stated as she approached the two, "or can anyone join in?"

"You're always welcome, Doctor," Matty answered.

"So, Doctor," Jack said, pointing toward the body, "Which one did her in. Stab wound number one or somewhere farther down the line?"

"Hard to say, Detective," Meeker answered as she looked over her shoulder toward the body, "any one of them could have been the one that did her in but, of course, I…"

"… won't know until after the autopsy," Matty said, finishing the sentence. "Did you find the murder weapon?"

Meeker motioned for the two of them to follow her, "It's over here along with the tarot card."

The two followed Doctor Meeker to an area on the other side of the body. There on the credenza were two separate evidence pouches, one containing the blade while the other held the single tarot card.

"That's not much of the dagger," Matty stated as she picked up the pouch.

"It's not a dagger at all," Jack said, studying it while still being held up by Matty, "it's a very ornate letter opener. What does it say there on the grip?"

Matty held the bag closer to her face and turned it from side to side, "well what do you know, Krew of Comus."

"Does it have a date on it?" Jack asked.

Matty turned it one way then another to be able to see both sides of the grip, "no date, just engraved words 'Krew of Comus.'

"Do you think it's solid gold?" Doctor Meeker asked.

"Could be," Jack asserted, "with people like Derek Willow, it wouldn't surprise me." Jack leaned closer to the letter opener. "The tip of the blade is slightly bent," he mused, "as if someone used it to jimmy open a locked drawer or box."

Meeker leaned forward next to Jack. "There are a few nicks also. I'll make sure to take a closer look under our electron microscope."

Matty laid the evidence bag back on the credenza and picked up the bag containing the tarot card. She held it up where everyone could see. The card depicted a prostrated man with ten swords piercing his back.

"Don't need to be a tarot card reader to figure this one out," Jack sneered, "the man's been stabbed in the back."

"Ten times," added Doctor Meeker, "just like the victim."

"So," Matty interjected, "somebody thinks that Sheila went behind their back. I wonder who that could be?"

"Detective Kohl!"

Jack didn't have to turn around to know the gruff voice belonged to Detective Beachmen. Both he and Matty sighed as they turned and walked back to the outer office where the irritating voice had originated.

Waiting in the outer office were not only Detective Beachmen and Petersen but Special Agent Salton and her two cronies. He looked toward Salton; his glance was perplexed and opaque. "If you're looking for Matthew Wilson," he said with a straight face, "I can save you the trouble. He's not here."

Anger grew in the color of Beachmen's throat like a Midsummer day thermometer. "You two are dismissed," he said with a look of smug satisfaction, "We'll be taking over here."

"Like hell," Matty said, taking a step closer toward Beachmen.

"I'm the Senior Detective here, and I'm telling you to leave."

Jack lightly put his hand on Matty's shoulder, "If you're equating weight to seniority than you outrank us all put together," Jack said, "otherwise you should be out looking for Matthew Willow."

"I won't tell you again," Beachmen threatened, "we're taking over this case."

Jack moved closer to Beachmen, "Okay Detective," Jack said in a very quiet but stern voice, "here are the two reasons why you and Special Agent Salton will be leaving now. The first is that Derek Willow is our main suspect in the murder."

"Main suspect," Salton blurted out, "that's absurd!"

"That's correct," Jack said, pointing towards Willow's office, "this young lady was in his employ and is now lying dead across his desk, stabbed ten times with his letter opener. I think that gives me enough probable cause to bring Mr. Willow in for questioning."

"I'm Senior Detective," Beachmen insisted.

"That might be correct," Jack agreed, "but you two are a Senior Detective and a Special Agent who are both personal friends of Derek Willow, and that is enough to disqualify you from this investigation."

"That's ridiculous!" Beachmen said, almost shouting now.

"As ridiculous as it may sound," Jack said, pointing toward Matty, who was holding the receiver of the closest phone out toward Beachmen, "the second reason is that Captain Steel has assigned us this case."

Beachmen snatched the receiver from Matty's hands, "Detective Beachmen… Yes, sir, yes, sir, but… Yes, sir." Beachmen sighed as he attempted to hand the receiver back to Matty. Matty turned around without speaking and walked back into the crime scene, leaving Beachmen holding on to the receiver.

"Let's go," Beachmen said, throwing the phone toward the desk as he made his way to the elevator.

As the elevator door started to close, Jack waved toward the scarlet faced Beachmen, "Bye now," Jack offered, "let us know if you need any help finding Matthew Willow."

Beachmen pointed toward Jack and began to speak, but the closing elevator doors cut him off.

"Sweet," Jack said, chuckling out loud as he returned to where Matty was standing.

"The Bad Year Blimp leave?" Matty asked.

"En mass," Jack confirmed. "I hope he doesn't explode in that tiny elevator. He'll end up taking them all out."

"I hope you guys don't expect my crew to clean it up,"

Meeker said as she walked up to the two detectives.

"They may have to seal that elevator permanently," Matty quipped. She turned her attention toward Jack. "How did you know about Beachmen being friends with Derek Willow?"

"I didn't," Jack confessed, "it was just a calculated shot in the dark. I figured that their private meeting with him after we had met was an early indication, and now, the fact that Willow was not with them tonight was enough for me to float the suspicion."

Matty noticed the puzzled look on Doctor Meeker's face. "If Willow would've shown up with them tonight, we would have arrested him on suspicion of murder. They were protecting him from going to jail."

"I'd like to have another look at that desk," Jack said as he made his way back between the credenza and the desk. He slowly checked each of the drawers. He opened those that could be opened and checked the lock on the one drawer that he couldn't open. "No sign of anyone attempting a forced entry," he said to the two women standing next to him. He then got down on his hands and knees and looked under the drawers and the desk. He noticed that on the locked drawer, there was a small piece of paper that was sticking out between the drawer face and the drawer box. He carefully reached to pull it out, and that's when it happened. A single drop of the victim's blood fell from her finger and splattered on the back of his hand.

Even before he was able to stand erect, the nauseating pulse in the pit of his stomach told him he was entering the sepia tone world that was somewhere between life and death.

He then watched as the witch entered the room. She was as black as night and born from the shadow world. Jack did not believe she could have been more grotesque than when he had seen her at Justin Willow's home, but the seeping sores had grown larger and more distinct.

Following closely behind was the huge charcoal gray mutant carrying Sheila over his right shoulder. As the witch approached the desk, she flung her hand first to the right and then to the left. Every item that was occupying the top of Derek Willow's desk flew in one of two directions. When she finished clearing the top of the desk, she raised her unholy fingers and pointed one of the claws toward the desk. She then moved aside and allowed the huge hulk to deposit the young woman.

Sheila's body hit the desk like a side of beef, a loud grunt escaping her open mouth. *Christ*, Jack thought, *the poor woman is still alive, although in a semi-conscious state.* The huge charcoal gray hulk stepped aside, allowing the witch access to the body. She stepped forward, raising the cruel letter opener that seemed to glimmer in her slim hand.

"Ambo te ignosce me," Sheila begged weakly.

Jack translated the Latin instantaneously, "please forgive me." For the first time, Jack understood that Sheila was a witch. *She probably was a plant in Willow's office, Jack concluded and worked for the Black Witch all along. So, she not only betrayed Derek Willow but, at the same time, betrayed the Black Witch.*

"There is no forgiveness," the witch answered in Latin, "for those who betray me." The knife stabbed downward and left young Sheila quivering on the desktop. As the Black Witch thrust downward, again and again, the blade became a crimson stinger transferring the sorcerers hate into the frail body of the young woman. When she had stabbed the woman for the tenth time, she calmly handed the blade to her companion. The titan coolly wiped the blade on his sleeve and slipped it into his coat pocket.

Jack watched in amazement as the woman walked around the desk and, with a single motion of her hand, flung open the top drawer of Derek Willow's desk. She flicked her wrist, and the letter opener belonging to Willow jumped into her hand. He then watched in horror as she carefully slid the blade into one of the open wounds covering it in Sheila's blood. He noticed that there was enough blood on her hands to coat the handle of the blade.

The final part of the vision sent massive chills through Jack's spine. The witch seemed to turn to face Jack. Then staring at him, she held the blade out at arm's length, "Let those who have transgressed against me in the past and might contravene my will in the future," she chanted while dropping the blade to the ground, "die as vermin under my feet."

The place where the blood had hit the back of Jack's hand began to burn like fire. Instinctively he pulled his hand back toward his chest.

"Dammit Jack," Doctor Meeker said as she attempted to decontaminate his hand, "hold still you baby. I've got to make sure you're all right."

"It's just a small drop," Jack said as he retrieved his hand from her." Whatever she had used on his hand smelled grossly medicinal.

"Jason," Dr. Meeker called out while searching the

room.

A man across the room raised his hand in acknowledgment.

"Jason," she continued, "make sure we get a complete blood work-up on the victim. I mean everything!"

She turned to Matty, "When you leave here, take Jack over to Charity Hospital. Doctor Benson will be waiting there to draw a complete blood panel on Jack. Do not let Jack stop for a hotdog on the way."

"You got it," Matty answered with a smirk on her face.

Meeker took hold of his hand for a second time and pulled it closer to examine it again. "At least you don't have any cuts or abrasions on the hand," she said with satisfaction. "Now, go!"

Matty pushed Jack towards the door, "You know she's going to have you drawing blood for the next six months."

"I know," he answered quite satisfied that Meeker cared so much for him. "Damn Vampire," he quipped as they entered the elevator.

# Chapter Thirteen

Jack and Matty sat at Jack's kitchen table, each with a large cup of coffee and a handful of the photographs copied the night before. They had spent the morning with Captain Steele explaining in detail the incident with Beachmen and Salton. While Steele had not completely agreed with the manner that they had handled the two, he did conclude that Jack and Matty were correct. When leaving his office, he reminded them one more time that, at some point, he would no longer be able to shield them from Special Agent Salton.

As they were leaving the station, the photo lab technician handed them a large Manila envelope and explained that they had finished the copy work earlier than expected. With envelope in hand, the two grabbed a couple of large coffees and made a beeline for Jack's house.

Jack held up the photograph of Justin's trophy sailfish again. "I'm simply amazed," he said, squinting at the picture, "that the woman in question is either blurred or fuzzy in every one of these pictures."

"It makes identifying her," Matty said, sipping on her

coffee, "almost impossible."

"Even blurred as they are," Jack offered, "you can tell she is an attractive woman."

"Yeah, that'll help narrow the search," Matty said, "we need a better picture, or this is a dead end."

"Wait a minute," Jack said as he sprung out of his chair and headed toward the living room. Shortly he came back, waving another Manila envelope at Matty. "We almost forgot about the photocopies that were supplied by Sheila," Jack said as he handed Matty the envelope.

Matty took several pages out of the envelope and began studying the first one. "Believe it or not, Jack," she said, handing him the first copy," these are a lot better."

Jack studied the first picture. It was the one of Derek Willow and his three sons flanking the sultry woman. Jack leaned over toward the kitchen counter, opened the drawer, and fished out a large magnifying glass. With magnifying glass in hand, he began to take a closer look. *Christ*, Jack thought to himself, *It's her. It's definitely the witch.*

"Anything?" Matty asked, still fishing through some of the other photographs.

"She's much clearer. I can make out some of the facial features," Jack said, handing both the photograph and the magnifying glass to her.

Matty eyed the photograph with a critical squint, "You're right, much better." Matty looked through the magnifying glass a second time. Her usually expressive face changed and became almost somber, "Jack, this woman looks awful familiar."

"I thought so too," Jack lied, keeping the fact that he knew she was a witch to himself, "if she had anything to do with Derek Willow and the Krew of Comus, I'm sure we've seen her face dozens of times on the society page."

"Possibly," Matty mused, "we can go through the newspaper archives and see if her face and a name show up together."

"That sounds good," Jack said, picking up the second photocopy, "we should start with the newspapers during the last two Mardi Gras seasons."

Matty placed the photocopy and magnifying glass on the table as she stood. "I'm going to jump on this right away," she said, picking up her coffee and her keys, "why don't you go catch up with Doctor Meeker? I'm sure if nothing else, she'll want another blood sample from you."

"Perfect," Jack sneered as he tossed the photocopy in his hand onto the pile, "why don't I just have her put in a keg tap? It would make things a lot easier."

"Sounds great," Matty said, making her way through the house. "Speaking of a keg, I'll meet you around five at Tommy's."

"Yeah, whatever," Jack sulked as he studied the back of his hand with the magnifying glass. He put the glass down and began rummaging through the photographs one more time. He picked up the magnifying glass and restudied the picture. When he was satisfied that there was nothing else to be learned from the photo, he tossed it back on the stack and magnified the back of his hand one more time.

"That's the wrong side of your hand," Aisling said in a wonderfully low voice, soft and clear, "if you're going to start a career in palm reading."

Startled, Jack looked to the rear screen door of the kitchen, "Aisling, how wonderful."

"May I come in," she asked while glancing at his eyes for any sign of objection.

"Of course, you can," Jack said, springing from his chair and holding the door open. "What brings you to sin city?" Jack guided her to the chair that Matty had occupied, not thirty minutes ago.

"I had a batch of supplies to deliver to Clarice's pharmacy. When I finished, I stopped by your police station, and they told me you weren't in. So, I took one more stab at it and came by here."

"Well, I'm glad you did," he said, taking his seat, "Can I get you anything to drink?"

"You're on city water, aren't you?"

"Of course," he said a little baffled.

"Then I'm fine, thank you." She answered. "How is your work coming along?"

"Baffling as ever," he sighed. "I did have a run-in with the witch again last night."

"I'm sorry to hear that, Jack," her faint smile had a touch of sadness. "That means someone else has died."

"Yes, a young girl this time."

"Was there a tarot card?" she asked.

"Yes, the ten of swords."

Her expression turned to deep sorrow, "A betrayal then."

"We believe so."

"Was she a witch?" Aisling asked.

"How would I tell that?"

Aisling shifted in her chair as she moved closer to Jack. "Most people cannot tell, at least not until it's too late, but I believe you may be one of the few who could." Aisling reached out to Jack with her right hand, "Let me have your hand."

Slowly Jack reached out and laid his hand into hers. Aisling then overlaid his hand with her left. At that moment, something intense flared through Jack's body. There was an instant tingling in the pit of his stomach not at all like the nauseating feeling he got when transporting into the sepia tone world, but a warm, tender feeling as if some private memory of his childhood flashed into his mind in the form of a vivid recollection.

Jack let out a breath he hadn't even realized he was holding as his eyes rose to her face. There was a slight hint of an aura around her angelic face. Its intensity was far less than he had seen at Justin Willow's home the night they were introduced to the black witch, and anytime he tried to stare at it, the aura would simply disperse.

As Aisling looked up to meet his eyes, her own breath escaped soft and moist, an innocent sound, a thing of faultless perfection.

He noticed that her eyes were no longer the apple green he had come to know but shone like a matched pair of priceless emeralds.

As she pulled her hands away, a slight blush, like a shadow fled across her cheeks, "Of course, Jack, as you know," she said, diverting her eyes, "the Dark Witch will project a much more sinister apparition."

"You're telling me she won't be someone I'd want to ask out on a date," he said, attempting to ease his embarrassment as well as hers.

"Let's hope not," Aisling laughed. Suddenly her demeanor changed, "Jack, you must be extremely careful. Just as you can discover her true identity she can, in turn, see yours and trust me, she will not hesitate to kill you."

"So, the best course of action," Jack stated, "would be to avoid any physical contact with her."

"Yes, I believe so," Aisling nodded, "even an accidental contact could make her aware of who and what you are."

Jack mused over Aisling's warning, already trying to figure out the details. He did not doubt that he would eventually come face-to-face with this woman and would have to have a plan already in place when that happened.

"That's quite a large frown," Aisling said, trying to change his demeanor, "I think I know of a way to cheer you up."

"I'm all ears," Jack said, forcing a smile.

"I believe this is your city," Aisling said, "and I believe it's your turn to buy dinner."

Even with everything happening around him, he was powerless to resist. "That sounds great," he said, checking his watch, "I have a 5 PM meeting that should last no more than an hour and a half. So, if you would like to stay here, I'll be back by seven."

"That's not necessary," she said, standing, "I thought I had a good chance of bewitching you into dinner, so I told the girls at the pharmacy I would be using Clarice's home for the night."

"A woman who makes plans; I like that," Jack said as he also stood, "I'll walk you to your car."

"It's out front," she pointed.

"This way then," he said as he led the way through the house.

Aisling followed close behind as Jack made his way toward the front door. When they reached his bedroom, she stopped. "Jack," she said, studying the top of his dresser, "this Origami is beautiful. Did a secret admirer make it for you?"

"Hardly," he chuckled, "my partner, Matty makes them. She's really quite good."

"Good doesn't describe it," Aisling said, studying several

the pieces, "the angles are clean and so precise, did she study the art professionally?"

"The way I understand it," she taught herself while convalescing from an accident. If you like, you may have anyone you wish."

"You honor me with your offer, but at the same time, I'm a little disappointed that you would be willing to give one up."

"She makes them all the time," he said, moving again toward the front of the house, "I doubt she'd miss one or even care."

Aisling caught up with him at the front door, "You miss the point, Jack," she said, trying to hide her disappointment, "Matty made them for you. To just give one away wouldn't be right."

"You're right," he said thoughtfully, "I never considered it that way."

Aisling brushed a gentle kiss across his cheek, "See you at seven."

Jack watched her as she moved toward her car. Suddenly, a thought crossed his mind. "Aisling, why is it," he asked, trying to pull all the pieces together, "that you just kissed my cheek, and we didn't have the same experience we had in the kitchen?"

A huge smile suddenly appeared on her face. "You're working on a Ph.D. in psychology, and you don't know?"

she said, shooting him a conspiratorial wink, "I'll see you at seven."

# Chapter Fourteen

Matty was already seated at their usual table when Jack entered Tommy's. He had no sooner sat down when two cold beers appeared in front of him. Matty had two in front of her also; one was already empty.

"Any luck with the newspapers?"

Matty shook her head, "There's a lot of shit to go through," she sighed, "I didn't know so many people could have such high opinions about themselves.

"Sorry I'm a little late," Jack said with a devilish grin, "I had to shake Petersen. For some reason, he was following me."

"Interesting," Matty said, "I had Beachmen trying to tail me."

Jack picked up a beer and took a long pull, "How'd you lose him?"

"It wasn't hard. I just started jogging."

Jack spit beer down his shirt and onto the table. "What an ingenious way to lose a tail," Jack laughed, wiping his face with a bar napkin.

"Yeah," Matty said, "guaranteed to work on anyone 75 pounds overweight. How did you lose Petersen?"

"Oh, I just had a few of the girls in the Quarter keeping him busy while I ducked out."

"Well, where's my chair?" Doctor Meeker asked as she walked up to the table.

Jack jumped up and got the third chair. He waited until she was comfortably seated before retaking his chair. He shot Matty an inquisitive look.

"Oh yeah," Matty blushed, "I forgot to mention that Doctor Meeker would be joining us."

"Well, Doctor," Jack started to say before Meeker cut him off.

"Your blood work is fine," Meeker said as she dug through her briefcase. "I have some very interesting information on Sheila's autopsy."

Jack caught Tommy's eye and pointed toward Meeker. The bartender nodded his understanding and went back to work. "Well, don't keep us in suspense," Jack said with a mock tone of irritation.

In her usual, professional manner, Meeker went right to the heart of the matter. "The knife we found at the murder scene is not the murder weapon."

"I know I don't have to ask because you're going to tell us," Matty sighed, "but how do you know?"

Two more beers and a generous pour of white wine appeared on the table. "We studied each of the entry wounds and matched them against the letter opener," Meeker said, looking over her shoulder to make sure no one could hear them. "While the stab wounds were almost a perfect match, there were inconsistencies between the blade that was used and Derek Willow's letter opener."

"How so?" Matty asked while making a circular motion with a hand to prompt Doctor Meeker to just continue.

"As you know," Meeker continued ignoring Matty's rudeness, "Derek Willow's blade was damaged when he apparently tried to jimmy open a lock. A closer inspection of the blade showed that not only was it bent, but as we expected, the edge had been chipped and marred." Meeker took a small sip of her wine, causing her to wrinkle her nose. "On four of the puncture wounds, the blade struck the bones in her rib cage. The resulting scoring on the bones was smooth and clean."

"Meaning?" Jack asked, knowing it was his turn to keep Meeker going.

"Meaning," Meeker said, leaning closer to the others, "the damage to Willow's letter opener would've caused a different scoring on the bone."

"So," Jack stated as he placed his empty beer bottle back on the table, "right church; wrong pew."

"What?" Meeker asked.

"A Krew of Comus letter opener," Jack sighed, "was used to murder the girl, but it wasn't Derek Willow's opener."

"That's what I just said," Meeker protested.

"Well," Matty mused, "I'm pretty sure they didn't throw these things off a carnival float."

"I agree," Jack said, starting on his next beer, "I'm guessing they were handed out to a select group of people."

"Like Derek Willow and our mystery woman?" Matty offered.

"Mystery woman?" Meeker asked.

"There seems to be," Jack said, hesitating looking for the right word, "a woman who seems to be a common denominator between Derek Willow and his two dead sons."

"A woman we can't seem to identify," Matty added.

"The woman in the photos!" Meeker exclaimed.

"One and the same," Jack said, nodding, "now if we can just put a name with the face, we might have our first real lead."

"Yeah," Matty scowled, "I only have about eight more months of newspapers to go through."

Jack looked at his watch, took a long pull on his beer, and stood. "I've got to run ladies."

"Hot date?" Meeker asked. "I'm jealous!"

Jack leaned toward Meeker's forehead; his kiss was

surprisingly gentle, "if that were only the truth."

"It could be," Meeker sighed as she watched Jack walk out of the bar.

\*\*\*\*

In 1913 a small grocery store at the corner of Napoleon Avenue and Dryades was purchased by Frank Manale. With the proper renovation, Frank soon opened Manale's restaurant. From day one, Manale's restaurant was a family affair that would be a lasting part of their success. By 1969 Pascal's Manale was renowned for its signature dish, barbecue shrimp, its raw oyster bar, and some of the finest Italian cuisines in the city.

Jack and Aisling sat at a small table for two sharing a dozen raw oysters on the half shell. "That bar is absolutely gorgeous," Aisling said, admiring it from afar.

"That bar was installed in 1913 by the Dixie Brewing Company," Jack said, eyeing another oyster. "The company installed the bar negotiating that Dixie beer would be the exclusive beer sold in the restaurant."

"I noticed the large Dixie beer sign above the door when we entered," she said.

"It's no longer the exclusive brand sold here anymore, but it makes for a great tidbit of color and adds to the history of the restaurant."

"If there was one thing," Aisling said, pointing to the oysters, "that could entice me away from my farm, this would be it."

"What about me?" Jack asked, wiping a spot of cocktail sauce from his lip. "Aren't I enticing enough?"

"No," she answered, moving another oyster to her plate.

"No?"

"No," Aisling reaffirmed as she brought the half-shell up to her mouth, "but I'll admit, you are moving up on the list."

He grinned mischievously, "Then there's still a chance."

"Un petit."

"A small chance is better than none," he said.

"Que," she said, then changed the subject, "how are you doing with identifying the black lady?"

"Very slow," he admitted. "We have several pictures of her, but in every case, the photo is so blurred we can't make a positive ID.

"They're all blurred," Aisling asked, eyeing another oyster, "that's a bit strange, don't you think?"

"More like just plain old-fashioned bad luck," Jack sighed.

"Ever think it might be witchcraft?"

"Right," Jack answered, his lips twisting into a cynical smile, "I don't think she would take the time to dance around naked under a full moon for a couple of pictures."

Aisling's face became emotionless. "Why is it that people think that casting a spell takes a black cauldron, a full moon, and a bloody sacrifice to complete."

Jack's eyebrows raised inquisitively.

"Alright," Aisling admitted with a huff, "Some do, but very few."

"Okay," Jack smiled, "give me one example of one that doesn't."

Aisling's eyes sparkled brightly at the challenge. She looked down at the plate of oysters between them, "How many oysters are left on the plate?"

"Just one."

Aisling reached over and took Jack's hand in hers, "Do you want it?"

"I wouldn't mind having it," He admitted.

"Well then," she said as she squeezed his hand, "it's yours if you can take it, but I think you're going to prepare it with a healthy portion of cocktail sauce and gently place it in my mouth."

"Fat chance," he said as he speared it with his fork, dunked it into the sauce and brought it up to his mouth only to then slowly turn the fork toward Aisling and slide the tasty morsel into her mouth. "That's not right," he said as he watched her chew the oyster with a huge gleam of satisfaction.

Jack motioned to their waiter, "Another dozen, please," he said, pointing to the empty tray. "Can you do that all the time?"

"Not always," she admitted, "that was just the power of

persuasion and my overwhelming desire for that last oyster."

"With a slight mystical spin on it," Jack said while making a whirling motion with his hands.

"Maybe," she confessed with a wink.

Seeing the amusement in her eyes, he laughed. He couldn't remember the last time he had laughed so freely.

They both pushed back from the center of the table as the fresh plate of oysters on the half-shell were placed in the middle of them.

"So, you think the photos are bewitched?"

"Quite possibly," she answered, motioning for him to take the first oyster, "it would be easy enough to tell."

If that's the case," Jack asked slowly, "is there anything you could do about it?"

"I would first have to see the photos," she cautioned, "but more than likely, I could do something."

"Well then," Jack offered, "let's finish off this dozen and head back to my house for a digestif and a little skullduggery."

# Chapter Fifteen

In his current position, Matthew Willow looked more like a raggedy scarecrow than a human being. Both arms had been stretched out at a 90° angle from his body and fastened to a wooden beam behind his back. Secured as he was, his arms took all of his weight; therefore, his body slumped forward, and his head lay pointing downward on his chest. It was the narrowing of his air passage that caused his breathing to be choppy and uneven, causing loud snoring sounds.

Unconsciously trying to hold back a snort, his breath caught in his throat, causing him to cough and gag. His head shot up as if on a lever, smacking the beam behind him. Grimacing, he squeezed his eyes shut and coughed several times more. He attempted to slowly open his eyes. His vision was somewhat blurred, but he could tell that he was no longer in the root cellar but was in what appeared to be a large dining room.

There was no furniture anywhere to be seen in the room. The floor was aged and weathered. On several of the walls, paint and plaster had either peeled or pulled away to the point where the wooden lath strips were exposed. Light filtered into the room through four large floor to ceiling windows. Each window was covered with equally long sheer curtains that were similarly aged and deteriorating.

The last thing his waterlogged brain could remember was falling asleep in the root cellar. His leaving the cellar and how he had gotten into his current predicament was a complete blank. He slowly rolled his head between his shoulders to ease the tension.

"Good, I see you're finally awake."

The voice came from someone standing behind him. Although he could not see who was speaking, he was sure that it was a young woman in her early teens. "Where am I?" Matthew asked. "And who the fuck are you?" As the words slipped past his lips, he immediately regretted striking out at his yet unseen abductor, remembering that his escape and evasion instructor had warned them against alienating anyone that was holding them captive. "I'm sorry for the harsh words," Matthew said as an apology, "I haven't been sleeping well lately."

"I can imagine," she said, inching her way closer, "I hate it when I don't get to sleep in my own bed."

"I'd settle for a mattress," Matthew said frankly, "that damp hard floor in the root cellar is tough on my back."

The sound of her heels striking the floor told him she would soon be in full view. The first thing Matthew noticed when she entered his view was that she was not a young teen but a woman of some thirty years. She wore a navy-blue jumper with calf-high black boots. She was very slender, reedlike in appearance. Her features were dainty, her wrists small and delicate. Her hair was cut into a pageboy, jet black in color, and with a shine like polished glass.

"It's funny you should mention the root cellar," she said.

There was a lethal calmness in her eyes as if guarding a terrible secret. An oddly primitive warning began shrieking in Matthews's head as the misgivings of his situation increased by the second.

"I have here," the woman sadistically chuckled, as she pulled a nine-tail whip from behind her back, "something that will certainly make you forget about the damp hard old floor."

Matthew's first reaction was utter fear at the possibility of this whip tearing into his flesh; then, he somewhat relaxed, rationalizing that this frail young woman could not cause any real insurmountable damage. It was then that he heard the sound of large leather boots hitting the floor. With each step, the weathered floor cried out with creaks and groans under the punishment of the heavy leather soles.

Matthew felt needle-like pricks spreading through his stomach as the large man came into view. He was tall, rawboned, his shoulders seemed to be a yard wide and chiseled from solid granite. His legs were firm as tree trunks, and his pants were jampacked with muscles. His shark-like eyes were set deep into the skull separated by a broken, misshapen nose. He also sported a 5 o'clock shadow that was now into overtime. All of this, Matthew thought, made for an ingenuously appalling face.

Matthew watched in horror as the petite woman handed the whip to the ogre. "Remember now," she almost cooed to the giant, "the Misses does not want you to kill him." The woman turned her attention back to Matthew. "I'll be back in a little while," she said, sounding like a small child, "my Misses wants to send your father a few photographs."

"There's no need for this," Matthew pleaded, "my father will pay any ransom without delay."

The young woman moved forward, close enough for Matthew to smell her honeysuckle fragranced perfume. "This is not about a ransom," she said flatly, "this is about humiliation and revenge." She then turned and walked past the giant, gently touching his massive arm, "Remember, you are not to kill him."

The beast nodded his understanding shaking the whip to loosen the nine straps.

Matthew let out a whimper understanding that the hulk was well-versed in the handling of the whip. He clutched his buttocks tightly together, preparing for the strike. Matthew tried to hold a pleasant image in his mind, but the first strike of the whip replaced it with utter despair. It was a full second before the lash drove screams from his throat, screams he didn't know he could make. Tears streamed down his cheeks, matched only by the warm urine running down his leg.

\*\*\*\*

As instructed, Jack sat at the kitchen table with a single stack of photographs directly in front of him. Aisling stood behind him with her hands resting gently on his shoulders.

She had made her instructions clear. She would lean over Jack cupping her hand over the area that Jack wanted to be sharpened in the photo. As soon as she removed her hand, Jack was to study the area that had hopefully been clarified. She had made it clear that she was unsure of how much time Jack would have to study the results.

"Are you ready?" She asked.

"Yes." He nodded.

Aisling leaned over Jack's right shoulder and cupped her hand over the woman's face. Her breath was warm and moist against his face making it very difficult for him to focus on the task in front of him. She mumbled an incoherent chant and then quickly removed her hand.

Jack found himself staring at a crystal-clear image of the woman. He noticed that there was both a delicacy and strength in this woman. Her face was encapsulated by a wealth of long dark hair. Even though her hair was blown into disarray from being on the fishing boat, there was no other way to describe her than utterly beautiful.

Jack watched the image slowly return to a blur. "Can you do it again to the same photograph?" he asked.

"I'm not sure," Aisling said. "Let's give it a try and see."

Once again, she cupped her hand over the woman's face and mumbled her chant. Jack was ready when she removed her hand. "No change," he said disappointedly.

"Okay then," Aisling sighed, "it looks like you get one chance per picture then."

After going through several photos, Jack leaned back in the chair. Aisling, by not moving, now allowed Jack's head to rest between her breasts. Again, she placed one hand on each of his shoulders, softly massaging his neck.

"Well, what do you think?" Aisling asked, continuing to rub his neck.

Jack moved his neck from side to side in an attempt to reduce the stress that had been building. "I could definitely pick her out in a lineup," he assured Aisling, "the only problem being this woman would never end up in a lineup."

"Then," Aisling said, thinking out loud, "without a name, you're not much closer to finding out who she is."

"Not unless by some odd chance, I was able to run into her on the street." He sighed, letting out a deep breath and some of the tension.

"Would her initials help you?"

"It would be a huge leap from where we are right now," he confirmed.

"Then go back to the picture of the two of them wearing formal ball attire."

Jack leaned forward and started shuffling through the photographs, "Which one was that?"

Aisling leaned forward, pushing different photos out of the way. "There that one," she said, pointing to the picture.

Jack pulled out the pile and put it on top. It was a picture of Derek Willow and the woman both dressed in formal ballroom attire. The picture was made to represent a reconstruction of a formal ball during the Civil War. It was printed in the reddish-brown sepia tone that existed at that time of the Civil War.

Derek Willow was dressed as a Confederate general to include sash, sword, and feather plume in his hat. The woman was dressed in the most exquisite Victorian ball gown for the time. In Jack's mind, her attire was entirely authentic. As part of the charade, both of them stood fairly stiff. Jack remembered that this was necessary back in the eighteen hundreds to get a clear photograph. Because the lenses took so long to copy the image, a person being photographed must stand completely still so that their image would not come out shaky or blurred. This often gave those being photographed a kind of stiff appearance.

He was just about to ask Aisling about the initials when he spotted them. In the photograph, Willow was standing on the right, his left arm entwined with her right. In her left hand, she held a long lace handkerchief. There at the bottom of the handkerchief, even though it was blurred, Jack could see the monogram.

"I can't make it out," Jack said.

"Okay," Aisling said as she leaned over Jack's right shoulder, "let's try this again. I'm hoping that since the monogram is so far from her face and my hand didn't cover it, it wasn't affected by my last enchantment." She leaned over the picture, cupping her hand directly over the monogram, "Get ready, Jack," she cautioned, "it may only be clear for a split second."

"Ready," he confirmed.

As before, she cast the spell then quickly removed her hand. As she feared, the clarity only lasted for a few seconds. "Well," she asked, afraid that it had been too short of a period for Jack to catch the initials.

Jack sat there, not blinking, not moving. Finally, he closed his eyes and drew a deep breath, "M K M," he whispered, "it was M K M."

Aisling took one step forward, stopped, and inhaled a deep breath. "M K M," she repeated as she took a seat in the chair facing Jack, "are you sure about that?"

"Quite sure," he said with conviction. "Do the initials mean anything to you?"

Aisling suddenly paled. Nervously she moistened her dry lips, "Yes," she answered weakly, "the initials stand for Morgana Mista Kerr."

"You know her?"

Aisling shook her head, weakly, "I know of her, but I've never met her."

Jack gathered up all the photographs on the table and neatly placed them back in the Manila envelope. He then placed the envelope in the cupboard over the stove. While standing there, he placed a teakettle on the burner then turned it on. "If I remember right," he said, "you take lemon with your tea."

"Yes, that's correct," she said.

Aisling watched as Jack pulled a Mason jar from the

cupboard. It had a paper label that was marked simply 'Tea.'

The warmth of Aisling's smile echoed in her voice. "Where did you get that?"

"Clarice gave it to me," he answered as he scooped out the appropriate amount of tea and placed it into the tea strainer. Before placing the strainer into the pot, Jack poured some of the hot water from the kettle into the teapot and cups to warm them. After a few moments when he was satisfied that the teapot and cups were warm, he threw out the water and placed the tea strainer into the teapot and filled it with hot water from the kettle. He then placed the teapot and cups on the table.

After the appropriate steeping time, he removed the strainer, set it aside, and poured the tea for both of them. When he had added enough sugar, he brought the cup to his mouth, "Then tell me what you know of Morgana Mista Kerr."

"Well," Aisling sighed, "it is rumored that her family was from a nomadic tribe in the Great Steppe region of Eastern Europe. The tribe was known for its practice of Witchcraft. At some time in their history, it was believed that the tribe was destroyed, and its people scattered in an attempt to eradicate their magical beliefs. The few that survived the massacre fled Eastern Europe to settle in Belgium, France, and England. As my family did, some of them ended up coming to the United States."

"And today?" Jack prodded.

Aisling took another sip of her tea, gathering her

thoughts. "Morgana's family showed up here in the South sometime in the early eighteen hundreds."

"By in the South," Jack asked, "you mean New Orleans?"

"I'm not sure," Aisling admitted. "I do know that Morgana is the leader of one of the most private and secretive covens in New Orleans."

Jack placed his teacup on the table, "You forgot to mention that her coven practices black magic."

"Well," Aisling smiled weakly, "you and I have personal experience in the fact that she does." Her green eyes pierced the distance between them, capturing his, holding them as if in a trance. "Jack, when you finally confront her," she said sternly, "you will have to kill her quickly. There will be no second chance if you don't." Aisling held out her cup and allowed Jack to fill it. "You pour a nice cup of tea, Jack."

# Chapter Sixteen

Jack scurried down the hall of the precinct, barely holding on to the papers under his arm. Suddenly Matty appeared as she jetted out from an adjoining hallway.

"Any idea," Jack asked while still juggling his paperwork, "what this is all about?"

"Don't know," Matty answered as she helped Jack gain control of the papers, "but the captain sounds pissed."

"He always sounds pissed," Jack whispered as the two entered the meeting room.

Together they stopped at the door surveying those already in attendance at the meeting. It was the usual crowd of late, including Special Agent Salton flanked by her two assistants. Unfortunately, Detective Beachmen and Petersen were also seated. For some reason, it looked to Jack as if Beachmen had swallowed the canary, but in Beachmen's case, it looked like he'd also swallowed the cage.

He and Matty moved around the table and took their

seats. Jack locked eyes with Beachmen and nodded, "Hey Beachmen," Jack said with a huge smile of his own, "you losing weight?"

"No," Beachmen snarled.

"Didn't think so," Jack said nonchalantly as he studied the papers in front of him.

"Screw you, Kohl."

"You'll have to get in line," Jack smirked.

"Alright, Gentlemen and Ladies," Captain Steele said, addressing the group, "normally at this time I would ask for an update on each of your assignments, but today I'll start with a notification that our security has been breached."

"How so, Captain?" Matty asked.

"The murder weapon from the Justin Willow case has gone missing from the evidence locker." Captain Steel's eyes raked the room, waiting for someone to speak up. When no one volunteered any suggestions, Steele spoke again, "does anyone in this room have any knowledge of where that dagger might have disappeared to?"

Jack looked over at Matty and rolled his eyes as if to say, 'here we go.'

It was Matty who spoke up first, "Jack and I were the ones who signed it over to the evidence room. We've had no cause to go back and pull it out."

"That's what the log says," Steel confirmed, "but the fact is the blade is missing."

"Jack probably hocked it," Beachmen offered.

Jack leaned back in his chair, "All right, I admit it. I need the money to enroll Beachmen in a Dale Carnegie class."

"Asshole," Beachmen hissed.

"You should have saved your money, Jack," Petersen chuckled.

Beachmen looked at his partner with disbelief, "Watch yourself," Beachmen warned half-seriously.

"I know," Jack said to Petersen, "I should just get him that free pamphlet *I'm okay, you're still an asshole.*"

"Captain!" Beachmen pleaded.

"Alright, that's enough," Steele said, trying to keep a straight face. "I'll need statements from each of you. Before you leave today."

"Captain," Special Agent Salton interjected, "I am really enjoying this little sparring match, but can we move on."

"The second item," Steele said, raising his voice above the clamor, "Derek Willow is getting ready to press charges against us for stealing two boxes of photographs from his office."

Jack's heart slumped at the mention of the photographs. He looked toward Matty, who was able to keep a stone-cold face.

"Isn't Derek Willow the prime suspect in the latest

murder?" Jack asked, "I don't believe he has turned himself in for questioning as of yet."

"Mr. Willow turned himself over to me," Special Agent Salton informed them.

"Well, where is he?" Matty asked.

Salton made a sour face, "He's been cleared of the charges.

"Cleared of the charges?" Matty asked, dumbfounded by the claim. "Jack and I are the Investigating Officers, and this is the first time we are hearing about it. How can that be?"

Salton turned to Steele.

"As of this morning," Steele said, having a hard time clearing his throat, "the Governor of the State has requested that Special Agent Salton now head up the investigation. The mayor's office and the DA have agreed to hand over the case as requested."

"Really," Jack said as calmly as possible. He noticed that Beachmen's gloat could hardly be contained by the confines of the small meeting room. "Just like that, Derick Willow has all charges against him dropped."

"That's correct," Salton affirmed.

"And now he's suing the police department because someone allegedly stole a box of pictures from him?" Matty asked.

"Two boxes," Salton said, correcting her.

"Wouldn't it make more sense," Jack asked, "that the

young girl who was brutally murdered on Derek Willow's desk may have taken them?"

"Why would she have taken them?" Beachmen asked.

Jack leaned back in his chair, twirling his pencil between his fingers, "I haven't a clue, but the tarot card found on the body suggest the young lady had betrayed or, in simpler terms, indifference to you Detective Beachmen, she stabbed someone in the back."

"Did you bother," Matty asked, "to even check her home?"

"We're looking into that today," Special Agent Salton said as she motioned to one of her assistants to make a note.

Jack leaned forward in his chair, resting his elbows on the table. "You should jump right on that, Beachmen," Jack said, locking eyes with the detective, "finding those two boxes could break this case wide open."

"Who knows," Matty interjected sarcastically, "you may even find the dagger and a confession letter from the murderer."

"And if you're really lucky," Jack added, "you'll find Matthew Willow locked in her closet. By the way, Beachmen, how's that kidnapping case going?" Jack turned his attention toward Captain Steele before Beachmen could answer. "Captain, if this Crayola crap is over, Matty and I have some leads to follow up on."

Before Jack was halfway out of his chair, Salton

motioned for him to remain seated. "Detectives Wilson and Kohl," Salton said, mustering up her best authoritative voice, "the two of you are being removed from this case and will be reassigned as Captain Steele sees appropriate."

"Captain," Matty said, turning to her superior.

Captain Steele glared at Salton with burning, reproachful eyes before turning his attention to Matty. "Detective Wilson," his eyes softening, "you and detective Kohl will be reassigned tomorrow morning. Take the rest of the day off and report to me at 8 AM."

"And Jack," Beachmen said gleefully, "Petersen and I will need a copy of your work so far."

Jack followed Matty out of the conference room. "Not a problem," Jack said through clenched teeth, "I'll leave them somewhere where you're sure to find them."

"Like inside the candy machine," Matty added.

****

Matty and Jack sat on their favorite bench in front of St. Louis Cathedral and Jackson square. It was one of those perfect days in the square when there wasn't a cloud in the sky, and the humidity was low enough that you didn't sweat to death sitting in the shade. The two of them sat there, watching the tourists dart in and out of the many shops lining the outer edge of the square.

Jack's interest lay with the dayshift of the tarot card readers. Most were busy looking into the future of various tourists. They were laying out spreads, speaking to the vacationer about their past, their present, and oh, the possibilities of the future.

Matty sat on the bench, her legs stretched out and crossed in front of her. Her arms were similarly crossed across her chest. "Do you think it's time for us to go put in our applications at Maison Blanche?" she asked.

"Not yet," Jack said while his eyes moved from one card reader to another, "they will have to charge us or open a formal inquiry before they could fire us. It would take months for them to learn they didn't have a case."

"I know that," Matty hissed, "I thought that we should get a jump on employment before the holiday season gets here."

"I know for a fact that Sheila had the two boxes of photos in the trunk of her car." Jack continued to watch the readers as he maintained his thought pattern, "now her car was not at the Bank building, so I'm assuming that she was abducted from her house and taken there."

"And?" Matty prompted.

Jack's attention had narrowed down to a single card reader sitting in front of a folding table. From what he could make out of her sitting there, she was slender, had a pecan-colored tan, and blazing eyes that glowed and pierced his thoughts.

"And," Matty repeated her irritation starting to show.

"And," Jack answered without taking his eyes off the young lady, "I'm betting the boxes are still in the trunk of the car."

"So then," Matty proposed, "they will go to her house, find the car, open the trunk and find the boxes and we will be exonerated and put back on the case."

Jack continued to stare at the young reader. He noticed that her face was white beneath her otherwise tanned body. Her hair was a lush shimmering auburn color. "Not hardly."

"Why not?"

Jack took his eyes off the young woman just long enough to face Matty. "This whole thing about the dagger and the boxes of photos was just a stunt to give them an excuse to kick us off the case." Jack refocused on the young lady. She caught his eye and gently smiled. She raised her right hand off the table and, with just the tips of her fingers, motioned Jack to join her.

Jack turned back to face Matty. "They wanted us off the case, and they got what they asked for. There is no way we are going to get back in."

"That's total bullshit!"

"I agree," said Jack as he got up from the bench, "we'll just have to figure a way to work around it."

Matty sat up, "Where you going?"

Jack pointed toward the young reader, "I think it's time I have a card reading," he said as he walked toward the woman.

"And what am I supposed to do?"

Jack looked back at her as he continued to walk, "The hotdog cart will be open in a few minutes. Grab us a couple of the usual, and I'll be right back."

Jack took the chair opposite the young woman, "Good morning."

The young woman simply nodded and smiled with beautiful candor as she continued to shuffle the deck. Jack watched as the young woman placed the deck in the center of the table, then divided the cards into four separate piles. She then motioned for Jack to reassemble the deck.

Jack gave some thought to how he was going to reassemble the deck. "What type of spread are you going to use," he said as he reconstructed the four piles in front of him.

"There are times when less can be better than more," she offered, "the future is not set in stone but more like the shifting sands of an endless desert. We will be using a single card spread."

"A Touchstone Spread?" Jack asked.

"You know of such things?"

"I'm just learning," Jack said.

Jack watched as the woman made a symbol above the cards with her hand. He thought it may have been the sign of the cross but then figured that it was just his Catholic upbringing coming to the surface. She then, with a swipe of her hand, effortlessly spread the cards across the surface of the table. From Jack's perspective, it looked as if she hadn't even touched the cards.

"Choose."

With his index finger, Jack touched one of the cards, applied pressure, and pulled it away from the deck. The reader then turned the card over as if it were a page in a book.

"The Seven of Pentacles," she announced.

From where Jack was sitting, the card seemed to be upside down.

"At this time, the fruits of your labor are not as significant as you had hoped for," she said flatly, "it is as if you were waiting for something important to happen."

"That is possibly true," Jack admitted, "I had hoped to be farther along on a project that I am working on."

Jack watched as she moistened her dry lips. "Choose."

"How many choices do I get to make?" he asked.

"How many years," she answered thoughtfully, "were you in the service of your church?"

"In the service of my church," Jack said, thinking out loud. Suddenly the meaning came to him. "I was an altar boy for four years."

"Then that is your answer," she smiled, "choose."

Once again, Jack pulled the card away from the deck, and once again, the reader turned the card over.

"The Three of Pentacles."

As the last card was, this card was also upside down to Jack.

"There is a definite lack of teamwork on your project," she said frowning, "it shows that people are working against you. There are some whose intentions are to undermine you along the way. Even harm you if necessary."

"Tell me something I don't know," Jack laughed.

"Often, a tarot reading helps you to see your past," she said, her expression taught and derisive, "and understand your present so that you may face the future more objectively. Remember, the past and the present will help create your tomorrow."

Jack thought about the woman's words for several seconds before nodding his understanding.

"Choose."

Jack placed his finger over the deck moving from one end to the other. After reflecting for several seconds, he placed his index finger down on a card and removed it from the deck.

"The Nine of Wands."

For the first time, Jack felt a little better about the card he had chosen. For the first time, the card was facing upward. *I'm sure that right-side-up is better than upside-down*, he thought to himself.

"The man who represents you in this card looks somewhat weak and injured. Not only do you seem ready to fight another battle, but you also show a strong desire to win. You have a ferocious determination about you that will carry you into one last battle.

The Nine of Wands epitomizes you as someone who has undergone many trials, but through steadfast determination and willpower, you were able to overcome them."

Jack immediately thought of his fight with Daniel Jorgensen. "Will I be victorious as before?"

Across her radiant and exquisite face, a dim flush raced like a fever. "The conclusion is unclear," she said as muscles flicked angrily at her jaw, "as I said before, your past and your present will determine much but, remember there are other players who's past and present will intertwine with yours to produce the final outcome."

"Well, that's clear as mud," he sighed openly.

"Choose."

For the final time, Jack placed his finger on one of the cards and pulled it from the deck. As before, the young reader turned the card over, but to her amazement, the single card was actually two cards stuck together. She separated the two cards, placing both in front of him.

"What just happened?" Jack asked, not taking his eyes away from the two cards in front of him.

"Your selection has produced two cards," she answered as her brows drew together in an agonized expression, "it is very rare that something like this happens."

"So, what do I do," Jack asked, confused, "do I pick over?"

The reader was unable to face Jack's taunting smile; instead, she focused on the two cards lying in front of her. "You have chosen The Tower and The Star card. Both cards are facing upright."

Jack's gaze was drawn to the card marked "The Tower" mainly because he thought the card depicted so much destruction. The card was a picture of a towering spire dominating the top of the mountain. A large lightning bolt was striking the tower setting it on fire. People were jumping out of the windows as fire burst out of every windowpane. Jack had no doubt that in the end, the people would die, and the tower would be totally destroyed.

The young Reader noticed Jack's obsession with the Tower Card. "In order to make way for the new," she said in a calm, clear voice, "the old must be destroyed. Like the transformation of a caterpillar into a butterfly, change is a normal part of life that one has to embrace."

Jack stared into her eyes, "I suppose that with this card, death is not optional."

"No," she said, shaking her head.

"And this card?"

Jack studied the other card now. It showed a naked woman kneeling at the edge of a small pond or lake. He immediately thought of Aisling and her home in the country. The woman was holding two containers of water; one container she was pouring out onto the dry land while the other she poured into the lake.

"The Star brings new hope," The Reader said, "renewed power, and strength, but remember the trauma of the Tower card. There will be great suffering and death."

"Always death," Jack sighed.

The reader reached out to touch Jack's hand but then pulled her hand back as if she were afraid to touch him. "To have this card in your reading means that you will face a terrible life challenge. While you and others around you suffer, it is the strength of your bond that will ultimately bring inner peace to those that survive."

Jack did not miss the phrase "that survives."

The young woman collected the cards and placed them in a leather satchel by her side. As she prepared to leave, she looked at Jack one more time. "The Black Witch," she said in a tone just above a whisper, "is cunning and powerful. You must muster all of your strength to defeat her." The woman stood and began to walk away. "There is no easy path, Jack Kohl," she said while looking over her shoulder, "but there is a path."

Jack stood backing into Matty, who was cradling several foil-wrapped hotdogs in one arm and two drinks in her other. "Shit, Jack," she yelled, trying to hold onto everything, "catch the damn drinks before they fall."

Jack managed to scoop up the two drinks in one hand and steady Matty with the other. By the time he was able to look around, the young reader was no longer in sight.

# Chapter Seventeen

In the 19th century, the history-rich Esplanade Avenue was an important route of trade where many a cargo was carried between the Mississippi River levee and Bayou St. John, which was a direct link to Lake Pontchartrain and points beyond. In 1838, the Old U.S. Mint was built in the first block of Esplanade Avenue and was the only mint in the United States to produce currency for the United States and, during the Civil War and continued to mint coins for the Confederate States of America. It also has the distinction of being the only mint to reopen in the South after the war.

During the 19th century, Esplanade Avenue was home to many of New Orleans millionaires and was dubbed as a "millionaire's row" for the Louisiana Creole section of the city. The mostly whitewashed mansions were usually surrounded by ornate wrought iron fences, beautiful flower gardens, and neatly sculpted lawns.

The wide avenue was lined with large moss-covered oak trees divided by a grassy neutral ground. Where other cities would have called the dividing strips a median, the neutral ground is believed to have received its name from a time when the early Spanish and French settlers could conduct business between sections of the city while standing on "neutral ground."

Detective Jack Kohl now stood on the neutral ground staring up at one of the nineteenth-century mansions still lining the Avenue. The mansion, nicknamed Harvest Home, was constructed in 1844 by Rufus Kerr. It was said that Rufus built the home as a refuge away from the family's sugar cane plantation for his wife. During the sugarcane harvest, Mrs. Kerr would often become ill, which she blamed on the cutting of the cane, the processing of the cane syrup, and the subsequent burning of the spent cane stalks after processing. With New Orleans being only 40 miles from the plantation, it was a perfect place to build. Harvest home was now occupied by Miss Morgana M. Kerr.

Jack looked down at his watch to confirm the time. He had five minutes left before his 10 AM appointment with Ms. Kerr. The five minutes would allow him just enough time to cross the neutral ground and make his way to the front door. In New Orleans, it was improper to be too early and was definitely taboo to be late. At 9:58, Jack raised his right hand to ring the bell. He had forgotten that his right hand was now covered in bandages. To avoid shaking hands with anyone, he had Doctor Meeker wrap his right hand as if he had suffered a somewhat serious injury. It had taken him an enormous amount of time to dodge all of the questions that Dr. Meeker threw his way, but, in the end, she acquiesced. *"I'm just letting you know now, Jack,"* she said, her voice spiking upward as she struggled with the last fastener, *"I consider this a personal favor, and I expect a quid pro quo for the services"* She released his hand back to his control. *"And I'm not talking about a glass of cheap wine at Tommy's,"* she said *using carefully spaced words.* He reached over and with his left hand, pushed the buzzer.

Jack could see a slender figure approaching the door through its large crystal glass insert. The door was opened slowly, and he was now facing a very attractive young woman. She wore a simple black dress with a leather belt around her waist that further defined her slender appearance. A single strand of pearls graced her alabaster colored neck. Her features were dainty, her breasts small but completely proportional to her build. Her black hair was cut into a pageboy and shone like polished onyx.

Jack held up his identification, "Good morning," he said cheerfully, "I'm Detective Jack Kohl from the New Orleans Police Department, and I have a 10 o'clock appointment with Ms. Kerr."

"Yes, Detective Kohl," she said, the warmth of her smile echoed in her voice, "Ms. Kerr is expecting you. This way, please."

"Thank you."

As she moved through the house, she carried herself confidently, most certainly aware of Jack's appreciative glances. For a second, Jack thought that he had passed through some type of time warp that had taken them back to the eighteen hundred. The first thing to catch his attention was the fifteen-foot ceilings and the handcrafted crown molding. The floors were solid wood, polished to a lustrous sheen. The original Venetian plaster had been refurbished and looked as if new. Period floor-to-ceiling windows allowed the sunlight to stream in and burst into multi-colored shards of light as they reflected off the leaded crystal chandeliers. All of the furnishings, which were now antiques, were from circa eighteen hundred.

"You may have a seat here, Detective Kohl," the young lady offered, "Ms. Kerr will be with you shortly."

Jack remained standing as the young woman left the room. He continued to look about in amazement. Finally, he drifted over to the very large brick fireplace. Just above the mantel hung an oil painting whose length was just over four feet. It was an exquisite painting of a southern plantation, most certainly painted during its heyday. Jack smiled inwardly as he noticed that the lower right-hand corner of the painting had been signed and dated by the artist. The date was 1839. His eyes returned to the center of the oil, where he noticed a brass plate had been added to the frame. The engraving on the plate was simple, The Kerr plantation.

"It's been in my family since its construction in 1839."

The first thing Jack noticed was that her high, exotic cheekbones accented her feline features offset by her slightly almond-shaped eyes, the color closer to umber. Jack remembered that her ancestors were nomadic tribesmen from the Great Steppe region of Eastern Europe and wondered if some of her facial features were not inherent by nature. She had magnificent jutting breasts and a slender waist, which flared into agilely rounded hips and long, supple thighs. He envisioned her as a wild gypsy woman dancing around a camp bonfire. He didn't think the vision was that far off. "It's a marvelous painting," he said, his voice charming and smooth like molasses, "do you still own the property?"

"I should say so," her breath escaped softly through her

moist lips, "I could never let my ancestral home go."

Jack continued to study the painting, "Do you still spend time there?"

"Unfortunately, not," a dark shadow came over her face, "in 1862, the damn Yankee Cavalry torched our beloved home. My granddaddy and his men were able to save the home, but not before considerable damage was done to one section of the house."

"I'm sorry to hear that," his voice broke low on the words. "Was there any attempt to refurbish the home?"

The dark cloud still hung over her as a death sentence, "The damage broke my great granddaddy's spirit. He was unable to muster the strength needed to continue. Years later, he died a broken man."

"I'm so sorry…" Jack's words trailed off.

"Not to worry, Detective," she assured him, "I've been doing what I can when I can. One of these days it will be restored to its former glory." Ms. Kerr turned to face Jack, extending her hand. "Morgana Kerr," she said with a genuine smile.

Jack held up his bandaged hand, "I'm sorry I am not able to greet you properly," he said, "but a recent accident precludes me from taking your hand."

"Don't be silly," she said with a wave of her hand, "I was told you have some questions for me regarding Mr. Willow." Ms. Kerr moved toward a set of high backed chairs separated by a small table. She motioned for Jack to be seated in one of them. Once they were both seated, she reached out and plucked a small bell from the table. She rang it briefly and set it back down. "Some refreshments, Detective Kohl?" she asked sweetly. "We have some freshly brewed tea."

"Fresh tea, that would be nice."

The young woman who had shown him in walked into the room and stood next to Ms. Kerr.

"Delia, Mr. Kohl, and I will have a glass of iced tea."

Delia faced Jack, "You take sugar, Detective Kohl?"

"One spoonful, please."

Once the young lady had left the room, Ms. Kerr returned her attention to Jack. "I'm sure your questions are about the terrible incidences that have befallen the Willow family."

"Yes, that's correct," Jack stated flatly, "we are now in the process of asking the help of the family's friends and acquaintances."

"And where do I fall in?" she asked, offering Jack a thin-lipped smile.

"I would have to say," Jack answered truthfully, "you would definitely fall into the category of close friends."

The two stared at each other for several seconds.

"You're in several photographs displayed in the Willows offices," Jack stated. "Costume balls, vacation photographs, and other pictures."

Ms. Kerr finally smiled, "Yes, for a time, we were quite close."

"Oh," Jack interrupted, "I must say that I found you extremely beautiful in the photograph of you and Mr. Willow posing as a general and his lady. In that magnificent gown, you were the picture-perfect southern lady."

"Why, thank you, Mr. Kohl," she said, blushing in earnest, "that is most kind of you. I would dare say you would make a dashing young officer yourself."

The two exchanged smiles as Delia brought in the refreshments and placed them on the table. "Will that be all, Ms. Kerr?"

"Yes, Delia, thank you," Ms. Kerr said graciously, "please make sure that the detective and I are not disturbed."

"Yes, ma'am," Delia said as she left the room.

Jack picked up his glass and took a long sip of the tea. The thought did cross his mind that the drink could have been poisoned, but then Ms. Kerr had no way of knowing how many people knew where Jack was, and if anything were to happen to him, all fingers would be pointed at her.

"As I said," Ms. Kerr continued, "we were very close at one time. Mr. Willow and the boys were quite instrumental in helping me reconstruct the Kerr Plantation."

"Forgive me for asking," Jack prefaced, "in what way were they instrumental in the reconstruction?"

Kerr's eyes flared, "What are you inferring Detective

Kohl?"

"I infer nothing, Ms. Kerr, and I apologize if I was misunderstood. I was merely trying to understand what you meant by instrumental?"

"I see, thank you for clearing that up," she answered once again in control of herself, "I have started a nonprofit foundation; its sole purpose is to restore the plantation. Mr. Willow and his sons donated money of their own as well as encouraging other influential people to do likewise."

"You said that they helped at one time. Did something change?"

A pained look suddenly marred her face. "I've never spoken of this to anyone," she started, "but eventually, Mr. Willow began asking me to repay him for his help."

"Repay?"

"The man started asking me for sexual favors."

"He came on to you then," Jack asked bluntly.

"Yes, he flat out asked me to sleep with him," she said, repressing her rage under the appearance of indifference, "of course, I refused his advances."

"So, at some point," Jack continued, "he continued to pressure you, and you continued to deny his request. What happened then?"

"He and his sons pulled their support from the project."

"Was that it?"

"No," she continued, "other sources of funding began to dry up. I'm sure it was at the bequest of Mr. Willow."

Several emotions flitted across Jack's face, "So the project came to a standstill."

"Yes."

"Ms. Kerr, this is going to be a supposition on my part, but bear with me. The project stalled, and you were devastated because you were so committed to its completion."

"That's correct," she answered.

"So, you went back to him," Jack surmised, "and asked him to do the decent thing and help you finish the project."

"That's right."

"But you see," Jack said flatly, "I have come to know Mr. Derek Willow, and I understand that he is no better than a pig and would never do the decent thing."

She smiled at him, genuinely, "You do know the man, Detective Kohl."

"So, knowing him," Jack proposed, "he wouldn't back off of his offer of sex for money."

"No, you're right." She replied with contempt, "he decided to up the ante."

"How so?"

Ms. Kerr folded her arms across her chest, "For his agreeing to finish the project, I was to sleep not only with him but all of his sons. He said I would make a wonderful sex slave," she spat.

"Sorry for having to ask this," Jack said earnestly, "did you acquiesce.?

"I'll say it this way, Detective," she said the anger growing in her eyes, "the plantation stands unfinished."

"What happened next?"

She sat there deep in thought before she answered. "For months, it gnawed at me; the fact that I was so close to restoring the plantation. For months I agonized over what to do." She looked straight into Jack's eyes, "With the work stopped, the house began to deteriorate once again. Then after a lot of soul-searching, I decided that becoming his sex slave for a few months would be my personal sacrifice to the project."

"So, you took him up on his offer?"

An unwelcome blush crept into her cheeks, "I was going to," she confessed, "I was really going to, but then I read about the murder of Brandon Wilson, which was quickly followed by the murder of Justin."

"And?"

She looked at Jack tears in her eyes, "There was nothing for me to do. It was over. I knew if I went to him, he would've blamed me for the deaths of his two sons and gone out to the property and burned it to the ground with his own hands. I thought it best to just let it go. I hoped the police would solve the murders quickly, and things would get back to normal. Once these terrible events were behind us, I might once again consider asking Derek for his help."

Jack contemplated their conversation up to this point. He decided to press forward. "Ms. Kerr," he said firmly, "let me ask you a direct question. Did you or anyone you know have a hand in the murder of Brandon or Justin Willow?"

"No," she answered solemnly, "I would've gone directly to the police with any information I had about the deaths. Damn the plantation project, murder is murder."

Jack nodded his understanding. "I appreciate your truthfulness in this matter. I'm sure it hasn't been easy for you."

"No, not at all."

Jack took one more sip of his iced tea then stood. "Thank you for your time, Ms. Kerr," he said frankly, "may I call on you again if something else should arise?"

She stood facing him, a vaguely sensuous light passed between them, "You may call me at any time Detective," she said pointing toward the door, "it's not often that you find such a gallant young officer in this city. Your company would be most welcome."

Jack was strangely flattered by her obvious interest in him. He could see why someone like Derek Willow would desire her. "Thank you for your time," he said, exiting her home.

Morgana Kerr stood at the door and watched as Jack

disappeared around the corner. Delia approached and stood silently behind her.

"Delia," she said with a mischievous look plastered on her face, "make sure Detective Kohl meets with an unforeseen accident; a robbery would work nicely."

"Yes, ma'am."

"And Delia," she added, her index finger pointing toward the ceiling marking the afterthought, "make sure that whoever kills him can't be traced back to us. The sooner, the better."

# Chapter Eighteen

Directly behind and below where Kohl was sitting was the Washington Artillery Park and Jackson square. Kohl sat on the city-owned park bench atop the levee separating the mighty Mississippi from the New Orleans French Quarter. From this vantage point, he could see the Mississippi River winding off in both directions to his left and right. Just behind him and to his right was the old Jack Brewery constructed in 1891. As he watched smoke billowing out of the boiler chimneys, he listened very carefully, thinking he could hear the clinking of the amber bottles running down the filling line.

Out of the corner of the eye, he could see Detective Petersen slowly making his way toward the bench. Petersen's clothes hung loosely on his tall, lanky frame. It didn't seem to matter what the man wore; it always seemed two sizes too large. Petersen could trace his Creole heritage all the way back to the seventeen hundreds. He wore a Flatbush haircut trimmed close to the head. He probably hadn't changed his hairstyle since he left the police academy twenty-eight years ago. An interesting fact about Petersen was that he could speak Louisiana Creole, which is a French-based creole language spoken by fewer than 20,000 people across southern Louisiana. More than once, it had come in handy. With Jack's knowledge of French, he figured that if Petersen ever took the time to teach him, he could become more proficient.

Petersen sat down on the bench next to Kohl. "How's your day going, Jack?" he asked as an opener.

"Ah, you know," Jack answered, not taking his eyes off a large grain ship heading down the river, "if you put it in perspective, it's going a lot better than yesterday when that special agent bitch kicked Matty and me off the case."

"Well yeah," Petersen answered while dusting some dirt off his pants leg, "lot worse things could happen."

Jack turned to face Petersen, "Yeah, like what?"

"Well," Petersen shrugged, "you could be sleeping with the bitch."

The two of them threw back their heads and let out a great roar of laughter.

"Or worse yet," Petersen said with a trace of laughter still in his voice, "you could be forced to watch her and Beachmen screw on the steps of City Hall."

"Oh God, no," Jack managed to get out between burst of laughter and almost choking, "stop, no more."

The two sat on the park bench, not speaking until the laughter had died away.

"Petersen," Jack said as he wiped the tears from his eyes, "what the hell are you doing here?"

"I came here to cheer you up."

Jack was still smiling, "Well then, mission accomplished. Now that that's out of the way, what the hell are you doing here?"

Petersen leaned back on the bench and crossed his long legs. "This case is going nowhere fast."

"Sorry to hear it," Jack answered, still watching the grain ship make its way down the river.

"It might move along a little faster," he stated, measuring his word carefully, "if Matty and you were to lend a hand."

Jack turned his head to face Petersen, "Were you not in that meeting yesterday?" he asked, his expression darkening with every word, "Matty and I got our hands slapped yesterday. We could possibly lose our jobs!" Jack pushed himself up on the bench, "Does Beachmen know you're here talking with me?"

"Hell, no," Petersen answered uneasily, "I'd be looking for a new partner by sundown if he found out."

Jack's mouth dropped open. "So, you're out on this limb all by yourself."

"That's about the size of it," Petersen sighed, "between Salton's screaming and Willows threats, we're catching it from all sides."

Jack slid into a more relaxed posture, "So Derek Willow has finally admitted that his son has been kidnapped."

"Yeah," he said, the tension growing on his face, "over the last two days, he's become a raving madman. He's even jumping Salton's shit."

Jack looked upriver at another large ship, making its way downriver. Out of the corner of his eye, he spotted something he hadn't expected to see. Aisling was making her way down the river walk toward him. "I tell you what, Petersen," he said, keeping his eyes on Aisling, "I going to meet up with Matty in about fifteen minutes. I'll talk it over with her. I'll get back in touch with you once we've talked."

Petersen nodded his understanding. "Thanks, Jack," he said as he stood up and put out his hand, "I appreciate it."

Jack stood and took his hand. *Petersen had always been a straight shooter, he thought to himself. If he could help the man, he would.* "Keep this between us, okay?"

"No problem," he answered and started to walk away.

Jack kept his eyes on Aisling as she approached. He estimated the time it would take her to reach him and was glad to see that Petersen would be gone by the time she arrived.

"Oh, Jack."

Jack looked over his shoulder to see Petersen standing just a few feet away. "Yeah?"

"You and Matty watch your backs," he cautioned, "Salton has kind of put a bounty on you guys heads and Beachmen is aiming to collect it. I wouldn't put anything past that woman."

"Thanks for the heads up," Jack said as he waved goodbye."

Jack stood there, waiting for Aisling to catch up with where he was standing. She wore a long flowing skirt and a white blouse. A matching scarf hung loosely around her neck. In her hand, she carried a large straw hat. Her appearance was simple but somehow elegant at the same time. It was easy to imagine her as a subject of a Claude Monet painting. *Woman walking a levee* would be a good title, he thought.

"Good morning, Detective Kohl," she said with her usual bright smile, "I didn't expect to find you here."

Jack was a bit puzzled. "You didn't know I was here?"

Aisling stepped in so close Jack could smell the clean fragrance of her skin. "No," she said, shrugging her shoulders, "I had just made a delivery to Clarice's shop and decided to see if you were at the precinct. When they told me  that they didn't know where you were, I defaulted to my old routine."

"Your old routine involved walking along the levee?"

"Exactly," she beamed, "in the past when I had finished my deliveries I would either have dinner with Clarice or when she wasn't available, I use the time to walk along the river. This is one of the best places in the city."

"You're right about that," Jack agreed, "I often come up here to help clear my head."

"See, another reason for me to like you."

Jack pointed to the bench, "Would you like to sit?"

She leaned back on the bench, relaxing and immediately started soaking up the sun. Jack sat beside her and once again became mesmerized by the river traffic. For several minutes neither of them broke the silence, both wanting to soak up the tranquil scene around them.

Jack, taking a deep breath and let it out slowly. He spoke first. "I went and visited the Black Witch this morning," he said nonchalantly.

"I'd ask how that went," Aisling said, her eyes still closed, "but I noticed when I walked up that your body showed no sign of physical damage and you're still alive so it couldn't have been that bad."

"No, I guess you're right," Jack grinned, "but every time a car passes by me now, I have this terrific urge to start barking and chase it down the street."

She gave him a gentle nudge with her shoulder, "You're daft man," she chuckled.

Leisurely he stretched his long legs out in front of him. "Ms. Kerr had a very convincing story about Derek Willow and the boys."

"What was it?"

Jack stretched his arms over his head, "the usual," he said as a matter of fact. "Money for sex."

"Really," Aisling asked as she adjusted her head to face the sun more directly, "who was getting the money and who was getting the sex?"

"Does it matter?"

"No, not really," she answered, "what did she need the money for?"

"Lifestyle issues," he answered, "Matty is checking up on that part of the story as we speak.

Aisling nudged him again with her shoulder, "See, Jack," she said with a tinge of triumph in her voice, "that's another reason why I've chosen the simple, country life."

"You've chosen the country life," Jack reminded her, "because you're a Hedgewitch and are in your element."

"True," she admitted, "but what came first, the Hedgewitch or the lifestyle?"

"Ahhh," Jack beamed, "now you're playing to my psychology background." Jack leaned forward on the bench, in a controlled voice he asked, "If a Hedgewitch is in her environment with nature, does that mean a criminal psychologist must live in a world of crime?"

Aisling opened her eyes and rose quickly from her seat as if propelled by an explosive force. "Jack don't you even kid about that." she said, taking an abrupt step toward him, "No one can survive in an environment of so much hate."

Jack pushed himself to a standing position directly in front of her. Gently he wrapped his arms around Aisling's waist and drew her toward him. At the same time, she slid her hands inside his jacket until her hand felt the weapon suspended in the holster beneath his arm. Without looking away, she backed out of his grasp and walked a few steps toward the river.

Jack came up from behind her, his hands finally resting on her hips. He immediately noticed that her body was no longer receptive to his advances.

"We truly do live in two separate worlds, don't we, Jack?"

"Not really," he said, stepping closer until there was no space between them, "we live in the same world; it's just that we have different jobs to do."

Aisling reached down and grabbed each of Jack's hands and pulled them around her waist. "Is that all it is, Jack," she asked, leaning her head toward him, "just a job?"

Jack felt the undeniable magnetism building between them, "Well, up until now, it's been a big portion of my life; I mean being a detective and continuing with my education."

She gracefully performed a pirouette until she was once again facing him. This time she didn't bother sliding her hands up into his jacket but instead rested her hands on his shoulders. "That's right," she said, "you now have a master's degree in Criminal Psychology. What next?"

She was standing so close Jack could feel the moisture of her breath on his face; the sweet smell of her that was uniquely Aisling. "I've already been accepted into a program to receive my Ph.D."

Her eyes searched his face, "So what happens to poor Detective Kohl when you become a Doctor of Philosophy?"

"I guess Detective Kohl will join Captain Jack Kohl, US Special Forces somewhere in the annals of my past."

"So, you don't think that your new title will be, Detective Jack Kohl, Ph.D.?"

Jack sighed as he thought about her question. "Throughout my time on the police force, I meant it to be my field research in obtaining a Ph.D.; Now, I honestly don't know. I do love my work."

Aisling leaned in and whispered, her breath hot against his ear, "Do you think you could ever love something or someone else as much or more?"

"I… I," Jack stammered.

Aisling lightly pressed her finger to his lips before he could finish. She kissed him with her eyes then, removing her finger, quickly touched her lips to his. Her kiss was slow, thoughtful, her tongue sending shivers racing through his body. "You don't have to answer that now, Jack," she murmured softly into his ear before gently moving out of their embrace.

Jack's heart was hammering foolishly in his chest as the pit of his stomach began to churn. He watched as Aisling took several steps away before turning back toward him, offering him her hand. "Would you like to take me to dinner?"

****

The place Jack decided to eat was a small family-owned Italian restaurant that smelled of freshly baked bread and inexpensive Chianti. But in Jack's mind, the atmosphere was perfect. The dimly lit dining room was filled with small tables and booths for four. Each table was draped in a white and red checkered tablecloth topped by an empty Chianti bottle, covered in melted wax being used as a candleholder. Usually, mood music was supplied by speakers mounted in the ceiling; The songs a mixture of nameless Italian love songs as well as the occasional song sung by Dean Martin or Jerry Vale, but tonight the guests were being entertained by an older little man not much larger than the accordion he carried.

He would make his way from table to table entertaining couples with pleasant conversation and then would cap off his performance with a love song he had personally chosen for them. The conclusion of the recital always brought applause from several of the surrounding tables as well as a nice tip from the couple being serenaded.

Meals at the restaurant were served family-style, and it only took Aisling and Jack a few seconds to settle on Chicken Parmesan and Spaghetti. Freshly baked garlic bread had been served with their Ensalada Italiana, and a freshly opened bottle of medium-priced Chianti sat between them. The little man walked up to their booth, "Buonasera," he grinned, the smile on his face was warm and sincere as if Jack and Aisling were members of his own family. "How are you doing this evening?" He continued in Italian.

"Bene," Jack answered.

"What a beautiful couple," he said, switching to English, "yes, a beautiful couple."

"Grazie," Aisling blushed.

The little man raised a callused index finger into the air, "A match made by the angels themselves, I think," he grinned at them, "No?"

Aisling again blushed as a broad smile covered Jack's face.

"Tonight," the little man said as he adjusted his accordion, "I have a very special song for such a lovely couple."

He then skillfully began to play the accordion as he sang the Italian love song, Innamorata (Sweetheart).

Jack raised his glass of wine in a toast to Aisling. She, in turn, raised her glass and lightly touched his. The clinking of the glasses was barely audible above the accordion. Suddenly the memory of their kiss upon the levee came back to Jack, leaving a warm sensuous feeling throughout him. *Could he love such a woman as Aisling in conjunction with his job?* He wondered, *or would being in love with her require so much more?*

Gentle clapping around him broke his trance, and Jack instinctively began to clap with everyone else. He looked toward Aisling, focusing on her beautiful smile and moist eyes. As not to embarrass her, Jack turned his attention to the little accordion player, "molto bella," he said in Italian then repeated it in English, "very nice!" Jack palmed a five-dollar bill and shook hands with the performer, "molto bella," he repeated as the man nodded and moved onto the next table.

Aisling leaned across the table and placed her hand on Jacks, "He was wonderful," she said, her mood buoyant, "what a nice treat."

"He was great," Jack exclaimed with intense pleasure, "if the Chicken Parmesan is half as good as he was, we're in for a real treat."

Jack's statement about their meal turned out to be even better than expected. After a wonderful meal, a shared piece of tiramisu and a couple of cappuccinos, Jack and Aisling walked out of the restaurant arm in arm as Jack escorted her back to Clarice's home.

On their walk back to Clarice's home, Jack suddenly became painfully aware of the predicament he was walking into. They would soon be at the door of Clarice's home. He had no question that Aisling would be receptive to a goodnight kiss but, Jack worried that she may ask him to stay for a while. If he entered the home with her, there was a good chance that the two of them would end up in bed together. In Jack's mind, there was something inherently wrong with the idea of the two of them having sex in Clarice's bedroom.

While it was true that Clarice had broken up with him before leaving for Haiti, it didn't change the fact that he still had strong feelings for the Voodoo Queen. After a little soul-searching, Jack understood that he would always have feelings for Clarice, and she would always have a special place in his heart. Defiling those feelings would not happen. He quickly decided that he would have to be strong and say goodnight at the door.

When they turned the last corner onto this street where Clarice lived, Jack noticed that two of the streetlights had been busted out. Seconds after that, two men moved out from between a pair of houses and began following them.

Aisling stiffened on his arm. "Jack," Aisling said in a fearful whisper, "I think we're being followed."

Jack had felt it also and released his grip on her arm, "Keep walking," he commanded in a low tone. Before she could reply, he gently pushed her forward and turned to face the two men, "Hey guys," Jack said as he approached the two head-on.

Before he could finish his sentence, the man closest to him lunged at him, knife in hand. Two thoughts quickly passed through Jack's mind as he grabbed the assailant's wrist and pulled the knife hand and the attacker to his right. The first was that the men were amateurs and not professional assassins; the second thought was that the other attacker was just now pulling a small-caliber pistol out of his pocket.

As the first attacker, thrown off-balance by Jack's counterattack, moved past him, Jack raised his left arm and smashed his elbow into the man's ear. The force of the man moving in one direction, combined with Jack's elbow moving in the opposite direction, caused a devastating blow to the right side of the man's head.

As soon as Jack felt the man loosen his grip, he twisted the knife out of his hand and held the disoriented attacker in front of him. Almost as if on cue, the second man fired his weapon in a trio of blast. The pop pop pop from the small-caliber weapon was matched by the sudden jerking of the first assailant's body as each round impacted his chest. Jack threw the limp man forward into the second attacker disrupting his aim. Instantaneously Jack was upon him, forcing his gun hand downward and away. A fourth shot rang out, the bullet chipping the pavement at their feet.

The second attacker, confused, took two steps backward, trying to figure out what had just happened. He looked down at his chest, his eyes reflecting a crazy mixture of hope and fear. Jack had struck quickly and accurately, the blade of the first man's knife was buried all the way to the hilt, piercing the gunman's heart. The gunman shrugged slightly as if to hide his confusion and collapsed to the ground. The entire incident had taken less than forty-five seconds.

Jack turned back to face Aisling. She was several steps away, a look of horror on her face. With one quick forward motion, she was in his arms. "Jack, are you alright?"

"I'm fine," he assured her. "I need you to do exactly as I tell you," he said firmly yet with an overtone of great concern, "I want you to go to Clarice's house and stay there. Do not come out until I knock on the door."

"How long will it take?"

Jack shook his head. "I don't know," he answered, "it may not be until tomorrow morning. Now, please go."

Aisling nodded and headed toward Clarice's home. Jack watched her until she was out of sight. Then with the police sirens getting closer, he put his hands in his pocket and waited.

# Chapter Nineteen

The lights from the police and emergency vehicles flooded the street with shimmering flashes of blue, red, and white. Jack was leaning against one of the patrol cars as Matty sat on the fender, her legs dangling over the edge. Even though Jack had not discharged his weapon, he had voluntarily handed it over so that in the next few days, it could be forensically examined. He also handed over his jacket that had several bloodstains present. Since he had been personally examined by Doctor Meeker and given a clean bill of health, he can only assume that the blood had come from one or both of his assailants.

"Do you think it was our friend?" Matty asked as she stretched her shoulders by twisting from one side to the other.

Jack didn't have thinking about an answer. "No doubt," he answered flatly, "she didn't waste any time."

"I just thought that," "Matty mused, "she would have been smarter to take a little extra time and hire a professional."

"I for one," Jack responded, a touch of impatience in his voice, "am glad she rushed into things."

Matty offered him her version of the evil eye. "You know that's not what I meant."

Jack nodded his understanding. "What did you find out on her story of the plantation restoration?"

Matty placed her hands in her lap and began to swing her feet as if she were a little schoolgirl. "Pretty much what she said," she confirmed, "she successfully filed 1023 with the IRS and opened a nonprofit corporation about 6 months ago. Their charter is to help with the restoration of Louisiana plantations, which appear on the state historical registry."

"Of course, Kerr Plantation is on the registry."

"You bet," Matty answered, "I was also able to obtain a list of donors, and as you might expect, Derek Willow is one of the largest contributors."

"Followed closely behind by Brandon, Justin, and Matthew Willow," Jack added.

"Along with an impressive list of who's who in the state."

"Well," Jack sighed, "she's at least truthful about that much. Are the donations continuing to come in?"

"They slowed down to a trickle," Matty noted, "they've raised a total of just under $65,000."

Jack shook his head, "I know about restoring a home on the historical registry," he commented, "and $65,000 is just a drop in the bucket. Especially when you're talking about a plantation home that was partially destroyed during the Civil War."

"So, what do you think?" Matty asked.

Jack pushed himself off the patrol car, "As usual," he mused, "the truth usually lies somewhere in the middle. But whether there was an offer of sex for money or not, there is certainly a motive for Ms. Kerr to have killed the Willow brothers."

"That house means that much to her?" Matty asked.

Jack's eyes flashed a gentle but firm warning, "That plantation means everything to her. She would gladly kill a thousand men to see it restored."

Matty moved to one side so she could see around him. "Here comes the Captain."

Jack turned to face the man. "Captain."

"Matty, Jack," he said, nodding his salutation, "I've just spoken to the DA and Lieutenant Rogers from Internal Affairs. They both agree that this was a case of self-defense."

"That's good news," Matty said, sliding down off the fender of the car.

"Of course," Steele cautioned, "they still want your written statement, and they also want you checked out by the department psychiatrist."

"And, my weapon?" Jack asked.

"They are running it through ballistics tomorrow," Steele assured him, "you'll have it back in a couple of days. In the meantime, tomorrow, you can sign out another gun from the armory." Steele turned to face Matty, "After Jack's finished writing his statement tomorrow morning, I want the two of you to stop by my office."

"Not a problem, Sir," she assured him.

"In the meantime," Steele smiled mischievously, "why don't the two take the rest of the night off?"

Jack unconsciously looked at his watch. It was 2:48 AM.

**** 

Jack was at the precinct by 6:40 AM. It wasn't that he couldn't sleep. It was more of his self-training as a college student. He was never one to leave a term paper unfinished until the last moment, and he considered his statement from the night before nothing more than a small term paper.

After leaving the crime scene, he stopped by the precinct and phoned Aisling. While she was still unnerved by the incident, she was doing much better and refused Jack's offer to stop by. Instead, they agreed to meet at a restaurant located just off Interstate 10 at 5 AM. They shared a quick breakfast while discussing the event. In all, Jack felt quite good about their conversation and was even more encouraged when Aisling gave him a long kiss goodbye and made him promise to come spend Sunday with her in Gramercy.

Jack's fingers flew across the keyboard as he typed out his version of the incident. On the whole, the report was extremely accurate except for his leaving any mention of Aisling out. There was no reason in his mind that she should be brought into the case. The two assailants' entire purpose was to kill him as ordered by the Black Witch.

During the writing of the report, he had even considered going back to Kerr's home and questioning her a second time. The only purpose, of course, was to flaunt her obvious failure in her face. As appealing as it sounded, he reminded himself that he was not dealing with an ordinary person, and there was no way he could understand how she might react. Instead, he was sure that Matty and he would continue to keep the woman under surveillance until such time as they gathered enough evidence to arrest her.

Jack removed the finished page from the typewriter and neatly slipped in a new sheet of paper. Instantly his fingers began to slam the keys down as his anger steadily grew.

"Damn, Jack," Matty said as she walked up behind him, "you want me to get a fire extinguisher to put out the flames?"

"What flames?" he said, obviously missing her sarcasm.

"You're burning up those keys," she said in an attempt to clarify her statement, "personally I'm just a two-finger and a

213

thumb typist. With all the practice I've had, I've become pretty fast but nothing compared to you."

"Yeah," Jack said as his fingers continued to blaze out the report, "it's just a byproduct of pumping out seven years of college term papers."

"And you're gonna go for three or four more years?" she asked incredulously.

"If I'm lucky."

"You want to tell me who the girl was last night?" Matty blurted out.

Jack's fingers came to a dead stop, the typewriter probably needing the break anyway, he thought. "What, girl?"

"The one you took to DeMitri's last night."

Jack's first inclination was to deny the fact that he even had gone to DeMitri's for dinner last night but then thought better of it knowing that Matty had already checked up on it. "No one of consequence," he assured her, "I wasted twenty-two bucks on her, and I struck out. I won't be making that mistake again."

"So, she wasn't with you last night when you ran into the two perpetrators."

"Nope," he assured her, "after I crashed and burned, she went her way, and I went mine. And thank you so much for reminding me of that."

"I just can't figure out why you ended up where you did last night. I mean, your car was right there parked by DeMitri's."

Jack's eyes sparkled as though Matty and he were playing a game. "After I got dumped last night," he said as earnestly as possible, "I was headed back to my car when I noticed it was under surveillance by persons unknown.

Figuring it could have been a hit set up by Kerr, I decided to head in the other direction."

"What could you possibly gain from that?" Matty asked.

"Military tactics, my dear," Jack smiled, "if I would've gone back to my car, I would've walked right into their ambush and probably would have died last night. But, by avoiding the ambush sight, they would have either had to cancel their plans or hastily make an attempt at killing me somewhere else. That was the first sign that they were not professional killers."

"Professionals," Matty said, nodding her head in agreement, "would have aborted the hit and rescheduled it at a time and place of their choosing."

"Correct," Jack said triumphantly as he pulled the sheet of paper from the typewriter. He handed the small stack of papers to Matty. "Here, check this over," he said as he stood and stretched, "if you think it's good enough, we'll drop it off and go see Captain Steele."

Within a few minutes, they were knocking on the door of Captain Steele's office.

"Enter," Steel said flatly. When the man looked up and noticed it was Matty and Jack, he straightened up in his chair and, with a sweeping motion of his hand, offered the two to have a seat. "You feeling okay, Jack?"

"Yes sir," Jack answered, adjusting himself into the chair, "fine."

Steele glanced toward Matty. She nodded her assessment of Jack's mental state.

"Good," Steele said, picking up a piece of paper off his desk, "I got the initial ballistics back this morning, and it's all good. First of all, Jack's gun had not been fired, and furthermore, it was loaded with departmentally approved ammunition."

"That's good news, sir," Matty stated.

"And," he continued as he tossed the report back to his desktop, "Doctor Meeker has just called me and inform me that there are powder burns on the right hand of the one man.

"Proving he fired the weapon," Matty added.

"That is correct," Steele continued, "Also, the three rounds recovered from the other assailant's body were all twenty-five caliber APC."

"I carry a 9 mm," Jack stated for the record.

"That's correct," Steele answered, "the weapon found in the possession of the second assailant was indeed an old twenty-five caliber auto." Steele tossed the photograph of the gun to Matty. When she finished examining it, she handed it to Jack.

"This is just an old piece of crap," Jack commented, "The 25 auto is a terrible weapon. They jam more than not. The shooter would have been better off with a 22."

"Yep," Steel concurred, "it was probably stolen at some point. The serial number has been filed off. We're checking on that now."

"So, the bottom line is," Matty offered, "that we have two bungling amateurs who decided to rob the wrong guy."

"A mistake," Steele offered, "that they won't get to make a second time."

"Is that all you wanted to see us about?" Jack asked.

Steele got up from his desk, walked to the door, and closed it. "No," he said, returning to his seat, "I have an assignment for the two of you."

Jack's heart sank as he looked to Matty for support only to see a glazed look of dread parked squarely on her face.

Steel looked down at his desk, contemplating what he was about to say. "Matty, Jack," he said with firm resolution, "as you know someone has broken into one of the lockers in the evidence room and have stolen the dagger from the Justin Willow case. The fact that there were no visible signs of forced entry leads me to the one conclusion that it had to be an inside job."

"You don't think Sergeant Baker," she said, clearly surprised at where Steel was headed, "had anything to do with it, do you, sir?"

"Baker's a good man, sir," Jack said, his tone was even yet edged with steel, "I'd be really surprised if he had anything to do with it."

"Well," Steel answered as he leaned back in his chair, pointing his finger at the two of them, "that's why the two of you are going to look into it."

An oddly primitive warning sounded in Jack's brain as he chose his words carefully, "Sir, you know there's a good chance," Jack said, keeping his tone even, "that someone associated with the case is probably involved."

"That's right," Matty said, lending support to Jack's theory, "I doubt we're dealing with someone who was just treasure hunting. There is no doubt in my mind that they were after the dagger."

Steel nodded his agreement, "I reached the same conclusion two days ago and have been grappling with a solution ever since.

A chill ran down Jack's spine as he recalled the last time he was involved in a case with a dirty cop. It was the New Orleans, oil millionaire, Justin Trotter Case. He didn't care to go through something like that again.

Jack turned his attention back to the Captain. "Sir," he started slowly, "you understand where you're putting Matty and me on this?"

Steele chose his words carefully, "I understand where you're coming from, Jack, but you and Matty are the only ones I feel comfortable assigning to this case.

"Jack is right, Sir," Matty said swallowing hard, trying to remain composed, "We have just been kicked off the Willow investigation, how is it going to look if we start probing into the activities of the remaining members of that task force?"

"Discretion will definitely be the better part of valor." Steele smiled weakly.

"So," Jack said as he took a deep breath and let it out slowly, "we shouldn't drag Beachmen for questioning; you know, good cop, bad cop kind of thing?"

"Joke all you want in here, Jack," Steele said with an air of inevitability, "but once you walk out of that door, I expect you'll handle yourselves as professionals."

"Yes, sir," they responded in unison.

"Sergeant Baker. I've already set up an appointment for you."

"Tomorrow is Saturday," Matty reminded him.

"That's correct," Steele confirmed, "You'll be meeting him at his home. He will be expecting you at 10 AM."

Jack pulled lightly at his right earlobe, "The meeting him at his home is part of the whole discretion thing, right?"

Steele turned to Matty, smiling, "And you said that Jack could be a little dense at times."

# Chapter Twenty

Morgana Kerr sat in her sunroom at the rear of the house. Her lips were thin with irritation as she viewed one of the latest photographs of Matthew Willow. Even the aroma of her Jasmine tea could not break her out of her foul mood. She thought for sure that Derek Willow would have acquiesced by now, but his love of money was a hard mistress to deal with.

Delia quietly walked up behind her boss and stood in silence.

"Do you have an update on Detective Kohl for me?" Kerr asked.

"Yes, ma'am," the young woman said with a twinge of hesitation, "Detective Kohl was able to fend off the two attackers and is still alive."

"And the two men we hired to kill him ?"

"Both of the men are dead."

Kerr turned her attention back to the photograph of Matthew Willow. "I hope you had the good sense not to pay those buffoons in advance," she hissed.

"No, ma'am," Delia assured her, "they were to receive payment only after Detective Kohl was dead. Should we try again?"

Morgana Kerr was still holding the photograph of Matthew Willow, but her thoughts were on Detective Kohl. "No," Kerr said as she contemplated her next move, "I think another attempt on the Detective would only raise suspicion. As it is right now, they've probably credited the incident to a failed robbery attempt."

"That's exactly what our contact inside the eighth precinct informed me of this morning," Delia said.

Her expression stilled and grew serious, "and he and his partner are still off the case?"

"That's correct," Delia confirmed, "currently, they are performing administrative work for their Captain while their fate is decided."

For the first time this morning, a smile blossomed on Morgana Kerr's face. "That's good," the woman beamed, "for Jack Kohl being an errand boy is a fate worse than death." She then held the photograph over her left shoulder, "take this photograph and the cassette tape and make sure Derek Willow gets them as soon as possible."

Delia accepted the photograph from her hand and then recovered the cassette tape from the table. "he will have it today," she confirmed as she started for the door.

"Oh, and Delia," Morgana Kerr said as she picked up her teacup.

"Ma'am?"

"If the latest photograph and the tape of his son pleading for his father to save him does not loosen Willow's purse strings, we will start ripping the flesh off the young man's body until Papa agrees to finish the restoration."

Delia's eyes blazed with the anticipation of fulfilling her mistress 'request. "It will be my pleasure."

****

Jack and Matty sat at a picnic table in the back yard of Sergeant Baker's townhouse. Sergeant Baker had just over eighteen years with the New Orleans Police Department. He had spent the first fifteen years as a patrol officer and had planned to finish out his twenty years doing just that. That is until he and his partner had answered a domestic disturbance call one afternoon. As they walked up to the house, a drunk stumbled out on to the porch carrying a loaded shotgun. In the end, Baker's partner and the drunk were both dead, while Baker took a shotgun blast to his left hip and leg. The wound forced him off the street and landed him a job in the Evidence Room until he could retire.

Baker exited the rear door of the house, carrying three bottles of beer. While his limp was obvious to both Matty and Jack, the man's face showed no sign of pain. He placed the bottles on the table and sat on the attached bench. Awkwardly he managed to swing his legs under the table.

"Thanks, Bobby," Jack said as he picked up one of the bottles.

Matty handed one of the two remaining bottles to Baker and kept the last one for herself.

"I don't know what to tell you," Baker said while studying the beer bottle in his hand, "this has never happened before."

Matty leaned toward the center of the table, "First things first, Bobby," Matty said in a sincere voice, "neither Jack or I believe you had anything to do with the disappearance of the dagger."

"That's right, Bobby," Jack added, "We already have several leads of which none of them lead back to you."

Jack glanced toward Matty to see her response to the point about them having leads. Even though Matty knew that the two of them didn't have a single lead, she didn't dispute Jack's claim.

221

"What we need from you," Jack continued, "is help in closing out your end of the process."

"Sure, Jack, anything," Baker stated.

"Bobby, when was the last time you physically saw the dagger?" Matty asked.

"I guess that it was the day I logged it into the evidence room," he answered calmly, "as always, once evidence is released by the medical examiner it is given to me, and I log it in and assign it to a locker."

"You never laid eyes on it again?" Jack asked.

Baker shrugged his shoulders, "No, Jack; I wouldn't have any reason to."

"Then, when did you notice it missing?"

Baker thought about Jack's question while draining half his beer, "Early last week," he answered with confidence, "Detective Beachmen came to the evidence room with a request to sign it out. When I looked into the locker to retrieve it, it was gone."

Jack's right eye shot up almost to his hairline, "Beachmen asked for it?"

"Yeah, that's right. So, I looked in several of the other evidence lockers thinking that I may have misfiled it."

"And you didn't find it?" Matty asked.

"No, it was nowhere." Baker sighed, "I then turned the place upside down looking for it but still couldn't find it."

"What about the tarot card?" Jack asked, "was it still there?"

"Yeah, right where I put it."

"Did Beachmen ask for the terror card, also?" Matty asked.

Baker shook his head, "No, just the knife."

"Was Beachmen upset that you couldn't find it?" Jack asked.

Again, Baker shook his head from side to side, "You know Beachmen, Jack. The man doesn't give a shit about anything. He just said to give him a call when I found it."

Jack finished his beer and set it down on the table. "Is there anything else you can think of Bobby that might help us?"

Baker shrugged his shoulders, "This is kinda crazy," he said, exchanging glances with Jack and then Matty, "I pride myself at having a photographic memory. On every piece of evidence that comes across my desk, I can tell you something unique about it."

"For instance?" Jack prompted.

"Take that stupid tarot card," Baker said while closing his eyes, "it was the three of swords. The background was covered in gray clouds. There are three bluish-colored swords piercing a red heart. The bottom right corner has a blood spot on it."

"Wow," Matty exclaimed, "I didn't even remember seeing the bloodstain."

"So, what's the point, Bobby?" Jack asked.

Baker took in a deep breath and let it out slowly, "It's just that every time I try to remember anything about that dagger, I come up empty."

"Empty?"

"Yeah," Baker continued, "I can't tell you a damn thing about it. I try to visualize it, and it's just not there."

"Come on, Bobby," Jack said, laughing, "you have to remember the mother-of-pearl handle. It's was quite striking."

"Sorry, Jack," Baker said, tears forming on the lower edge of his eyes, "I can't remember."

"Earlier," Matty prompted, "you said you guessed the last time you saw the dagger was when you logged it into the evidence room?"

"Yeah, that's right."

"But you're not sure, you don't remember logging it."

A single tear now crested the man's lower eyelid and ran freely down his face. "No," he said, wiping the tear away, "I don't."

"But the tarot card?" Jack urged.

Baker offered Jack a warm smile, "Like it happened twenty minutes ago."

Jack and Matty exchanged a quick glance. "Thanks, Bobby," Jack said as he stood, "if you can think of anything else, please let us know."

"Not a problem," Bobby assured them.

"Thanks for the beer," Matty said as she stood next to Jack.

The two made their way toward the gate.

"Hey Jack," Bobby said as he limped toward the two of them.

"Yeah, buddy," Jack smiled.

"This isn't going to affect my retirement, is it?" Bobby asked, trying to maintain control of his emotions, "I mean, I've only got two years to go."

Jack placed his hand softly on Bobby's shoulder. "No worries, Bobby," Jack assured him, "they'll have to kill me first to get to you."

Bobby's face brightened, "That sounds good," he said, chuckling, "I hear you're a hard man to kill."

"Count on it." Jack winked.

"I think he's telling the truth," Matty asked as she entered the car on the passenger side.

Jack stuck the key in the ignition and started the motor, "Or what he remembers of the truth."

"Yeah," she sighed, "the poor man didn't remember much about the knife, did he."

Jack nodded his head in agreement as they pulled away from the curb, "did you notice he didn't remember that the handle of the dagger was made out of black obsidian, not mother-of-pearl as I described it."

"Yes," Matty answered, "he remembered the tarot card in fine detail but couldn't recollect a single thing about the dagger. Do you think he was drugged? Someone could have slipped something in his coffee."

"I don't know of a single drug," Jack sighed, "that could cause selective amnesia. I mean, I've heard of drugs that could make you forget you were even born, but nothing that could make you forget a solitary item."

"What about hypnosis?" Matty asked.

"Maybe," Jack thought, "I've read articles where hypnosis has been used in the cure of battle fatigue or combat neurosis, but in all those cases, the subject is aware that they are going to undergo hypnosis and were in acceptance of the treatment."

"Did you notice how he reacted," Matty asked, "when either of us mentioned the dagger. His face seemed to go totally blank."

"Yeah, I was going to mention that," Jack stated, "in the case of battle fatigue many times a patient is given a trigger that when activated makes them forget their anxiety or depression."

"A trigger?"

"From what I've read," Jack continued, "sometimes when a patient is under hypnosis, they're given a trigger word or an action that takes her mind away from the real issue. I've heard of one case where a patient had been hypnotized to quit smoking. Every time he thought about a cigarette, he would snap a rubber band that he wore around his wrist."

"Did it work?"

"I guess so," Jack said, shrugging his shoulders.

"Well," Matty sighed, "none of that is going to help us."

"What about Beachmen?" Jack asked.

Matty's jaw clenched, her eyes narrowed slightly, "What about him?"

"What reason did he have," Jack asked, his brows drawing together in an agonized expression, "to go to Sergeant Baker and ask to sign the dagger out?"

"You're right," Matty agreed, "if Beachmen hadn't asked to see the dagger, no one would've ever known it was missing."

"So, in a sense," Jack offered, "Beachmen triggered the investigation into the missing dagger."

"Do you think he did it on purpose," Matty spat, "I mean knowing all along that the dagger was not there."

Jack shrugged matter-of-factly, "It's certainly possible, but there's no way we could ever prove it."

The two sat in silence, knowing the conversation had played out. Both keeping to their own thoughts. Jack, of course, was thinking about Aisling and spending Sunday with her.

"You got a hot date tomorrow?" Matty asked, grinning like a Cheshire cat.

Jack recalls Aisling's last kiss. The prolonged anticipation of seeing her again was almost unbearable. "The hottest," he grinned.

"The same chick from DeMitri's?" Matty prodded.

A frown covered Jack's face, "I told you that I crashed and burned with that one.

"I thought that the mighty Jack Kohl," Matty teased, "never struck out. Or, if he did, never gave up."

"I've become wiser in my old age," Jack joked, "one of the most useful things I learned in college is the 'Law of Diminishing Returns.'"

"Well, don't keep me in suspense," Matty chide, "what does it mean?"

"It simply means that at some point, the level of profits or benefits gained is less than the amount of money or energy invested."

"So, what you're saying," Matty said, "if they don't put out, you're out."

Jack slowly shook his head as he considered her description, "Yeah, I guess that qualifies as a crude layman's definition."

"You're such a pig, Jack," Matty said thickly.

Jack didn't bother to answer, trying to swallow the lump that lingered in his throat. The Playboy persona was not something that he particularly liked, but it helped distance him from the women he worked with. He remembered the advice one of his early mentors had given him. *Jack, my boy, the mentor had said, don't ever dip your pen in the company ink.*

# Chapter Twenty-One

When Jack pulled up to the front of Aisling's home, the usual greeting committee was not waiting for him. In fact, there wasn't a soul in sight. None of the three geese were posted at their usual lookout at the top of the truck. Jack shrugged it off and stepped out of his car and started for the front door. He hadn't taken but a few steps when Abigail, the Snow Goose, came racing around the corner.

"Ah, Abigail," Jack said as he bowed at the waist, "it's good to see you."

To Jack's surprise, the bird stopped, spread its wings out fully, and bowed her head to the ground.

"I see you've made Abigail's friends list," Aisling chuckled, as she came out onto the front porch, "not many have obtained such as high honor."

"Did you see that? "Jack asked in amazement, as Aisling walked up to him and gave him a playful peck on the lips. "I bowed to her, and she curtsied back."

"Well," Aisling answered as she looped her arm with his and lead him toward the front entrance of the house, "that would be the polite thing to do, don't you think?"

"Yeah, but," Jack started to say, changing in midsentence, "wow, what smells so good?"

"That is your lunch," Aisling said with a slight giggle as she squeezed Jack's arm, "we have chicken and dumplings, fresh green beans sautéed with onions and bacon and for dessert, the American favorite, homemade apple pie. There might even be some vanilla ice cream in the refrigerator if you have room for a pie ala mode."

Between Aisling's description and the aroma of the food, Jack's mouth began to water. "Would it be rude of me to ask when lunch will be served?"

"It's ready now, Jack," Aisling said, leading him into the kitchen.

Lunch was a mixture of great food, wonderful conversation, and several moments of vaguely sensuous glances passing between them. Jack finally made the sensible choice of leaving half of his pie ala mode on the plate. Together they cleared the table, and Aisling washed as Jack dried.

"You up for a walk around the lake?" Aisling asked as she handed Jack the last dish to dry.

"That would be wonderful," Jack said as he accepted the dish and begin drying it.

"Perfect," Aisling said as she attempted to remove the apron from around her waist. "Dammit," she cursed lightly as she continued to fidget with the strings of the apron.

"What's the problem?" Jack asked as he walked up behind her.

"These apron strings are wet," Aisling said, looking down toward her waist, "and now they're in a knot, and I'm having trouble unfastening them."

"Let me see what I can do," Jack said as his arms encircled her and began working on the knot at her midriff, "there, that's got it."

"Thank you," Aisling said as she managed to turn in his arms and place her hands on his shoulders.

Jack's hand slipped up her back, bringing her closer. Their eyes met for a second before their lips met in a kiss that sent new spirals of ecstasy through the two of them.

Reluctantly, Aisling broke their embrace, "I think we better take that walk now," she said, her lips still moist from their kiss, "I believe we have a little more than just lunch to walk off."

Jack sighed as he stepped back, wanting more, "Lead the way ma chérie."

Aisling took him by the hand and lead him out through the back door and down the trail leading to the small lake. Jack's senses seemed to explode as they neared the lake. The sun was warm on his face while his eyes attempted to take in the magnitude of colors offered by the different varieties of plants and flowers. As they reached the path, Jack became keenly aware of the bees buzzing from one flower to another. Their melodious buzzing inviting him to relax and enjoy the moment. Suddenly, a hummingbird zipped into his view, hovering not six inches in front of his face.

"I think this little guy," Jack said, "is checking me out."

Aisling squeezed his hand, "probably so," she mused, "you're a stranger to his little world."

"Do you think I'll pass muster?"

"There's a good chance of that," Aisling assured him.

The hummingbird continued to flit back and forth in front of Jack's face just out of Jack's reach. "What makes you so sure?"

"Because," Aisling said reassuringly, "if you pass muster with me, they will except you. You forget Jack Kohl that this is my environment. Everything you see around you is bound by a homogeneous state. Including me."

"Ah," Jack said, reaching an understanding, "this is all about you being a Green Witch."

"That's right."

"If my recent studies on Witchcraft served me well," Jack said confidently, "A Green Witch predominantly communicates with the world and works with the natural energies of Mother Earth."

Aisling's face was radiant, "This," she said with an embracing gesture, "is where I can be as one most strongly with nature. It is here that I have the greatest ability to venture into the Otherworld and communicate with the spirit realm."

"Now, you're talking about the practice of a Hedge Witch."

"Yes Jack, if you like," Aisling agreed, "but you can try to compartmentalize what I am, a Green Witch or a Hedge Witch, or what I actually am and spend the rest your life trying to tuck all those loose ends into a nice box and still not understand what I practice."

"After dealing with my own affliction, I wouldn't dream of trying to pigeonhole someone into a specific title. Hell, I can't even explain what happens to me, and you've seen it firsthand."

"First of all, Jack," she sighed heavily, her voice filled with anguish, "what you have is not an affliction; it's a gift."

Jack picked up a flat stone and skipped it across the smooth surface of the lake, "That's the same thing Clarice would tell me."

"Maybe that's why she and I are kindred spirits," Aisling smiled.

Jack locked eyes with Aisling and smiled. He then decided to change the subject, "Did I tell you that someone stole the Athame Dagger from our evidence locker?"

"No," Aisling said, "but it doesn't surprise me."

"No, why not?" Jack asked.

"Because Jack," Aisling sighed, "it is the Black Witch's main ritual implement used in any ceremony she would conduct. It makes all the sense in the world that she would want it back."

"I'm not nearly as troubled," Jack frowned, "with why she wants it as much as how she got it back."

"It's like you said," Aisling shrugged, "she stole it back."

"And there lies the problem," he said triumphantly, "the evidence room is secured with limited access. Everything that goes in or goes out has to be placed in the logbook."

"Have you spoken with the keeper of the log?"

"Yes," Jack grinned as he thought of Sergeant Baker as the 'keeper of the log,' "Sergeant Baker keeps a tight rein on everything to do with the evidence room."

"Is he above suspicion?" She asked.

"Matty and I spent time with him yesterday." Jack confirmed, "the funny thing is he has no recollection of the knife at all."

Aisling's face tightened, "No memory? He can't recall handling the blade?"

"No," Jack confirmed, "he doesn't even remember what it looked like."

"I see," she said as she awkwardly cleared her throat. "Jack, why do I have the feeling that you are about to ask me if a Witch is involved in the disappearance of the dagger?"

"Well," he said with detached inevitability, "the dagger belongs to the Black Witch, and we both believe she would want to back, but we both know she couldn't just walk in and ask for it."

"And you believe that she would have to have help from somebody on the inside?"

"That's correct," Jack answered, thinking of Beachmen's asking to sign the blade out.

Aisling looked up at Jack from beneath questioning brows, "but why a Witch? Why couldn't the Black Witch just bribe someone within the Precinct to help her?"

"I'm working on that angle also," Jack assured her, "but the most puzzling of the pieces is the fact that when it comes to the dagger, Sergeant Baker seems to have selective amnesia. He can remember the tarot card in infinite detail but comes up with a complete blank on the dagger itself."

"I see."

"And," Jack continued, "I know of no drug that can produce specific memory loss for a single item."

"So, you think that there may be a potion that could produce this type of forgetfulness?"

Jack picked up another stone and tossed it into the water, "I guess I'm asking you if such a potion is possible?"

"Yes," Aisling answered after she thought about it, "it's possible but would be a very complicated potion. But then we're dealing with a witch with tremendous knowledge and power."

"So, she could have had someone slip a potion into the man's coffee."

Aisling thought about Jack's statement for several seconds, contemplating an answer. "It wouldn't be that simple," she confirmed, "the person would have to be a witch."

"Really," Jack spit out without thinking.

"Yes," Aisling nodded, "giving him the potion is one thing, but it would have to be quickly followed up with an incantation."

"Incantation?" Jack mused as he pulled lightly at his right earlobe, "An incantation like a set of instructions? Like 'Forget everything you know about this dagger.'"

"Yes," Aisling giggled, "I love the way you trivialize magic, Jack."

"What do you mean? I was serious."

Aisling hugged his arm affectionately, "I know, Jack, but combining a potion and a spell is not something for an amateur."

"So, you're saying is," Jack said, thinking again about Beachmen, "you couldn't have given me the potion to administer to Sergeant Baker."

"Not hardly," she confirmed, "even a novice witch couldn't pull off an incantation like the one required to do what you said happened."

Jack thought about the information Aisling had just given him. If the Black Witch had been present to perform the ritual, someone in the building would have remembered her. A gorgeous woman like Ms. Kerr would have turned every head in the building. The watercooler talk would have reached his ears by now. Even her assistant would have caused quite a stir. They couldn't have made every police officer in the building forget that she was there.

An agonizing pain grew in his gut as he thought about spilling everything he knew to Matty. Matty and he were on polar sides of the argument during the case with Danial Jorgensen and his use of Voodoo. Several times Jack thought that he had pushed Matty to the breaking point on the voodoo case. Hell, he thought, he was dumbfounded that she hadn't asked for a new partner after the case was closed.

Jack closed his eyes and shook his head slowly. I need Matty's expertise, he thought, regretting he hadn't brought her in earlier.

"Jack," Aisling said, interrupting his thoughts, "are you alright?"

"Yeah," he said, unconsciously rubbing his stomach.

"You seem to have drifted off," she commented.

One corner of his mouth twisted upwards as he attempted to glaze over his predicament. "It's just this damn case is getting me down."

"But you're so close," Aisling insisted.

Jack couldn't tell her that the closer he got, the more isolated he became. "Sometimes, it doesn't seem that way," he answered truthfully.

His thoughts were interrupted by the honk of Abigail flying overhead. The goose circled the lake twice and then glided down to the water and landed with the slight splash. A random thought popped into Jack's mind, "Are there alligators in this lake?"

Aisling's gentle laughter rippled through the air, instantly lightening Jack's mood. "No, Jack," Aisling said as she continued to chuckle, "the geese make sure that the lake is alligator free."

"You know," Jack said thoughtfully, "I was thinking, I should get a couple of geese for myself."

There was something warm and enchanting in the manner of Jack's statement that brought a huge smile to Aisling's face. "Come on, Jack," she said with a glint of humor still in her cheeks, "I'll walk you back to your car."

Jack was admittedly a little disappointed that Aisling had not invited him back into the house but didn't show it. Together they arrived at Jack's car, still locked arm in arm. As

Jack reached for the door handle, Aisling gently placed her hand on his shoulder.

"Jack," Aisling said, searching deep into his eyes, "there are many things that I've come to love about you, but I'm still torn about how a serious relationship could work for us."

"I understand," he said, then for an instant, a wistful thought stole into his expression, "somehow I'd like to think that things could be different between us."

With a deliberately casual movement, Aisling closed the gap between them, her face inches from his, "deep in my heart," she said almost reverently, "I hope for the same thing."

His large hand gently brushed her cheek. The kiss that followed was surprisingly soft.

\*\*\*\*

At 10:39 PM on Sunday evening Derek Willow may have been the only person in the National American Bank building. He sat behind his desk, staring at the latest photograph of Matthew that he had received earlier in the day. With a cold twinge of disappointment, he studied the photograph. A curse fell from his mouth, wondering why his son had not managed to escape by now. Hadn't he spent thousands of dollars on escape and evasion training for the three boys, he thought. He was furious at Matthew's vulnerability.

He breathed in shallow, quick gasps as he again studied the photograph. It was obvious that the boy had endured great pain, and of course, this was obvious by the cassette tape that had accompanied the picture. He clenched his jaw tightly in order to kill the sob in his throat.

"Am I interrupting anything?" Morgana Kerr said, leaning against the office door frame.

Willow's eyes suddenly filled with fierce shimmering hate as in a single fluid motion, he removed the revolver from the desk drawer, stood, and aimed it at Morgana's head.

"Shooting me won't get your son released," she said matter-of-factly.

Willow noticed that the transparent black shirt she wore heightened the firmness of her bare breast beneath. The woman's shirt was tied off above her midriff while her pants rode low on her hips, offering an unobstructed view of her firm belly and lower abdomen. He began to lower the revolver until he once again quickly leveled it at Morgana's head.

"I should fucking kill you," he hissed, "right here, right now!"

Morgana Kerr pushed herself off the doorframe and move toward the desk. "Do you mind," she said as she took the chair in front of his desk. "You won't kill me," she affirmed as she adjusted the neckline of her blouse.

He could clearly see the curvature of her firm breast as the continued to point the gun at her face. "You're stupid if you don't think I would get great pleasure in splattering your brains all over this office."

"That's probably true," she sighed, "but of course, the pleasure would be short-lived."

"How so?"

"Well," Morgana started, "my assistant waiting for me in the car would inform the police of our sexual relationship and figure that you killed me in a lover's quarrel. Then as you sat rotting in jail, you would get the sad news that your son Matthew's body was found floating face down in Lake Michigan. All the evidence in his death would point to the fact that he had stolen drugs from his Chicago crime partners.

When they discovered his treachery, they tortured him and killed him, dumping his body in the lake."

"You wouldn't," he hissed.

"Before going to the electric chair yourself," she continued as if she hadn't heard Derek's comment, "you would have to live with the fact that, in the minds of everyone you knew, your baby boy was a dead drug dealer." She straightened up in the chair, "Is that how you want Matthew to be remembered? Is that the legacy you want for your family?"

Derek Willow lowered the gun to his side. "What do you want, Morgana?"

"You already know what you have to do," she spat, "just do it."

"If I start funding your project again, you'll release Matthew?"

Morgana Kerr's eyes flared, "No, of course not."

"What do you mean, No," he repeated with contempt.

"You don't get Matthew back," she said, pointing her index finger at his face, "until the project is finished. I won't have you pulling the funds the second you have your little boy back."

"If I don't get Matthew," Derek hissed through clenched teeth, "you don't get a dime."

"As I've already said," she stated, her nostrils flaring, "Matthew will be my guest until the project is finished. Of course, he will be well looked after. The pain and suffering will cease, and he will receive medical care and proper nourishment. You'll get regular updates to include pictures and voice recordings."

Derek swallowed hard, trying to manage the rage he felt. "I have your word."

"Of course," she confirmed.

"Alright then," he acknowledged, "I'll start the process first thing in the morning. The money should hit your account by Wednesday." He searched her face for a sign of affirmation. When he couldn't detect it, he spoke again. "Is that soon enough for you?"

Morgan stood and began to walk around to Derek's side of the desk. "Wednesday will be fine," she said as she stood over him. "But I will need certain assurances tonight before I leave."

Uncertainty crept into his expression, "What else can I give you other than my word?"

With a single motion, Morgana removed her blouse, allowing it to fall to the floor. "I'll let you know when I feel… well assured," she leered as she wiggled out of her pants.

# Chapter Twenty-Two

Jack was already in a foul mood when he entered the Precinct. The fact that the first two people he came across were Detective Beachmen and Special Agent Salton only made it worse.

"Hey Jack," Beachmen almost sang as they passed in the hall, "how's that paperwork going?"

"Just great," Jack responded with a forced smile, "you find the Willow kid yet?"

"We are working on it," Salton shot back.

"You find the killer of the Willow boys yet?"

"Working on it," Beachmen parroted.

"That's wonderful," Jack said as he passed. As an afterthought, he turned back toward the two. "You know the street department has been working on a sewer problem at the end of my street for almost 6 months now. Every time I see them, they tell me they're working on it. The bottom line is the project stinks, and they're no closer to finishing than they were six months ago. Sound familiar?"

Beachmen and Salton continued down the hall with Beachmen holding his finger up over his head as his only response.

"You guys have a great day," Jack shouted after them and continued to his desk.

By the time Jack reached his desk, his mood had sunken to a new low. He sat there staring at the pile of paperwork all the time, tapping the eraser of his pencil on the desk.

"Someone didn't get laid this weekend." Matty offered as her morning greeting.

"Is that a confession?" He shot back.

"Wow, Jack," Matty said, taking the two cups of coffee and four doughnuts from the sac she carried, "you're going to have to find some easier women to date. If you like, I'll help you pick some out."

"And how did you become an expert on easy women?" He said, reaching over the desk and pulling a cup of coffee back in front of him."

Matty tossed a doughnut in his direction, almost knocking his coffee over, "here, stuff this in your mouth."

"Thanks," he said sheepishly.

"I have some news that might cheer you up," Matty said, taking a seat at her desk.

"What happened, Beachmen fell in the hallway, and they can't get him up?"

"Even better," Matty said through a mouth full of doughnut.

"Well," Jack huffed, "you going to tell me, or do I have to wait for the trailer of the movie to come out?"

"Man, you are wound tight." She observed.

Jack peered at her over his coffee, giving her the 'And?' look.

"One of my contacts at the National American Bank informs me that first thing this morning, Derek Willow put in for a $20,000 wire transfer to the account of the Kerr Plantation Restoration Fund."

Jack rose fluidly from his chair, leaned over the desk, grabbed another doughnut, and slid gracefully back into his seat. "That is good news," he said, studying the doughnut, "too bad we're not working the case."

"So, when did mere details ever stop us?" Matty asked.

"True," Jack conceded, "but how do we confront Willow with it? If we step one foot into Willow's office, Captain Steel and Special Agent Salton will jump deep into our shit."

"I got the information," Matty said, shrugging her shoulders, "you could at least come up with a plan on how to use it."

Before Jack could answer, one of the uniformed officers from the front desk walked up and handed him a small envelope.

"Thanks, Roger," Jack said as he opened the envelope.

Jack studied the message carefully. It was simple enough, *Brewery park bench - one hour.*

He handed it to Matty, "One of my informants," he advised her, "we may have an opening yet."

****

Jack sat on the bench overlooking the river. It was a beautiful morning and actually, he thought, he wouldn't mind if Petersen were a little late. Hell, he thought, he didn't care if the man showed up at all.

That thought went up in smoke; the second Petersen took a seat next to him on the bench. "Why do I feel like a secret agent in some cheap spy movie?" Jack asked.

"Because," Petersen said as he stretched out his legs and made himself comfortable, "you always have had an active imagination.

"Well then, imagine me telling you to fuck off."

"I said," Petersen offered, "that you had the active imagination, not me. Hell, I'm just a simple cop trying to do my job."

"Is that why we're sitting here?"

"Jack," Petersen started as he awkwardly cleared his throat, "this case has turned into a real shit storm."

"And you didn't bring your raincoat," Jack interjected.

"Yeah, something like that."

"Petersen," Jack said, shaking his head regretfully, "I really don't have time for fifty questions, so what the hell is on your mind?"

"Derek Willow wants a private meeting with you." Petersen blurted out.

"A meeting with me?" Jack asked as casually as he could manage, "What for?"

Petersen looked around the area, making sure no one was in listening range. "He feels that he's getting the runaround from Salton. Quite frankly, he's tired of her bullshit and lack of results."

"Well, if there's one thing I know about Derek Willow, he's a man that demands results. Oh, and the other thing I know about Derek Willow is that he's a womanizer."

"Yeah, that might be true," Petersen agreed, "but he's a man that also knows how to spot someone who is going to get the job done."

"Oh, stop it," Jack teased, "you're going to make me blush."

"No bullshit, Jack," Petersen continued, "he wants to meet one-on-one with you. He told me to tell you that he's willing to lay it on the table if you'd only help."

Jack hesitated, sizing Petersen up for a moment. "Why do I feel like you're trying to get me to walk into a sting operation?"

"This is no bullshit, Jack. He said you choose the place and time, and he would be there."

"No one else?"

"I swear," Petersen answered, pulling a scrap of paper out of his pocket. "Here's the number to his private line in his office. Give him a call and allow him enough time to get to your meeting place."

Jack took the piece of paper and studied the phone number. "I have one more question for you."

"What's that, Jack?"

"Why are you doing this? What's in it for you?" Jack demanded.

Petersen cleared his throat as he adjusted his tie, "Hopefully, I get my partner back."

"Beachmen?"

"Yeah," Petersen answered, "the dirtbag has been acting really funny lately. It's like I don't even know him."

Jack sat up on the bench. "How so?"

"I don't know Jack," Petersen sighed, "it's like he's not all there. He's become very unstable and," Petersen said as a gazed look of despair spread over his face, "he's become unreliable."

Jack saw the opening he was looking for, "Why did Beachmen go to the evidence room to sign out the dagger?"

"What the hell are you talking about?" Petersen asked, "There would be no reason for him or me to sign out that dagger."

"Sergeant Baker says otherwise," Jack said flatly.

Petersen shook his head from side to side, "Well, if he did, he did it when I wasn't around."

Jack knew that Petersen and Beachmen were together ninety percent of the time. If Beachmen farted, Petersen was there to complain about it. There was a good chance, Jack thought, that Petersen was telling the truth. "Do me a favor then. Ask Beachmen about the dagger the next time you get a chance. I'd be interested in hearing what he had to say."

"You'll meet with Derek Willow then?"

"Just talk to Beachmen and get back to me. I'll handle Derek Willow," Jack stated as he stood and prepared to leave.

Jack walked down levy toward Jackson square, wondering if he had just made the biggest blunder of his career. If, in fact, this was a sting operation, Jack would be up on charges and out of a job. He had already made the decision not to involve Matty. As it stood right now, Matty could claim plausible deniability. It would at least save her job until they figured out a plan to get her.

As he walked around the square, his eyes darted from one card reader to another. There was a good crowd of tourists for a Monday, and most of the card readers were busy. Subconsciously Jack searched for the young woman who had read his cards just a few days ago. He openly sighed when he could not find her.

After walking around the square for a second time, Jack decided he should head back to the precinct and catch up with Matty. His face changed and became almost somber when he thought about how he would handle Matty. There would be no doubt that she would ask him about his meeting with the informant. His mouth thinned with displeasure at the thought of lying to her. He already told her enough lies in the last few weeks to last him a lifetime, but telling her that Morgana Kerr was a Black Witch and was using magic against the Willow's was out of the question.

As he made the left turn in front of the St. Louis Cathedral, he noticed that the crowd had become denser. There were now people shopping amongst the street vendors at the entrance to Jackson Square, as well as several tourist groups getting ready to enter the Cathedral. The tourists waiting for the church tour were required to mill around out in front of the Cathedral until the morning mass had ended. Church patrons were now exiting through the front doors making for an even larger crowd outside. This didn't particularly bother Jack as he was used to large crowds in the French quarters. So, he carefully began to methodically weave his way through the groups.

It was then that he was bumped from one side to another by several of the people headed in no one particular direction. This was also not an unusual occurrence among crowds of tourists, but this time the jostling had been followed by a sharp, burning pain on his right side just above his belt. Instinctively Jack inserted his left hand under his jacket to search out the pain.

He became instantly alert at the sign of the blood on his fingertips. He cocked his head as the pulled aside his jacket to see where the blood had come from. There, just above his belt, was a thin cut penetrating his shirt. There wasn't much blood, but it confirmed that his skin had also been cut. He relaxed when he figured out that the cut was not a puncture wound but merely a scratch. He stood on his tiptoes, searching the crowd for anyone that might look suspicious. When the search failed, he assumed that when he had recently been knocked about by the crowd, someone's umbrella or another sharp object had nicked him. He made a beeline to his favorite hotdog vendor.

"Hey, Jack," the vendor said as he approached, "two of the regular?"

"Not yet, Nickie," Jack said, reaching for the napkin dispenser, "I just need a few of these if you don't mind."

"Sure, Jack," the man grinned, "anything for one of my best customers."

Jack walked away, applying the napkins to the wound, "Thanks, Nick, I'll see you later."

He covered the last few blocks to the station and went immediately to the men's locker room. He opened his locker then quickly removed his jacket, exposing the cut in the shirt. Within seconds he had stripped down to the waist allowing him to examine the small cut. Jack fished through the upper shelf of the locker, where he kept his personal items until he found a small abused looking tube of Neosporin®. Standing in front of one of the sinks, Jack washed the wound and applied an ample amount of the antibiotic to the area. Still leaning to one side, he was able to unwrap a Band-Aid® and stretch it over the small cut. Looking in the mirror, he smiled with satisfaction at his field dressing. He walked back to his locker and retrieved the shirt. He quickly found the hole and stuck his finger through. "Damn," he cursed out loud, wondering if he would be able to get the bloodstain out and sew the small hole. He lobbed the shirt into the locker and removed one of the two clean shirts he had stored there.

He was just finishing tucking in his shirt as he walked out of the door to the men's locker room.

"There you are," Matty said as he exited, "I was beginning to worry that we might miss our lunch date."

"Lunch date?"

"Yeah," Matty confirmed, "Dr. Meeker is going to meet us at Mama Billy's. You really got her hooked on Red Beans and Rice Mondays."

"I can't take all the credit," Jack said, "Let's head out the back."

They had gotten about a block away when Matty asked the question Jack had been dreading. "So, how did your meeting with your informant go?"

Jack swallowed hard, "First of all, let me say that my informant is a little out of the ordinary."

"What informant isn't?"

"Good question," Jack said as they walked side-by-side, "this one is a little bit different."

"How so?" Matty asked.

"The informant is Rupert Petersen," Jack blurted out, preparing himself for the repercussion.

Jack and Matty walked in silence for what seemed to Jack to be an eternity.

"I'll grant you," Matty said evenly, "Detective Petersen is a little bit different on a good day, but the real question Jack is, can the man be trusted?"

"My gut tells me yes," Jack answered, "but I still hear alarm bells going off all over the place."

"What information was he willing to share with you?"

"First of all, he confirmed what we already know. Their case is going nowhere. Beachmen has seemed to have gone off the rails, and Agent Salton isn't helping."

"There's a big surprise," Matty snorted, "what else did you learn?"

"He informed me that Derek Willow wishes to meet with me one-on-one."

Matty took a while to formulate her next question. "Are you going to meet with him?"

"Not sure," Jack answered truthfully, "that's why you and I are talking about it now. What do you think?"

"Well, the first thing to jump out at me," Matty said sarcastically, "is that the whole thing is a setup."

"That was my first inclination also."

"If it is a setup," Matty said, thinking out loud, "you could lose your job."

"Right," Jack sighed.

"But, if it's a genuine offer," Matty said, "it could be a major break."

"And that's the part that keeps tugging at my gut," Jack admitted.

They again walked in silence until they had reached the front entrance of Mama Billy's. Matty stopped just before the door. Jack followed her lead.

"You want me to go along with you?"

"No," Jack said uneasily. "If it is a setup, I like to know I have at least one person in the precinct that would be on my side."

Matty's dark, earnest eyes locked with his, "You can always count on that."

Jack's face beamed with tenderness, "And the thought of that makes what I have to do just a little bit easier."

"Now, let's go inside and eat," Matty insisted, turning away from Jack to wipe the tear away, "I'm starving."

As soon as they entered Mama Billy's, both of them spotted Doctor Meeker sitting at their usual table. The fact that she was almost standing and waving at them also helped.

"Hey, Matty, Jack." Meeker beamed.

"You been waiting long?" Jack asked.

"About ten minutes," Meeker confirmed, "I had to fight one guy off who wanted to invite himself to lunch with me."

"What did you tell him?" Matty asked, laughing.

"I told him," Meeker said, her voice holding a steely edge, "that I was still contagious and didn't think that would be a good idea."

"That's great!" Matty said, almost choking on a sip of water, "I'll have to remember that one."

Meeker turned to Jack and suddenly glanced at him with a professional scowl, "You feeling okay, Jack?" She said as she turned his head from side to side, "you look a little pale?"

"Yeah," Matty said, chiming in, "I kind of thought so too."

Jack backed away from Meeker's touch, "Are you going to charge me for a full exam or just the consultation?"

"Don't be an ass, Jack," Matty ordered, "Cynthia's just concerned."

Meeker leaned over and put the back of her hand to Jack's forehead, "You're a little warm."

"Well, considering that I just walked four blocks on a hot, muggy day might have something to do with that."

Meeker leaned over and picked up her purse from the floor and began to rummage through the center pocket. "I have a sample of ibuprofen here in my purse I want you to take a couple with a glass of water?"

"Will I then be able to eat my meal in peace?" Jack asked.

"Here's a blister pack of twelve pills," Meeker said, ignoring Jack's comment, "take two now and then repeated every four hours."

Jack turned to face Matty, "Who knew that one of my best friends would turn out to be a drug pusher."

"Quit being such a baby," Matty said.

Knowing that the lunch would not return to normal until he followed Meeker's directions, Jack pop two of the pills in his mouth and drank half of the water in his glass. He had to admit to himself that the cold water felt good going down his throat. "Can we order now?"

Meeker turned to Matty, "Keep an eye on him."

Matty shook her head, "Every single day," Matty sighed.

# Chapter Twenty-Three

When it came to covering his ass, Jack was no amateur. He decided that the best place to meet Derek Willow would be at Tommy's. Matty was at that moment, sitting in a meeting with Captain Steele. By now, she would inform the Captain that he had gone home because he was not feeling well. The truth was he wasn't feeling well. It felt as if he was going to have one of those nasty summer colds. When he had first sat down, he had the waitress, Maggie bring him a glass of water, and he took two more of the pills Dr. Meeker had given him.

Earlier, he had a Dancer he knew make a phone call to Derek Willow from the payphone at one of the strip clubs on Bourbon Street. He had instructed her to tell him the time and the place to meet. She was to have him repeat it back to her then hang up. His cover would be that he was sitting in Tommy's by himself having a drink when unexpectedly, Derek Willow entered the bar and sat down with him. Both Tommy and Maggie would swear that's how it came down if there was trouble.

Like clockwork, Derek Willow showed up at the prescribed time. It only took him a few seconds for his eyes to adjust to the dim light before he spotted Jack.

"Mind if I sit down," Willow asked.

Jack motioned to the chair across from him.

"Thanks for seeing me," Willow said as he took his seat.

Jack also knew that if by some chance, Derek Willow was wearing a wire, there was very little chance that it would be able to pick up their conversation. The music in Tommy's was loud enough to distort any conversation that a wire may try to capture, along with the fact that Tommy's was located in a building that was very unfavorable to electronic transmissions. Jack figured that unless the receiver was sitting on the table next to them, there was little chance of anybody hearing or recording their conversation.

"Jack," Maggie smiled as she walked up to the table, "would you like a beer now?"

Jack motioned to Willow, "Beer?"

"Yes," Willow said, "that would be great."

Jack looked up at Maggie, "two beers, darling."

"You got it," she said as she began to walk away.

"Oh, Maggie," Jack said, catching her attention.

She turned and nodded, "Yeah, Jack?"

"This will be on his tab." He instructed her.

Jack studied Derek thoughtfully for a second, "I'm surprised to see you here," Jack smiled, "one doesn't see many people of your… stature in a place like this."

"Jack, I've been in some shit holes that would make your hair curl, Mr. Green Beret."

"That's ex-Green Beret," Jack informed him, "it's now simply Detective Kohl."

"Good," Willow grinned, "I'm in need of a good detective."

Matty placed the two beers in the center of the table, "Anything else, Jack?"

"No, Maggie," Jack said, "just keep an eye on the beers."

Willow stared at Maggie as she walked away. "Nice tits," he said, turning back to Jack.

"The best money can buy," Jack replied, taking a sip from his beer. The beer was cold enough but tasted flat. "I'm surprised you need a Detective," Jack said, returning to their previous conversation, "I understand you have several at your beck and call."

"None worth a shit. Agent Salton and that buffoon Beachmen seemed to be going around in circles."

"Wow," Jack chided, "I guess money can't buy everything."

"Look, Jack," Willow said with mounting impatience, "if you want to belittle me or berate me publicly, you can do that after you recover my son."

"Fair enough," Jack conceded, "I like to hear your side of the story before we continue."

"My side of what story?" Willow asked.

"Your... acquaintance with Morgana Kerr for starters."

Willow's breath seemed to have frozen in his throat, "You know about Morgana Kerr? You know she's got, my son?"

"Yes," Jack nodded, "that and the fact that she killed both Brandon and Justin."

"Son of a bitch, Jack," he said, his lower lip trembling with rage, "you know all this, and you've done nothing about it?"

"What would you have me do?" Jack shot back. "I've been framed for stealing evidence. My partner and I have been kicked off the case and are facing disciplinary action;

we might even be losing our jobs, and the other night two thugs tried to kill me. Sorry, but I've been a little busy. Besides, what makes you think anyone in the eighth precinct would give me ten seconds to explain what I know?"

"I...I," Willow stammered.

"Besides," Jack continued, "what I know and what I can prove are two different things entirely."

Willow seemed to be allowing Jack's words to sink in. "Sorry, but this whole thing has got me on edge. What would you like to know about Morgana?"

"Start at the beginning," Jack prompted, "When did you first meet her?"

"It was about four years ago," Derek sighed, "at one of the Comus balls. We were introduced by another one of the members."

A half-smile crossed Jack's face, "And how long was it until you began sleeping with her?"

Derek's face brightened at Jack's question. "That night," Derek confirmed.

"You don't waste any time, do you?"

"Have you seen that woman?" Derek's eyebrows raised inquiringly, "she's incredible."

Jack had to admit to himself that there was something about Morgana Kerr that was irresistible. Her persona and sexual demeanor were like flowers to a bee. "So, what happened next?"

"Things went along like that for some time," Derek confessed, "until I found out she was screwing my son, Justin."

"Man," Jack said, drawing his lips in thoughtfully, "that must've been uncomfortable."

Derek Willow thought about his answer for several seconds, "Not really. Frankly, I was glad for the relief." Derek leaned closer to the center of the table, "Jack, the woman is insatiable. She never seems to get enough, and quite frankly, when we finished having sex, I was usually exhausted."

"There's a pill for that." Jack smiled.

"It wouldn't help with her," Derek offered, "it felt like after a while, she was literally draining the life from me. Hell, it's the first time I've ever been scared to go to bed with a woman."

"So, you and Justin started tag teaming her?"

Willow nodded, "Something like that."

"So, when did Brandon make it a three-ring circus?"

"About three months after she started sleeping with Justin."

"Were the boys able to keep up with her?"

"No," he admitted, "they had the same weird complaint that I did."

Jack nodded his understanding. "When did the money become a factor?"

Derek's expression stilled and grew serious. "That was my fault," he confessed, "in several of our conversations she lamented about how the Kerr Plantation was literally rotting into the ground. I then offered to help her."

"You started giving her money."

"Not only that, but," he said, "I showed her how to open a 501 c tax-exempt non-profit company."

"That means that all the money she raises would be tax-free."

"Correct," he corroborated, "we could then donate money to help rebuild the plantation while receiving a nice tax deduction."

"So, let me get this straight," Jack said, his eyes glowing with amusement, "the three of you were taking turns screwing this woman while in the meantime, you and your friends were donating money to her restoration fund?"

"That's correct."

"Personally," Jack said, turning up his smile a notch, "I don't see how anything could have gone wrong with that plan."

Derek met Jack's eyes, "She kept wanting more."

"More?" Jack prompted.

"Yes, more money," he sighed, "and more sex. I mean, Justin came down with strep throat. The family doctor said he was totally exhausted and malnourished."

"I'm thinking that the three of you had a meeting and decided to cut her off, both monetarily and sexually."

"Something like that," Derek stated, "I mean it didn't happen overnight."

"But all in all," Jack continued, "she caught on to what you were doing. What happened next?"

"She confronted me, and when I told her it was over, she threatened me."

"She threatened physical violence?"

"Not in so many words," Derek recalled, "but it was easy enough to read between the lines."

Jack took another sip of his beer, winced at the taste, and pushed it aside. "So, what drove her to murder your two sons?"

Derek's eyes became hard and filled with hate. He swallowed hard, "She found out that Brandon was having an affair with another woman. "She came to my office and confronted me about it."

"And, of course, you lied and said you didn't know anything about it."

Derek managed a slight nod, "Yes."

Maggie dropped off two more beers at the table and picked up the empties. "Jack," she said, noticing his beer was almost full, "something wrong with your beer?"

"It tastes flat, Maggie," he said.

"No problem, sugar," she said as she started to move away from the table, "I'll get you a good one."

"So," Jack continued, "this is where the shit hit the fan, and you now have two dead sons."

"You know Jack," Derek scowled, "you can be a real asshole."

"Yeah," Jack agreed, "people tend to tell me that when I confront them with the truth. You want to continue?"

"That's it," Willow said bluntly.

"No," Jack corrected, "now we're up to the point where your youngest son Matthew was kidnapped. Why didn't you admit it that day in your office?"

"Morgana threatened to kill him if I brought in the police."

"Well, obviously, that didn't stop you from calling your friends in Baton Rouge."

"I figured I could control them; I mean, with my political influence and all. Besides, it was a better option than having you and your partner run around like a couple of cowboys trying to find Brandon and Justin's murder."

"Well," Jack sighed, "that didn't work out very well, either, did it?"

"No," Derek said flatly.

"So now for the $64,000 question," Jack said as he picked up his napkin and wiped the sweat from his brow, "so why come to me now?"

Derek Willow reached down and pulled several photographs out of his leather briefcase. He didn't bother to look at them before handing them to Jack. "She's been sending me these regularly."

Jack thumbed through the three photographs of Matthew Willow's. It was obvious that the boy had been under a regular regiment of torture. "Of course," he said, still looking at the photographs, "she promised that the torture would stop once you began funding her project again."

"Yes." Was all Derek could manage to say.

"Is that why you had the twenty thousand dollars wired to her this morning?"

"You know about that?" Derek asked in amazement.

Jack handed the photograph back to Willow. "Of course, you understand," Jack said, "that once you finish funding the project, she intends to kill Matthew. There's no way she can leave him alive."

Derek Willow shook his head. "I came to that resolution last night," he said, heat stealing into his face.

"You know where she's got him locked up?"

"All I know is, she owns several pieces of property scattered about the city. One or two of them are warehouses down by the wharf, but she's never mentioned anything about Matthew until last night."

"When she gave you the ultimatum, start the funding, or see your son die."

"That's correct," Willow confirmed.

Jack really started the feel the symptoms of his cold. Not only was he cold and clammy, but a doozy of a headache was starting to build. He figured spending time with Derek Willow wasn't helping. He promised himself that as soon as he got rid of Willow, he would head straight home.

"One more thing, Derek," Jack said, "I want you to come to grips with the fact that there is a very good chance that Morgana will be successful in killing your son. There's a small possibility that Matty and I may be able to stop her, but don't count on it. We'll do my best, and that's all I can promise."

"I understand," Derek said, nodding his head solemnly, "all I ask is that you give it your best try."

"This may come as a surprise to you, Derek," Jack said as he weakly got to his feet, "when it comes to my job, I always give it my best."

Derek stood and offered Jack his hand, "Thank you, if you need anything, you have my private number."

Jack looked down at Derek's outstretched hand, "Normally, I would shake hands, but I'm in the grips of a summer cold that I'm afraid is going to kick my ass."

"Normally," Derek said, "I would say you didn't want to shake my hand because you hate me, but all in all, you do look like shit." Derek instead patted him on the shoulder and began to walk toward the bar. "I can pay my tab at the bar, right?"

"Sure," Jack said, wiping his forehead on his sleeve, "and don't forget about that big tip you are going to leave for Maggie."

"Big tits; big tip, right, Jack?" he winked.

"Yeah, something like that," Jack answered as he headed to the door.

When Jack reached his car, he was forced to lean against it heavily, unable to keep his balance. He had planned to call Matty before heading home but decided that the call would be best made from his house. It took an enormous effort for him to reach his destination without wrecking the car. As soon as he entered the door, he began to peel off his clothing, leaving a trail all the way to his bedroom. He removed two more tablets from the blister pack he was holding and swallowed them down with some water from the bathroom. Unsteadily, he returned to the bed and collapsed. *I'll rest for a few minutes*, he thought, *then catch up with Matty.*

Much to his dismay, he did not fall fast asleep as he had planned. Instead, he was plagued with restless spurts of darkness often fused with flashes of disturbing visions. The images came randomly, many of them making no sense. He dreamt of the Voodoo Queen, Madam Justine, as well as her daughter Clarice. Then, of course, there were the nightmares of Daniel Jorgensen, the Voodoo killer, and the women he had slaughtered. Then there were the visions of Morgana Kerr.

It brought back the images of her as the Black Witch. As before, the whites of her eyes were dark as coal; her irises were a burning scarlet red. Her skin seemed to be stretched over her face distorting her features. The one feature that Jack would like to have forgotten was the large, crater-like scar protruded on an area of her left cheek. As before, the skin inside of the crater was raised and covered in small holes that at one time could have been regular pores, but now they seemed more grotesque than before. Microscopic parasites wove in and out of the holes. They seemed to be busy trying to enlarge the infected area. To Jack's horror, the black witch touched the inflamed area allowing the parasites to cover her fingertip. Then slowly, she reached out toward Jack. He tried desperately to back away from the ever-closer finger but was unable to move. Then with a quick flick of her wrist, Morgana struck at Jack's cheek, slashing a deep gash across his skin. Jack screamed as the parasites began entering the bleeding wound.

Jack lurched forward on his bed, gasping for air. His hand quickly went to his cheek, frantically searching for the wound. When he was convinced there was no cut, he lowered his hand

and fell back onto the bed. The sheets were cold and wet, but he couldn't force himself to get up. Within seconds the nightmares returned. The photographs that Derek had shared came to life, and he was forced to watch as the black witch tortured Matthew Willow. The young man reached out to Jack pleading, 'Help me,' he cried as he was struck again and again, 'stop the pain!'

Jack attempted to move forward and intervene in the boys beating but was unable to advance even a single step. Jack studied the interior of the room, trying to discover a way to intervene. There was no furniture anywhere, nothing he could throw at the Black Witch. The floor was aged and weathered in several spots charred by fire. Even the beam that held Matthew firmly in place showed its age. Jack continued to look around the room for something he might be able to use. Jack noticed that on several of the walls, the plaster had either peeled or pulled away to the point where the wooden lath strips were exposed. Again, nothing there that would help. He attempted to look outside through one of the four large floor to ceiling windows. His view was blocked by long sheer curtains that melted into the images of willowing ghosts that seem to be enjoying the boy suffering.

"God, make her stop," Matthew shrieked as a whip cut into his chest again.

Jack attempted to push forward again this time he was able to take a few small steps toward the boy. *If I can just reach the expose wooden lath strips,* he thought, *I could pull myself along.* Suddenly Jack stopped as he stared at the plaster wall. He concentrated on the wooden strips. *Lath strips,* he said to himself. What was it about the wooden strips that churned in his brain? They were not an uncommon item if you were involved in any type of restoration work in New

Orleans as he had been. Lath and plaster was a building process used to finish mainly interior dividing walls and ceilings. It was commonly used throughout the city in the eighteen hundreds until the early nineteen hundreds when it was replaced with modern-day drywall. The process Jack knew consisted of narrow strips of wood (laths), which are nailed horizontally across the wall studs or ceiling joists and then coated in plaster. He had restored several historical homes using this method.

He once again sat up in bed, his mouth taking in a deep breath of air, his eyes staring into the darkness. His face took on a hard, clammy look as he managed a cold eye smile.

"I know where he is," he mouthed as he staggered up from the bed and made his way to the shower.

# Chapter Twenty-Four

After downing four more ibuprofen and a quick cold shower, Jack had made the trek to Gramercy with no delay. He had to admit to himself that most of the trip was made on autopilot. He couldn't recall even the simplest task like stopping at the stop sign at the corner of his street or which on-ramp did he take to get onto the I-10. But he was finally turning into Aisling's driveway, making his way up the dirt road.

His reception in front of the house was anything but normal. As he exited his car, all three of the geese came charging out of the dark directly for him.

"Whoa," Jack screeched, holding both hands out in front of him, "come on guys, it's me, Jack."

The three geese were relentless and forced him up against the car. Any attempt to move forward was met with all three geese nipping viciously at his feet. Once, Spencer, the Canadian goose, grabbed on to his pants leg and shook it violently.

"Jack?" Aisling asked with an arched eyebrow indicating that it brought her great amusement to see his current standoff with the three geese.

"Aisling," Jack almost begged as the three geese continued to lunge at him, "I'll be geese food if you don't do something."

Aisling raised her lantern, "Vous trois. Partir," she commanded in French.

"Yes," Jack managed to parrot her command slurring his words terribly, "the three of you begone."

Instantly the three geese broke off their attack and waddled off to the backside of the house.

Jack continued to lean against the car for support as Aisling stepped closer. It wasn't till then that Jack noticed that she was wearing nothing but a short nightshirt and a very small pair of panties. Normally a striking figure like hers would have aroused him instantly, but it was all he could do to stay on his feet.

"Jack," she said, moving up next to him, "it's three in the morning. Not that I'm not happy to see you, but what are you doing here?" Aisling placed her lantern on the hood of the car then carefully slid her hands inside of his jacket to give him a hug.

Jack cried out in pain as her hand touched the wound at his waist. "Oh my God," he winced, pulling away from her touch while protecting his right side.

"Jack," she cried out her eyes sharp and assessing, "have you been shot?"

"I only wish," he said, taking a deep breath. "I've been shot three times," he confessed, "but none of them felt as painful as this."

Aisling picked up the lantern as she bent down in front of Jack. Slowly she began to pull back his jacket. Instinctively he tried to pull away. "Easy, Jack," she almost cooed, "I'm not going to hurt you." She again gently pulled back the coat.

Even Jack's nose picked up the vile stench emanating from the wound. If the site and smell the wound bothered her, she didn't show any outward sign.

"Can you walk?" She asked.

Jack thought about the question before shaking his head.

"Let's get you inside." She said softly, "Rest your left hand on my shoulder.

Jack followed her instructions and walked to the front porch and through the front entrance of Aisling's home. Jack stood in the middle of the living room, looking like a lost child. "What should I do?" he asked, his eyes darting around the room.

"Come with me into the kitchen," she said calmly leading the way.

Jack managed to follow her without stumbling too bad.

Aisling pointed to the kitchen table, "Can you sit on the edge of the table, Jack?"

Without speaking, Jack eased himself onto the table. Aisling quickly slid the chair under his feet, relieving the pressure on his abdomen. "First things first," she almost whispered, "Let's remove your coat."

With a lot of effort and an equal amount of support from Aisling, they were able to strip off his jacket.

"The gun is next, Jack," she said, pointing to his shoulder holster.

This took a much greater effort, and several times Jack winced with pain. Aisling started unbuttoning his shirt and gently slipped it over each of his shoulders and down the arms. After the shirt was removed, Aisling started to inspect the wound, but Jack stopped her.

"Here," Jack said as he gingerly reached behind his back and brought forth a knife from his hiding place in the small of his back.

"Heavens," Aisling gasped her eyes wide with amazement, "You planning on skinning the bear?"

A devilish look crossed Jack's face, "No, just a very bad witch."

Aisling didn't comment as she began to assess the wound. "Alright, Jack," she said evenly, "I'm going to attempt to remove your bandage without hurting you."

"Attempt?" Jack barked.

Again, Aisling did not answer but instead placed her hand over the bandage, and closing her eyes mumbled an enchantment. As soon as she finished, she peeled back the corner and cleanly removed the bandage.

Tears flooded Jack's eyes, but he did not make a sound.

"Stay right there," she said as she left the room, "I'll be right back."

"I'll be right here," Jack assured her, "unless I pass out and fall off the table."

Aisling immediately returned with what looked like a leather suitcase. She set it on the table about a foot away from Jack's perch. When she opened it, Jack didn't recognize many of the items but could tell that it was a very impressive looking first aid kit. Aisling slipped on a pair of latex gloves and began to examine the wound. Jack stared down at her as she worked. Even from what he could see, the wound was now scarlet red, the jagged edges of the cut were lined with pus. The wound itself was seeping a translucent colored liquid.

Aisling began to unfasten Jack's belt.

"What are you doing?" Jack asked, holding her hand.

"I'm going to remove your pants so I can work unencumbered on your wound."

"But," Jack protested "I'm not wearing any underwear."

The statement didn't seem to faze Aisling as she continued to unzip his trousers. "Didn't your mother ever tell you that you should always have clean underwear on in case you had to go to the emergency room?"

"I wasn't planning on a trip to the ER."

"They never do," Aisling chuckled as she walked over to the counter. She returned, throwing a large dishcloth at Jack's chest. "Here," she said, her eyes glowing openly with amusement, "if you're going to be squeamish about this, put this over your private parts."

As gently as possible, she removed his trousers and laid them over the back of a chair.

Then Aisling removed a device from her kit that, to Jack, looked somewhat like a knife, although the blade itself resembled a metal tongue depressor more than a blade and set it next to his side. She then removed a very old looking candle and a small square of granite. Aisling placed the granite block on top of the table, and with a quick flick of her wrist, a flame appeared on the wick of the candle. She tilted it until the flame rested against the wax of the candle, allowing the melted wax to hit the granite. Quickly she set the candle down on top of the melted wax, securing the candle to the block.

She then retrieved the metal tongue depressor. Skillfully Aisling placed the device under the wound and was able to scrape up some of the liquid onto the flat surface of the blade.

"You may want to turn your head away, Jack." She instructed him, "I'm pretty sure the stench is going to be overpowering."

When Jack continued to watch what she was doing, she proceeded with the next step. She began a chant as she held the blade just above the tip of the flame. Soon the heat of the flame beneath the blade caused the liquid to bubble and burn.

Jack gagged several times but refused to turn away. When the liquid was all but gone, what remained on the blade began to smoke.

Jack's eyes widened as he watched a green-colored smoke rise from the knife-edge.

Aisling removed the tool from the flame and seemed to physically relax, "Well," she sighed, "at least that's good news."

"Green smoke is good news," Jack asked skeptically.

"Yes," Aisling said as she again assessed the wound, "while the poison was concocted using black magic, its main purpose is to disable a person."

"It won't kill me then?"

"I didn't say that," she answered as she rummaged through her kit, "left unattended you would eventually die, but it would be a long, painful death."

"And that's good news?"

"I think so," Aisling answered as she took several ingredients from the kit and walked over to the stove. "At least it's treatable," she said as she dug additional jars and canisters from the cabinets above her head, "and you should recover fully."

Jack watched as she began to mix the ingredients into a small saucepan. His eyes dropped, and he stared at her butt, barely covered by the skimpy panties she wore. He finally forced himself to turn away.

Aisling soon returned to Jack's side, carrying a teacup in one hand and a small clay bowl in the other. "Alright, Jack," she said as she placed the clay bowl on the table and held out the teacup toward him, "I want you to drink all of this."

Jack looked into the cup, noticing that the liquid was clear but had a slightly pasty consistency. The smell was... earthy, not unlike pure dirt. "Don't you have something with a strawberry flavor?" He said, not taking his eyes off the brew.

"Sorry," she answered, handing him the cup.

Jack peered into the clay bowl sitting next to him. The paste was thick and dark green. Its smell was unpleasant, but nothing like the smell of the stuff seeping from his wound. "What are you going to do with that?"

"First, I'm going to clean up your wound and then apply this Poultice." She informed him. "Now drink up while it's still warm," she instructed, "I suggest you drink it as quickly as possible."

Jack brought the cup to his lips and took a large sip of the liquid. He gagged and spit liquid back into the cup. "Christ," he complained, looking into the cup, "this tastes like shit." The liquid had a strange metallic taste with hints of organic aftertaste.

"That's why I told you to drink it as quickly as possible," she reaffirmed as she poured a bluish liquid onto a gauze she was holding and gently applied it to the wound, "now drink."

Jack built up his courage and again brought the cup to his lips. This time he began to drink, forcing it down his throat until it was gone. It wasn't an easy task; his throat resisting every step of the way. "Can I at least have a glass of water?"

"In a second, darling," Aisling said as she applied the poultice to the wound. When she finished, she wrapped gauze around Jack's abdomen, holding the poultice in place. "That should do," Aisling said as she walked to the refrigerator. She returned, holding a glass out toward him, "Your water."

Jack down the liquid as if his life depended on it. He exhaled and held the glass for her to take. "Alright," he said, looking around, "help me get my clothes back on."

"What for?" Aisling demanded.

Jack reached for his trousers hanging over the chair next to him "because I can't go around outside naked."

"Jack," she protested, "you're not going anywhere."

His voice was heavy with sarcasm, "Are you going to try to stop me?" He challenged.

He could tell that Aisling was angry, but he watched as she forced herself to settle down. Jack slowly worked his way down off the table, still holding the dishtowel around his groin. As soon as both feet touch the ground, his knees buckled. Aisling was there to catch him.

"Jack," she said, holding up the dishtowel he had dropped, "you are in no shape to go anywhere, dressed or undressed."

Jack leaned heavily against her, his breathing erratic. "I've got to go." He protested.

"The only place you're going, Jack Kohl," she said, helping him into the living room, "is to bed. In a few minutes, that potion I gave you is going to take effect."

"And next," he said sarcastically, "you're going to warn me that I shouldn't drive or operate heavy equipment while taking this medication."

"I won't have to," she confirmed, moving him into her bedroom, "if I don't get you in the bed before you pass out, you're going to be sleeping on the floor where you fall."

"Where's my towel?" he slurred.

"You're not going to need it," she assured him as she lowered him to the bed as gently as she could. "Color optimus," she ordered in Latin. The light in the room began to slowly dim. "Satis," she said softly when the light had reached something closely resembling dusk.

Jack's glassy eyes came up to study her face, "I didn't…"

"Sleep, Jack," she whispered softly, covering him with a blanket.

Jack thought her suggestion was a good one as his eyes fluttered, then closed.

****

While Jack floated somewhere between the present and the netherworld, he was not totally unconscious. It was a new sensation for him, and he planned to fully explore its regions. The first thing he noticed was that his sense of hearing was muted. It was as if someone had turned down the volume on his ears. If he concentrated, he could make out some sounds but was unable to respond.

His sense of feeling was also greatly diminished. It was if all of his nerve endings had been marginalized. He felt no pain, but then neither did he feel hot or cold. He tried to touch his index finger to his thumb but was unsure that he could accomplish the task, or if he had managed to connect the two digits, the weakened sense of touch did not register the link.

The sense of sight was totally obliterated. The lead shields that were Jack's eyelids were unmovable. There were no shades of gray, only the total darkness of black.

He had only wished that his taste buds would have followed the lead of his other senses. Unfortunately, a metallic, earthy taste filled his mouth. While it somewhat resembled the nutty, earthy taste associated with truffles, the heavily organic and unpleasant metal mouth feel could never be mistaken for the savory taste of truffles.

The one sense that was truly on overload was his sense of smell. The area about him seemed to be impregnated with the salacious aroma that was purely Aisling. The scent of her brought back many pleasant memories of their brief times together. He wouldn't be alive now, he thought if it weren't for her. Was he still alive, he wondered, or had he truly passed into the spirit world?

The fresh scent of her presence filled the air begging him to open his eyes. With extreme difficulty, he was able to partially open his fluttering eyelids. The more light that seeped in, the more he was encouraged to open them. Blinking heavily, he was able to focus on his surroundings. He was in a bedroom, not his… Aisling's, he thought? Yes, he had stopped at Aisling's home, where she had attended to his wound. It was her bedroom that he was in.

He looked around the room, not particularly focusing on any one item, that is until he saw Aisling. She was sitting in a large rocker, her legs crossed under her. Her head was back, and her eyes closed.

"How do you feel?" She asked, not opening her eyes.

"I'm, I'm not sure," he was able to answer through parched lips.

"Do you feel any pain?" She asked, finally opening her eyes and offering a sweet smile."

Jack took a quick inventory of his body, "No," he thought out loud, "no pain."

Aisling unfolded her legs from under her and leaned forward. Gently she placed the back of her hand on his head. "Your fever has broken," she informed him. "Other than drugged," she asked, "how do you feel?"

Jack's eyes darted around the room as he thought about her question. "Hungry," he finally answered. *I must've given her the right answer, Jack thought as her face was beaming.*

"I've made some vegetable soup," she informed him, "would you like some?"

"Do I have to get up?" He thought out loud.

"This one time," she said, her eyes sparkling, "I'll make an exception and bring it to you."

"Thank you," he said in earnest.

Within just a few minutes, he was now sitting up pillows propping his back up against the headboard of the bed. Aisling had brought in a breakfast tray and had positioned it in front of him. As promised, she had brought a bowl of vegetable soup that was more like a stew. Two slices of homemade bread and a tall glass of iced tea accompanied it. Jack fished out a small chunk of carrot and gingerly placed it in his mouth. "Oh my God," he said, "this tastes wonderful."

"You really like it?"

Aisling was sitting on the edge of the bed. Jack laid his left hand on top of hers. "My mouth feels like I've been chewing on a piece of copper forever," he informed her. "This," he said, pointing to the bowl with his spoon, "is heaven-sent."

"Thank you," she said, acknowledging his compliment. "When you finish will see if we can get you up and walking. There will be some after-effects of the poison and the medication. So, the sooner we get you up and get your blood circulating, the better you'll feel."

"Oomph," he responded with a mouth full of soup, "you're a miracle worker."

"Jack," she said, her mouth twisting dryly, "you were heavily in the clutches of that poison."

"You don't have to tell me," he said hungrily, chowing down on the bowl in front of him, "I thought I was a goner."

"A few more hours," she confirmed, "and you would've been."

"I feel great now," he repeated.

Aisling took his left hand into hers, "it's too early to tell what type of damage that poison may have done."

The spoon in Jack's hand stopped midway been between the bowl and his mouth, "damage?"

"Yes," she said, moistening her dry lips, "there could be some residual damage left behind by the poison."

He set the full spoon back into the bowl as his appetite suddenly left him. "What type of damage?"

"I don't know," she said quite frankly, "it could manifest itself in many different ways."

"Well," he sighed, "why don't you give me the top ten possibilities."

She drew her lips in thoughtfully, "loss of strength from time to time," she said, "reoccurring pain in your abdomen or something as minor as dry mouth. We'll just have to keep an eye on you for a while."

While the possibilities made him frown, he was determined not to let it slow him down. "What time is it?" he asked.

"Around one o'clock."

"Good," he said, "I still have most of the day."

Her expression stilled and grew serious, "that day is gone, Jack," she informed him, "it's one in the morning. You've been in bed for almost 24 hours."

His voice was heavy with doubt, "it can't be," he stammered, "I just laid down a few minutes ago."

Aisling removed the food tray and started to pull the cover down. "Let me check your wound," she said.

Jack help push the blanket down to his lower abdomen and then stopped it from going any further.

"You're still not playing Mr. Modest," she said as she lightly applied pressure to the area. "are you?"

Jack merely stared, tongue-tied at what he saw. "You can hardly tell that it was a seeping wound just one day ago." He then released the sheet from his grasp, "And yes," he said softly, his eyes narrowing in jest, "some of us still believe in modesty."

Aisling continued with her examination. "Well, it's too late for that," she grinned.

Jack's eyes narrowed, "What do you mean?"

"I took advantage of your deep sleep," she informed him as a flash of humor crossed her face, "and gave you a sponge bath."

"Without my consent?" He said, trying to keep a straight face.

"You're in my bed, and you stank fiercely," she informed him, "I didn't need your consent."

Jack suddenly remembered his conversation with Derek Willow. "Aisling, have you ever heard of a witch using her powers to drain the life out of someone?"

"There are some old stories," she shrugged dismissively, "but they're only stories."

"I talked with Derek Willow yesterday, and he swore that Morgana Kerr, somehow during sex, left him feeling weak," Jack relayed, "and in his words, it felt as if she were draining the life out of him. He says his two boys corroborate the claim."

"She was sleeping with all three of them?"

"Apparently," Jack confirmed, "during the same period."

Aisling stood up, offering Jack her hands, "Come on,"

she said, "the quicker we get you up and moving around, the better you will feel."

# Chapter Twenty-Five

Jack paced from one end of Aisling's kitchen to the other in the pre-dawn light. He continually flexed the fingers in both hands and occasionally shook his finger loose when they became stiff. As part of his new ritual, he rotated his head from one side to the other while shrugging his shoulders forward and backward. Sporadically he would stop his pacing and swivel his hips as far as he could at the waist, then resume his pacing.

Aisling was busy preparing breakfast for the two them and would periodically be required to maneuver around Jack so that the two did not collide. "Are you ready to eat Jack?" she asked as she brought a bowl of home fries to the table.

He nodded perfunctorily and returned to his pacing. When Aisling sat down at the table, Jack ended his stretching routine and joined her.

"You feeling better?" Aisling asked as she passed Jack a plate.

"Not bad," he said as he dug into the bowl in front of him, "I start to stiffen, but I'm able to shake it out quickly." Jack took a sip from the cup of tea Aisling has set in front of him. "Is this medicinal?" He asked.

"Does it taste medicinal?" she asked as her left eyebrow rose a fraction.

Jack took another sip from the cup, "No," he answered, "it tastes rather good."

"Then enjoy it."

Jack's appetite was insatiable. He went back for seconds on both the potatoes and the sliced ham. "You know," he said, allowing his food to go down, "you never did answer me about Morgana Kerr draining the life from Derek Willow?"

"I most certainly did," Aisling said, her eyes full of remoteness.

"No," Jack countered, "you said there were rumors, but you never confirmed or denied the possibility."

Aisling glared at him over her teacup, "You know Jack, sometimes I dislike the fact that you are a detective."

"A very minor flaw," he assured her.

"That depends on the perspective," she shot back, "to an ant a bowl of sugar is a mountain.

"To a detective," he retorted, "a brushoff is not an answer."

"What was your question?" Aisling asked.

"Has there ever been," Jack said slowly and purposely, "an instant where a witch was ever accused of drawing the life out of a victim?"

Aisling nodded her understanding, "and I answered your question."

"No," Jack insisted, "you skirted the answer. I believe you said, and I quote: 'There are some old stories, but they're only stories.'

"See," she smiled smugly, "I did give you an answer."

Jack returned to his meal, picking through the food on his plate. He refilled his teacup from the pot in front of him and made a silent offer to refill Aisling's cup. She held out her cup, and he politely filled it.

"I assume," she said, breaking the silence between them, "you are waiting for me to answer your question."

"Only if you feel like it." He shrugged.

Aisling contemplated, formulating an answer. "Alright, Jack," she said, exhaling heavily, "what I'm about to tell you is completely hearsay. I have never received the information firsthand, nor has it ever been corroborated by anyone I know. It is, for lack of a better term, a witch's tale. Whispered in the dark, told around campfires."

"I understand."

Again, Aisling hesitated as if sorting the facts into a logical order. "Do you remember when I told you that Morgana Kerr's tribe came from the Great Steppe region of Europe and that her clan was almost totally obliterated for its practice of witchcraft."

"Vaguely," he answered, "but yes, I do recall it now."

"Well, The Eurasian Steppe extends thousands of miles, starting at the mouth of the Danube and going east almost to the Pacific Ocean. The only thing we need to concern ourselves with is the Western edge of the Steppe. A very small area that is now known as Romania."

"Romania," Jack repeated, "okay, continue."

Aisling's eyes turned cold and reserved, "Stories say that her tribesmen were one of the first group of witches to immerse themselves into black magic. It was said that one particular family discovered how to literally rob a person of their life force."

"You mean what Derek Willow thought he felt during sex with her?"

Aisling nodded, "Yes, it was rumored that the transference of a person's life force was easier to steal during a person's heightened emotional state."

"Amazing," Jack gulped, "so do these victims die when their life force is stolen?"

"I believe that would be true," Aisling confirmed, "if the attacker didn't break off in time, I'm sure the victim could die. But, again, I believe that in most cases, only a small amount of the victim's life force would be taken at any one time."

"That way," Jack surmised, "the victim could be used time and time again like Derek Willow and his sons."

"Correct," she said, "the attacker's motive could thus be concealed."

"I bet," Jack huffed, "having a stack of dead bodies around usually will start to draw a crowd."

"Exactly."

"So," Jack's right eyebrow raised inquiringly, "what does someone like Morgana gain from the experience?"

"Well," Aisling started slowly, "if you were to take the stories to be true, then the attacker would need the victim's life force to survive."

"So." Jack concluded, "someone like Morgana would need the life force to continue living."

"Yes."

"Would it be possible then," Jack asked, "that performing this ritual would keep her young?"

"It makes sense," Aisling concurred, "if you were able to constantly resupply your life force, then a person could theoretically live for a long, long time."

"Imagine being able to literally be able to suck the life…" Jack's eyes grew the size of small saucers as the shock of discovery hit him full force, "wait a minute, Romania, sucking the life out of a person. Are you talking about vampires!"

"Slowdown Jack," she cautioned, "we're talking about the fifteenth-century campfire folklore. I don't believe there is such a thing as a blood-sucking vampire, but it makes sense that stories of people being able to 'suck' the life out of someone could have morphed from the stories of Morgana's tribe."

"I see your point," he said, "and this ability to steal someone's life force is the reason why surrounding tribes decided to annihilate Kerr's people."

"I believe so."

"Wow," he said, his mouth dropping open, "Morgana Kerr is already one of the most dangerous people I've ever met and now pile this on top, and she moves straight up to the top of the list."

"I should hope so," Aisling said, crossing her arms over her chest.

"One more thing," Jack asked sheepishly, "I almost hate to ask."

"What is it?"

"What about driving a wooden stake through their hearts. Is that also true or just conjecture?"

Aisling shook her head, "No, from what I've heard. When the other villages raided the Kerr camp, those that were not killed outright were gathered together and impaled on long wooden pikes; then burned at the stake, so to speak. That's where it's believed the myth of the wooden stake killing a vampire originated."

"Damn," Jack barked. "They didn't mess around, did they?"

When he had finished his tea, Jack took his plate over to the sink and rinsed it. Without speaking, he picked up his holster and weapon. He methodically went through the motions of adjusting the straps until the weapon lay just beneath his armpit. In a single fluid motion, he removed the gun from the holster and released the clip allowing it to fall in his left hand. He inspected both the weapon and the clip, and when he was satisfied, he reinserted the clip into the handle of the gun until it was seated with a noticeable click. He then picked up his knife, and using both hands behind his back, seated the blade in the leather sheath.

Aisling stared at him in astonishment. "You know, Jack," she said her coolness evidence that what she was saying was somewhat of a surprise, "this is only the second time I've seen the warrior side of you." She stood and moved toward him, "the first time was when those two men attacked you in the French quarter. That time you were defending yourself."

There was a stillness in his voice, "And now?" he prompted.

"Now," she replied, "you are the aggressor. You have an air of authority and the appearance of someone who demands instant obedience."

"But I think you're wrong," he said, with an affable understanding. "I am still the defender. Although my actions may become aggressive, I am still only interested in defending the rights of others. In this case, those of Matthew Willow. And you might think that I am setting out for retribution for the deaths of Brandon and Justin, but that is not my motive either."

"Then what is?" Aisling asked, hanging on Jack's every word.

"My true motivation is justice," he said, leaning lightly into her, tilting his face toward hers, "it's all about Newton's Third Law of Motion."

"What does Newton's law have to do with what you're about to descend on?"

"Easy enough," Jack smiled wickedly, "in every interaction, there are forces working on two interacting objects. If the forces are equal, then the situation becomes stagnant. Neither side wins. So, for one side to overcome the other, its force must be greater or, as people usually see it, become more aggressive. If I want to free Matthew Willow and bring Morgana Kerr to justice, I will have to be more aggressive than the Black Witch. She is not, as they say, going to come along quietly."

"Is that," Aisling asked as she quirked her eyebrow questioningly, "your Criminal Psychology in action?"

"No, my Lady," his lips brushing against hers as he spoke, "It's one of the fundamental laws of nature, and as one who communes with nature, you know it to be true."

"Jack," she breathed lightly between parted lips, "you had better come back to me."

"I fully intend to," he said as he backed out of her embrace. He then scooped up his coat from the back of the chair and put it on as he moved toward the door. "Besides," he said as he opened the door, "I'm looking forward to my next sponge bath."

Aisling moved toward the back door. "Jack," she called after him. She waited for him to turn and face her. "So am I, so don't be late."

****

Jack made his way around the lake to a small trail that, as Aisling had promised, led to the rear of the Kerr plantation house. Jack checked his watch. By now, Aisling had phoned Matty and told her of Jack's movements. A permanent sorrow seemed to weigh him down as he considered the actions he had taken. If he had called Matty when he first arrived, he reminded himself, he would now, more than likely, be in the intensive care unit at Charity Hospital. Between Matty and Doctor Meeker, they would have every sensor, probe, and toxicology test being run on him for something he knew they could not solve. No, Jack convinced himself for the hundredth time, it would be better if Matty would arrive with the Cavalry.

Jack continued to make his way to the backside of the plantation using the deteriorated slave quarters for cover. Off to his left was the family cemetery. It, unlike the rest of the house, had already been restored to its former glory. A well-kept black wrought iron fence surrounded the dozen or so above-ground tombs. In the center was a singularly large mausoleum that Jack was sure was the final resting place of the builder of the plantation and his wife.

The home was not nearly in as good shape. Of course, Jack had come up from behind the home to conceal his presence. He had hoped that if anybody were keeping an eye out for trespassers, it would be from the front side of the house, thinking that somebody would be stupid enough to come up the main entrance drive.

As majestic and grand as the front entrance of most plantations were, the back of the homes were usually very plain. In the case of the Kerr plantation, the bottom floor was made of stone while the rest of the home was covered in wood drop siding. There were two doors on the first floor, separated by a row of three windows. At first glance, all of the openings on the first floor were covered with plywood sheets, probably to prevent vandals from breaking into the home. He made a mental note to check each of them for the possibility of being pried open.

The second-floor windows seem as if they were all ceiling to floor in length and had no plywood covers. He noticed that several of the small glass window panes making up the huge windows were cracked or broken. These individual window panes had been covered with some type of plastic covering to keep out the weather. Those windows would be his best chance of gaining entrance to the house. *Now,* he thought, *he would just have to figure a way to climb up to the second floor.*

His break came as he started around the left side of the home. There, already constructed, was a three-story scaffolding. Some workers had been doing restoration work on the wood drop siding. It was obvious that the work had been stopped some time ago, but the scaffolding remained in place.

Jack quickly made his way up the scaffolding, being careful to stay between two windows. It would not bode well for him if he ascended the scaffolding directly in front of a window only to be seen by someone inside the house or to have his shadow announce his arrival. When he reached the second level, he hugged the wall until he was just inches from the window. Quietly he got down on his knees and carefully peered into the bottom pane of the window.

The window shears blocked part of his vision, but after several minutes he convinced himself that there was no one in the room. He again stood and tried the security of the window. It was firmly locked in place and could not be budged. He then searched along the window frame for a locking device. He quickly found what he was looking for. The latch was securely fastened. He removed his knife from his belt and tried to jimmy the lock. When it wouldn't budge, he came to the conclusion that he would have to break the windowpane to reach in and unfasten the bolt. The thought of breaking the window made him cringe. In an empty room such as he was looking at, the sound of the glass breaking would be nothing short of shouting through a megaphone.

He then moved to the second window and began the process again. His eyes took on a sheen of purpose as he discovered one of the windowpanes closest to the latch was in serious disrepair. The glazing compound that was used to hold the glass pane within the frame showed signs of obvious decomposing. Jack broke a small piece of the compound away from the frame and was able to crush it between his fingers. He once again removed his knife from the sheaf. His jaw clenched, his eyes slightly narrowing as he began digging away at the powdery compound. In just a few minutes, he had removed most of the glazing and, with the tip of the knife, was able to pry the windowpane free. It neatly fell into his open hand and carefully related down on the scaffolding.

Jack rechecked the room, making sure it was still vacant. He then put his ear up to the opening and carefully listened. When there was no sign or sound of anyone nearby, he delicately slid his arm in through the hole until he was able to reach the latch. In opening the window, he was forced to use his knife as a wedge in several places where the wood had swollen due to moisture. He smiled to himself even though the fact of entering the home sent his pulse racing.

*I sure hope Matty and the backup arrive sooner than later,* he said to himself as he lowered his leg into the room.

# Chapter Twenty-Six

The first thing to grab Jack's attention was the dank, musty smell permeating the room. It immediately brought him back to the times he spent at his favorite aunt's home, where he would sometimes play in the basement while she restocked the shelves with homemade canned goods. He closed the large window and quickly secured the lock.

He made a quick assessment of the room before taking another step. The two windows, covering most of the wall behind him were the only source of light. The morning sunlight fought hard to break through the grungy windowpanes that were covered with 100 years of history. He doubted that the windows had ever been cleaned since the Civil War. The translucent light stained the walls and ceiling with a dirty eggshell color. In the dingy light, the floor looked more like ancient Egyptian scrolls instead of wooden planks. The floorboards were covered in dirt except for the few that had pulled up and were now bent and twisted, pointing like arthritic fingers toward the ceiling. In two areas of the room, the floorboards had simply rotted away, exposing the joists beneath.

Jack looked up at the ceiling above the damaged floor. He discovered that water damage from a leak in the roof had caused the ceiling to collapse and, over time, disintegrate the floor below. He carefully walked closer. As he suspected, a new roof was in place, no longer allowing water to damage the interior of the home. A new roof would have been the first thing needed in the restoration; any work on the inside of the house needed to be protected from the outside elements.

Jack, as quietly as possible, made his way to the door. As soon as he attempted to peek out of the room, a monstrous fist grazed his forehead, sending him spiraling back into the room. Jack lost his footing, crashing to the floor. In a moment of horror, Jack watched his weapon sliding across the floor, heading for one of the large holes. He stretched out his hand toward the weapon as if that would be enough to stop it. He moaned softly as the gun teetered on the edge of the gap then slipped out of view.

He quickly scrambled to his feet, moving away from the door. He stood unsteadily, shaking his head, attempting to clear the ringing in his ears. The metallic taste of blood filled his mouth. As he looked back toward the door, he quickly forgot about his injuries. There blocking most of the doorframe was one of the largest men he had ever seen. A wave of uneasiness washed over Jack dampening his spirits as he sized up the monster in front of him. The massive shoulders of the man filled the coat he wore stretching the seams to their splitting point. His stance emphasized the force of his muscular thighs. He would not be easy to topple. Jack considered taking out his knife but decided against it. Seeing the blade, the man would change his tactics to compensate. It would be better, Jack thought, *to save the blade for a surprise attack at some point.*

Jack took several steps to his right to see how his adversary would respond. The behemoth didn't move but merely adjusted his gaze to follow him. Jack stared at the man's massive hands. They were big and square, reminding Jack of a matched pair of pile drivers. The grazing wallop the man had given him earlier had nearly knocked him unconscious. Jack knew that one wrong move would cost him his life.

The man suddenly lunged forward, his right hand cocked back and ready. Jack braced for the attack. The massive hand flew through the air passing through the empty space where Jack had been standing only seconds ago. He studied the creature as he slowly turned around. *Thankfully,* he thought, *speed and motor control weren't the beast's strong suits.*

Jack teased his opponent by stretching out his right-hand beckoning, daring his enemy to come at him a second time. His adversary changed his stance to one more akin to a wrestler. He hunched down, his legs spread apart, his arms stretched wide, fingers ready to grab him. Jack, with a little false bravado, smiled, motioning for him to engage. With a low growl, the man again moved forward this time; his stance was more like a giant gorilla. Jack waited to the last second, then dived to the ground, performing a shoulder roll between the man's legs. Jack quickly regained his feet, his lanky leg kicking out, driving the heel of his foot into the man's knee.

The behemoth's knee buckled but did not break, and the man hobbled to the other side of the room. "Shit," Jack said under his breath, "I've just managed to piss off a seven-foot-tall giant!" Jack was very pleased, though, to see that his attacker was now favoring the leg. He quickly checked his surroundings preparing for the next attack. For the first time, he felt the nauseating sinking feeling of despair as he noticed that he was now trapped between his assailant and the large gaping hole in the floor. The position gave him very little maneuvering room, knowing that the giant would not allow him to slip between his legs a second time.

His assailant readied himself for a new attack. Growling long and low, the beast moved forward at a reduced speed, keeping his eyes on Jack. Again, Jack waited until the last second feigning a move to the right. Instinctively his attacker compensated to the right, and Jack, with a quick spinning motion, using the man's own body as a pivot point, skirting the man on the left thrusting his blade between the ogre's cervical spine and the base of the skull as he passed.

Jack staggered back and waited. The giant stood motionless for several seconds before crashing into the hole in the floor. The man's weight carrying him down into the hole almost to his waist. When the giant failed to move after several minutes, Jack walked over to the body and gave him a swift kick. When he still didn't move, Jack began a search for his knife. Soon he let out a sigh, then gave a resigned shrug accepting the fact that he had lost both his gun and his knife.

As he approached the door, he reminded himself that getting sucker-punched just once was one time too many. This time he followed a tried and true method of searching the hallway. Jack got down to his knees and laid flat on the floor. Then he slowly inched out just far enough to look down the hall in both directions. The hall was empty. He jumped to his feet and began meticulously checking the other rooms on the second floor.

After a careful but thorough search of each room, Jack became convinced that Matthew Willow was located somewhere on the first floor. He had considered checking the attic, but then he remembered that the photographs of Derek showed that the room was a finished living area. The attic would be bare of any plaster walls or curtains.

Jack approached the black wrought iron railing that overlooked the grand foyer of the house. Where he stood at the center of the second-story balcony, twin staircases on both his left and right spiral down to the first-floor landing. The landing was bare of any furniture, although it did look as if it had been recently cleaned up. He stood leaning over the balcony, searching below. There was no one in sight, and after several seconds of silence, he figured that he may be the only one left in the house. *It would be very fortunate,* he thought to himself, *if he had already taken out the only caretaker in the building.* Now he would be free to search the rest of the house for Matthew Willow. Not wanting to throw caution to the wind, he crept down the staircase as quietly as possible. He decided to start his search with the first room off the foyer to the right.

He walked into the room and was greeted by Morgana Kerr.

"Hello, Detective Kohl," she said, her tongue heavy with sarcasm, "I would've thought you'd be dead by now."

"No," Jack replied, checking himself over in a mock examination, "no, still here. How have you been?"

"Until now," she sneered, "I've been well." Morgana Kerr took a few steps toward him, "I thought the exterminators had taken care of all the vermin in the house," she said in a cool, aloof manner. "Now I see," she continued as she pulled out the Athame dagger, "there is still one that I must dispatch myself."

"Oh, thank God," Jack said, ignoring her comment, "I see you found your dagger. I was afraid some lowlife had stolen it."

Kerr's eyes flared, Jack noticed as she was obviously irritated by his mocking tone. "Have you had a chance," she asked, "to examine this blade up close?"

"No," Jack retorted, "but I'll have plenty of time to study it later when you're on trial for kidnapping, extortion, and... oh yes, murder."

"Why wait on something that may never happen," she chided as she suddenly flew across the open space, separating them.

Jack was taken aback by the attack. The woman seemed to glide across the floor at a humanly impossible speed. Jack's eyes bulged at the phenomena. He watched as she raised the dagger, and suddenly screaming plunged it toward his heart. The dagger struck his jacket right at the breast pocket. As the blade penetrated the cloth, there was a sudden shower of dazzling sparks. The space between he and Morgana exploded in a blinding white light. The two of them were thrown into the air and forced apart by several feet. Jack hit the ground hard and rolled. As quickly as possible, he staggered to his feet, looking for his adversary. She, too stunned by the blast, was just now regaining her feet.

For several seconds Jack and she stared at each other; total bewilderment shared by both. Suddenly Jack smelled a light whiff of smoke. He quickly looked down at his jacket, inspecting the gash caused by Morgana's dagger. The cut was located in the top portion of the chest pocket. As he would have expected, it was a clean puncture with sharp edges, but the smell of the smoke became more intense. He pulled back the jacket and peered inside. The smell of smoke was stronger, and it was coming from inside the inner breast pocket. Jack kept one eye on Morgana Kerr as he peered inside the pocket with the other. He reached in and slowly pulled out a piece of paper. Holding it out in front of him, he suddenly recognized it as one of the origami Sheriff stars that Matty often made. He held it out in front of him and threw it to the ground as it burst into flames.

Jack looked toward Morgana. She looked just as befuddled as he was, but he sensed that she recognized what had just happened.

"Clever boy," she hissed at Jack, "I should have known that there would be those that would try to protect you."

Jack spotted the dagger lying on the floor just 10 feet away. *If I can keep her talking*, he thought, *maybe I can get to the dagger before she does.* "So Morgana," he said, "just how old are you? One hundred, one hundred and fifty?"

Morgana Kerr parted the lace at her throat to allow the hollow of her neck and firm breasts to show. "Do I look 150 years old, Jack Kohl?"

"No," Jack admitted as he moved closer to the dagger, "but you made a major mistake when I was at your house."

Morgana Kerr's finger lightly stroked the cleavage between her breasts, "How's that?"

Jack made a slight shift in his stance, "When I was admiring the painting of this plantation, you told me it was built by your *grandfather* in 1839." Jack made a quick glance down at the blade and continued with his explanation. "Well, if it were built by your grandfather, which I'm inclined to believe it was, then that would make you over 100 years old." Jack crept closer to the blade, "and believe me," he lied, "you don't look a day over forty-four."

The warmth of her smile echoed in her voice, "Why, Jack Kohl," she stated with a heavy southern drawl, "aren't you the flatterer." Morgana suddenly dove for the blade. Jack was half a second behind her.

Morgana Kerr reached the knife first, but Jack's hand gripped her wrist, pinning it to the ground. Morgana then flipped on top of him using her free hand to beat his face. Jack felt the change over to the sepia tone world between the hammering blows of Morgana Kerr. Grabbing her free hand with his, he bucked at the waist throwing the lighter woman over his head. He released her hands while she was in midflight and rolled out from beneath her. As he stood, he readied himself for her next attack.

Standing before him, not moving was the Black Witch. She was wheezing heavily, the dagger still in her right hand. Her appearance was worse than he remembered the night he had first seen her at Justin Willows home. Her skin still had the same look as bad leather. The crater-like scar on her left cheek had grown in size, housing more of the small blood-filled pores. He noticed that there was a new smaller crater now infecting her right cheekbone. It seemed to be the home of some type of parasite.

Jack readied to charge but stopped when Morgana Kerr, with a wave of her hand, shouted in Latin, "The pain!"

Jack doubled over the agony, the right side of his abdomen feeling as if something was trying to crush his insides. He kept a watchful eye on the witch's right hand as his own hand rested on the small scar at his hip.

"That's better," Morgana Kerr said, still trying to catch her breath, "you didn't think I would stick you with a simple poison, did you, Jack?"

Jack tried to slow his breathing as he attempted to straighten. He consciously had to force his hand to release the wound. "No, Morgana," he said as he removed his jacket and threw it to the ground, "I don't guess anything is easy with you."

"Some things are," she said wickedly, "but I'm afraid that you'll never enjoy those pleasures."

"Is that nasty face of yours," Jack said, pointing toward her, "part of those pleasures? What are those scars, the holes filled with puss and those nasty little creatures? Is that all part of the Witches Rule of Three?"

Morgana's hand shot up to her face but stopped short of touching the source. Jack figured that the fact that he could see her as she really was surprised her. "What do you know of the witches' rule?"

"I know that you have to be one nasty bitch to look that fucking bad. No matter how old you are." He said, continuing to berate her, "If everyone could see you as I do, you couldn't get a donkey to sleep with you!"

As a shattering scream escaped her mouth, she charged toward him, dagger held high over her head. Jack was ready for her this time and blocked her downward thrust with his elbow as he delivered a powerful blow to her solar plexus. She staggered back several paces, not showing any effect of the blow. She instantly attacked again, thrusting the knife out in front of her. Jack turned his body, allowing the knife to pass by harmlessly but not before he was able to grab her wrist with his left hand and follow through with a right-handed knife strike to her elbow.

The blow caused her arm to bend at the elbow, forcing the blade upward. Jack staggered backward, holding the dagger in his left hand. He quickly moved into a defensive stance protecting the blade as he expected her to charge again. Oddly enough, though, Morgana stood back, a terrible smile on her face.

"You were good at disarming me, Jack," she sneered, pointing to his left shoulder, "but not good enough."

Jack glanced at his left shoulder. The gash in his shirt was a good two to the three inches long. Blood was already starting to seep into the fabric of the material. The grazing blow must've happened when he twisted the dagger out of her hand.

"I can promise you," she tittered, "your death will be long and agonizing."

"Then," Jack stated matter-of-factly, pointing the blade toward her, "there's no reason that I shouldn't take you with me."

As the last word spilled over his lips, he charged directly toward the woman.

Again she held out her hand and shouted the curse to force the pain to take Jack. "Dolor," she commanded, and Jack doubled over in overwhelming pain. He couldn't move forward or stand up straight. He just stood there doubled over.

"That's better," Morgana grinned, "the poison from the blade will start to affect you shortly, and you'll stop being a problem."

Jack let out a moan in response.

Morgana stepped in closer, preparing to retrieve her dagger. "I'll take that," she said as she motioned for Jack to surrender the blade.

As she reached for the knife, Jack unfolded like a catapult, the finely-honed blade slashing through the air toward Morgana. The blade caught her just above the left side of her jaw and neatly made its way across her cheek and on to the bridge of her nose.

Jack stumbled back, still holding his gut with his left hand. The dagger clattered to the ground when he could no longer hold onto it. He stared at Morgana, who was now bent forward, both of her hands clutching her face. Blood trickled between her fingers splashing on the tile below.

Morgana stood up, her hands held out in front of her. Rivulets of blood ran down her horrific face. "Look what you've done, you bastard!"

Jack sank to his knees, his legs no longer able to hold him upright, "I guess sex is out of the question then?" he asked, staring at her through eyes that no longer could be trusted. He suddenly recalled that Meeker had warned them that the poison on the blade contained an unknown hallucinogenic. For a moment, he shook his head, clearing his vision, and stared intently at Morgana's face. The blade had sliced through the crusted scar on her left cheek, slicing the pulpy center wide open. Small insect size crustaceans were scampering to get out. At first, he thought they were searching for a way to escape, but then he realized that they were hungrily devouring her flesh. She screamed a second time holding her hands in front of her terrified face as she was forced to watch the creatures busily destroying her lovely fingers. Jack was able to keep his eyes open as Morgana crashed to the ground like a discarded mannequin, silent and immobile.

He weaved from one side to the other, still able to maintain a kneeling position. The sound of high heels striking the marble floor drew his attention to the door on the opposite side of the room. Again he was forced to shake his head and blink several times to clear his view. There standing just inside the door stood Special Agent Salton.

"Thank God," Jack slurred in a mocking tone, "the police."

Without speaking, Salton walked over and gazed down at the body of Morgana Kerr. "Nicely done, Jack," she said, picking up Morgana's dagger.

"Here for souvenirs?" he asked weakly."

"Not hardly," she shot back, pointing the dagger toward him, "I have to confess that I thought for sure she would've killed you and then I would have been forced to kill her to take over the coven." She took a few more steps closer to Jack. "But now," she grinned, "with her dead, and this dagger buried in your chest, everything will be neatly tied up."

Jack's mind fought the effects of the poison in the hopes of mounting one more battle with Salton, but trying to move his arms was futile.

Salton held the dagger out in front of her, "When it came to magical poison's," she said, studying the blade, "Morgana was an artist."

"I purr fur Moe nay," Jack slurred.

"I'll make sure to mention that," she said, readying her strike, "on your epitaph. Goodbye, Jack,"

Jack heard the pop, pop, pop from behind his head, and watched as Salton's chest jerked with the impact of each bullet. Three crimson flowers sprung upon the woman's blouse and began to spread. Jack had to smile as he noticed that the three bullet holes could have been covered by a silver dollar.

"Matty," he said, crashing to the floor at the same time as Salton.

Jack watched as Matty knelt next to him. Her hands gently rolled him over onto his back. Jack choked several times, and his breath came in ragged gasps, "Matty?" he coughed, "my shoulder…"

To Jack, the sound of her ripping his shirt sounded like thunder rolling across his chest."

"Shit, Jack," Matty exclaimed as she examined the wound.

"Sssshit," Jack parroted his eyes rolling.

He was not surprised as Matty produced a blade of her own. He was used to the woman being well-armed. He was surprised, though, when Matty held the blade in the palm of her hand with a quick motion sliced a gash across it. "Matty?" he said. He watched as she then placed her bloody palm directly on his wound. Her action seemed to rejuvenate him slightly. Matty began to chant under her breath.

"Remove your hand from him."

Jack looked over to see Delia, Morgana's assistant standing close by. Even more troubling, he thought, was that she now had possession of the Black Witch's dagger.

"Remove your hand, I said," Delia commanded.

"I can't," Matty shot back, looking at the woman while she continued her connection to Jack, "he'll die."

"Remove your hand," she demanded as she held the dagger out toward Matty, "or I'll kill you along with him."

"No," Matty shot back, tears in her eyes.

Jack watched helplessly as Delia prepared to follow-through with her threat.

Unexpectedly a blinding beam of light shot across the room, pinning Delia in place. Jack was able to turn his head enough to follow the beam back to its source. There standing like a pillar of Solomon was Aisling, her left hand held out in front of her, projecting the beam.

"You're both traitors," Delia screamed, still unable to move.

Jack tried to sit up but was held down by Matty, "Lie still Jack," she whispered softly, "this will be over quickly, one way or another."

Jack's eyes turned back to Delia, who was still pinned by the light. Struggling, the woman managed to hold the dagger out in front of her and began what sounded to Jack like a sing-song nursery rhyme.

"Stop her!" Matty screamed toward Aisling, "Don't let her finish."

Jack turned his attention to Aisling in time to see her lift her right hand and wave it across the beam from left to right. He heard Delia's neck snap more than he saw it. The woman and the Athame Dagger fell to the ground.

Aisling made her way to Jack's side. He looked from one woman to the other. "Shhhit," he slurred.

"What, Jack?" The two women asked in unison.

Jack sucked in a deep breath, "four dead bodies," he wheezed, "I'll be writing this report until I'm fucking retired."

# Chapter Twenty-Seven

Jack was semiconscious when, strapped to a stretcher, the EMTs rolled him out of the front door of the plantation. He noticed the two medevac helicopters sitting some 30 yards apart. *Was one of the women still alive*, he wondered? *If so, which one?* He quickly reached the conclusion that he really didn't care. He then heard the second gurney coming up on his left side. He waited to see who it would be. A smile beamed across his face when he saw that the stretcher was occupied by Matthew Willow. The young man turned to face him, smiled weakly, and nodded his gratitude.

Matthew Willow was loaded into the first chopper as the blades began to whip up to speed. *Well*, Jack thought, *money does have its privileges.* One of the EMTs covered Jack's eyes as the first helicopter left the ground. When he could see again, he looked to his right, noticing that Matty and Aisling were quietly chatting. He was surprised to see the two women closed the distance between them and hug for several seconds.

Jack couldn't trust his senses as he was still locked in the grip of the poison. He had never seen Matty hug anyone and chalked it up to part of his delusion. The gurney began to move again, and while he was being loaded into the helicopter, both women smiled and waved. Also, Aisling threw him a kiss as they closed the helicopter door.

The poison had a tight grip on him. The hallucinations came and went, or at least that's how he perceived it. None of his senses seemed to be reliable. The eyes and the ears seemed to be most susceptible to the intruder. Distorted vision, random flashes of light, and his entire color spectrum were faulty. His hearing was no better as sounds would become earsplitting, and then seconds later, he wasn't sure that he had not gone deaf. The voices of the helicopter crew were either muffled or grossly misleading.

It seemed that different parts of his body were short-circuiting randomly. He had just finished a short period of the sweats when suddenly he began to shiver uncontrollably. Unexpectedly air was everywhere around him except in his lungs. His mouth slacked open, strings of saliva rolling down his chin as he fought for the smallest breath.

"Weee reer looosing himmm," someone shouted in his ear over the sound of the helicopter's jet engine.

"Increase fluids," Jack heard clear as a bell.

His eyes rolled loosely in their sockets, unable to focus on anything for more than a second.

"His blood pressure is still dropping," someone said in a squeaky little voice that sounded like a cartoon character from a kid's show.

"Push... Epinephrine..."

Jack's eyes popped open. Suddenly he was lying on the hard, cold metal deck of a Huey helicopter, the deck plates were vibrating so hard that his vision was jumpy. The sound of the blades was deafening.

The soldier hovering over him was covered in blood.

"Hang in there, Lieutenant," the soldier shouted, "We're almost home."

Jack watched as the young man looked at the person across from him. Jack gasped, as the soldier reluctantly shook his head.

"Clear!" The nurse shouted.

Jack focused on the woman hovering over him, holding the paddles.

"What have we got?" she asked impatiently.

"Nothing!"

"OK, clear!" the nurse said as the paddles came toward him.

The explosion of the mortar round knocked Jack head over heels into the foxhole.

"Lieutenant!"

"Yes, sir," Jack answered.

"Charlie has set up a couple of mortars on our left flank." The voice said with authority. "I want you to get your men and take them out!"

"Yes, sir," Jack said as he crawled out of the foxhole. He had taken but a half dozen steps when another mortar round landed close, throwing him into the air.

"Detective!" Jack heard over the roar of the helicopter engine. Jack opened his eyes to see the nurse staring down at him.

"There you are," the nurse smiled at him, "We lost you there for a moment. Glad to see you back with us."

Jack could only nod before his eyes became too heavy to keep open.

"Jack?"

His eyes fluttered, not wanting to open.

"Jack,"

He heard it a second time. With an over-exaggerated motion, he was able to force his eyes open. "Cynthia?" he asked, weakly, confused as ever.

"Hi Jack," Doctor Meeker said as she walked alongside the gurney, "stay with me."

"Am I dead?" he asked in earnest.

"No, Jack," she said, laughing out loud, "You're not one of my patients yet. We're in the main hospital. "We're going to get you better. Do you understand me?"

"Better," he repeated.

"That's right, Jack," she smiled, continuing to hold onto the gurney as it traveled down the hallway. "This is Doctor Remi," motioning to the man on the other side of the gurney, "he's one of the best toxicologists in the South."

Jack was able to move his head slightly to look at the man. He then turned back to Doctor Meeker. "Thank God," he said slowly, "are we still in the South?"

"Yes," she giggled nervously, "you're at Charity Hospital. Remember, Charity?"

Jack managed a weak nod.

"Matty phoned in," Meeker explained, "she says they believe the poison is a derivative of a fungus known as Ergot. Doctor Remi can definitely help."

Jack's eyes floated over to Doctor Remi. "We're going to fix you up, Jack," The man assured him.

Jack smiled and mouthed the words, thank you, before slipping into the abyss once more.

****

Jack slowly opened his eyes and blinked. It took him several seconds to clear his vision enough to see Petersen sitting next to him in a gray metal chair.

"Hey, Jack," Petersen said softly, "How ya feeling?"

Jack wet his lips, "Where am I?"

"Charity Hospital," Petersen stated while placing a drinking straw in Jack's mouth, "take a little of this."

Jack sucked on the tube, grateful for the cool, cleansing water. "What day is it?"

"Wednesday," Petersen confirmed.

"How long have I been here?"

"Eight days Jack," Petersen said, "it was touch and go for quite a while. That Dr. Meeker was very present, though. I don't think she left your side for more than a pee break."

"Where's Matty?"

"She left about an hour ago. Captain Steele kicked her out of here...told her to go home get some rest."

Jack nodded his understanding before closing his eyes.

After what seemed only to be a few seconds, Jack opened his eyes again. He stared at the small menagerie of Origami animals occupying the table next to his bed. He glanced to the left to see Matty dozing in the chair. He cleared his throat, "You want to switch places?" He asked.

Matty instantly sat up in the chair, "Jack... you, okay?"

"Water,"

She poured a fresh glass of water, inserted a straw, and held it up to his lips. "Easy, not too much."

"Where's Petersen?"

"He hasn't been back since Wednesday."

Confused, Jack's eyes wandered restlessly around the room. "What day is it?"

"Friday morning," she confirmed as she placed the water glass back on the table.

Pieces of the event at the plantation house flashed through Jack's mind. "You, okay?"

Matty nodded, "Yeah, partner. I'm good."

"Matthew?"

"Doing good. He's back home already."

"When am I getting out of here?"

Matty shook her head, "Don't know," she said, "not for a while.

Jack's eyebrow shot up, "Why not?"

As casually as she could manage, she brushed his hair out of his eyes. "Jack, you're still eating your meals through a tube. They're still running blood panels on you every day. Whatever that bitch Morgana stuck you with, it was some crazy shit.

Jack nodded in agreement. Suddenly his breath caught in his throat as he felt his heart begin to pound, "She's dead," he asked, "right?"

"Morgana, very dead," she assured him.

"You shot Agent Salton?" It was more of a question than a statement.

She regarded Jack quizzically for a moment. "No, Jack," she said, struggling with the uncertainty of the words. "Agent Salton was shot three times by Morgana's assistant, Delia. She had just fired the third shot when I was able to grab her and disarm her."

"She's alive… Delia, I mean?"

Matty locked eyes with him. "No, Jack, I was forced to kill her. I broke the woman's neck."

Jack nodded his head, accepting her words although he wasn't sure he understood. Suddenly another flash of insight hit him. He gently picked up Matty's hand, turned it inside up, and examined her palm. He blinked several times when he didn't see the knife wound; he was sure that Matty had self-inflicted one upon herself. He was going to ask about Aisling but thought better of it.

Matty picked up the glass of water and gave Jack another sip, "You just lie back and rest," she said when he had finished with the drink, "one of us will be checking up on you as much as possible."

"Okay," he said, thinking Matty's suggestion was a good one. As his eyelids began to close, Matty leaned forward and kissed him on the forehead.

# Epilogue

Jack winced, sucking air in through his teeth as he exited the car. Rubbing his left shoulder, he looked around Aisling's front yard, waiting for the geese to show up. Within seconds Abigail came around the corner of the house. She came within a few feet of Jack and as before curtsied.

"Hello, Abigail," Jack said, placing his hand over his stomach and bowing slightly at the waist, "you don't know how glad I am to see you." It was just enough to cause pain in his side, but it seemed to satisfy the bird. She quickly turned and headed back around the side of the house. When Jack did not follow her, she turned to face him, honked several times, and then started again.

"Ah," Jack said quickly, understanding, "you want me to follow."

Jack made his way around the house and quickly spotted Aisling sitting in the gazebo. He waved to her when she looked up.

Aisling quickly approached several tears rolling down her cheek. Jack gathered her into his arms and held her snugly. Gently the two rocked back and forth.

"It's good to see you," Jack whispered into her hair.

She backed up just enough to allow her lips to meet his. Her kiss was slow and thoughtful. "I've missed you, Jack," she confessed.

She slipped her hand around his waist and guided him toward the gazebo. She led him to a chair, "Sit here, Jack," she said softly, "what would you like to drink?"

Jack eased into the chair, trying to make it look easy. "Some water would be fine?"

Her eyebrow rose a fraction, "Water? You?"

"Yes," he confessed as he took the glass from her, "Doctor's orders."

Aisling took the chair next to his, "How's the recovery going?"

"Not bad," he said, hoping the truth didn't show on his face, "I'm feeling better every day."

"Good," she smiled, not pushing the issue, "I noticed you're not carrying your gun today?"

"No," he confirmed, holding open his new jacket, "I'm on medical leave."

"I should say so," she winked, "I've prepared a sort of a buffet for lunch. There's sliced ham or turkey, potato salad plus three other types of salads, baked beans, and two different types of homemade bread. We'll discuss the dessert after you finish your meal."

"I know what you're trying to do," Jack said, wearing a wily smile. "You're trying to get me well."

"Doctor's orders," Aisling said as she stood, leaned over, and kissed Jack on the forehead, "I'll bring the trays out here, and we can enjoy this beautiful day while we eat. You need anything?"

"Yeah," Jack said, "how about a new body?"

"Let's just fix up the one you've got," Aisling answered as she moved back toward the house, "I kinda like this one."

They spent the rest of the afternoon and into the early evening casually dining between snippets of conversation. Jack didn't know if they had completely avoided talking about the events at Kerr Plantation on purpose or if they just had more pleasant things to talk about.

"Oh, Jack," Aisling said, "I understand you missed your graduation. I'm so sorry."

"Nothing lost," Jack assured her as he nursed the glass of iced tea in his hand, "I'll make it up when I get my Ph.D."

The sun had completely disappeared behind the trees, only to be replaced by the most stunning full moon.

"I don't think I've seen a moon like that," Jack commented, pointing up to the large silvery desk, "since, as a kid, my dad would take me camping."

"It is beautiful," Aisling agreed as she stood taking Jack's glass from him and set it on the table. She offered Jack both of her hands, "Would you like to take a walk around the lake?"

Unconsciously Jack's brow furrowed. He wasn't sure he could make it all the way around the lake. "Alright," he beamed, "let's give it a try. Do you have a flashlight?"

"We won't need one," Aisling assured him as she led him toward the path, "you'll see."

Slowly, they started down the path with all three geese in tow.

"Reste ici," Aisling ordered. The three geese stopped but weren't happy about being ordered to stay. The three honked loudly as they returned to the house.

"I wish I could do that with some of the people at work," Jack said.

"Forget about work," Aisling said as she intertwined her arm with Jack's. "Let's just enjoy the evening."

Somehow Jack had forgotten how tranquil the lake area was. It was as if he was entering into a heightened awareness of the subtle world around him. It was as if the area had an energy all its own.

Jack's mouth took on an unpleasant twist as he looked off to the horizon. In the past weeks, he had small fragments of hallucinations that came and went just as quickly, so naturally, he questioned many of the things that he now saw.

"Aisling," he said softly, trying to maintain his composure, "is it just me, or is that the sun rising in the north?"

Aisling stopped alongside him and looked to where Jack was pointing. The horizon did have the distinctive hues of red and orange, much like a sunrise.

"That's not the sunrise," she said peacefully, "it is a fire at the Kerr Plantation."

"A fire," Jack almost screamed, having no idea how serious his voice sounded, "we should go. Offer some assistance."

Aisling gently held him in place, "no assistance is needed, Jack," she said, her voice trying to lull him into a relaxed mood, "it is the burial pyre for Morgana Kerr."

"Burial fire," he quipped, "it looks like the whole plantation is burning down."

"You are correct," she informed him, "in Morgana's last will and testament she requested that she be cremated inside the home. Her ashes were then to be placed in the family crypt."

"She turned the whole manor into a funeral pyre?"

"Yes," Aisling confirmed, "that was her final wish."

Jack's eyebrow shot up in a questioning manner, "How do you know about this? Is it some kind of a 'witch' thing?"

Aisling chuckled softly and lightly kissed Jack on the cheek, "No darling," she said faintly, "I read about it in the local newspaper. Tonight is a full moon, the Hunters Moon it's called. Its apex will happen shortly."

"So," Jack said knowingly, "it's the full moon. She's hoping for a new beginning."

"Yes," Aisling answered, "I hope she finds it."

Jack's eyes were hooded like those of a hawk, "She's not going to try and come back from the dead, is she?"

"How many times do I have to tell you," Aisling said firmly, "I've never heard of anyone coming back from the dead. In death, their life force is given back to the universe. Dead is dead."

"Alright," Jack said nervously, "I'll defer to your knowledge on this one."

They continued on the path around the lake, the huge moon lighting the path. Jack finally decided that there were things he needed to discuss with her.

"Aisling," he said as they continued to walk, "I've been doing a lot of thinking over the last few weeks."

"And," she prompted.

"I've spoken to Captain Steel and the Police Commissioner," he said, "and I won't be going back to my old job."

"I can't say I'm sorry to hear it."

"I've talked them into giving me a new position."

"They must think a lot of you, Jack, to do something like that," she remarked.

"Well, that and the fact that I've had the support of the State Attorney General and the Governor," he confirmed.

"How did you swing that?"

"I did have a little help from Derek Willow," Jack confessed, "I think the man felt that he owed me some type of gratitude for saving his son."

"So, what are you going to do now?"

"I'll be working with the detectives in the capacity of an advisor on their more serious cases," he informed her.

"Serious meaning murders?"

"Yes, the bulk of my time will be spent working on my Ph.D. in Criminal Psychology. I will use that degree and my experiences on the force to help the other Detectives."

"Sounds like a win-win to me." She answered.

"I was hoping that it would be a win-win-win."

"And the third win would be?"

"Well, the big win," he said, smiling affectionately at her, "would be if you and I could spend more time developing our relationship."

Aisling's face became serious, "Jack, I won't leave here," she said, "I know you don't understand, but I can't leave here."

"I would never ask you to do that," he assured her, "I know how important this place is to you." Suddenly, Jack grabbed his right side, groaning in pain.

"What is it, Jack?"

He straightened up as best he could. "I just got a stitch in my side."

Aisling eyed him, warily, "You don't get a stitch in your side from walking, Jack."

"No?" he asked innocently.

"No," she confirmed, "and I'm willing to bet that the pain is directly over the area where you were poisoned the night you came to my house."

"Kind of," he answered.

"And the shoulder," she asked, "still experiencing intermittent pain there?"

"I wouldn't say intermittent."

"What would you say then?" she asked.

Jack stopped and turned to face her, "I'd say more excruciating," he confessed, "I'm to the point where I'm afraid it may never permanently go away."

Aisling didn't answer but studied him intently.

"Any suggestions," he asked.

"There might be one cure that I know of," she answered.

"Anything," Jack said, rubbing his right side.

Aisling studied his face, finally locking eyes with him, "a sponge bath," she offered.

"What?" Jack asked, unsure of her meaning.

"A sponge bath," she repeated, "right here and now."

"I don't know about you," Jack said, "but I didn't bring my sponge with me."

Aisling put her arms around his neck. Her kiss sent the pit of Jack's stomach into a wild churning eddy. At last, hesitantly, they parted a few inches.

"I didn't bring a sponge either," she said as she backed away from him. Quite neatly, Aisling dropped her dress from both shoulders allowing the garment to fall to the ground. She now stood naked before him. "I guess this will have to do," she said, slowly backing into the water.

Her naked body had a sensuous luster that seemed to glow in the moonlight. Jack was amazed that her golden hair looked to have been spun by Rumpelstiltskin himself. He continued to watch as Aisling went deeper into the water.

Aisling compellingly motioned for him to enter the water with her. Jack took off his clothes and timidly stepped into the lake. He was surprised that, being October, the lake water was amazingly warm and soothing. He continued to walk toward her. Aisling slowly disappeared under the surface as he approached. When he had reached the spot where he had last seen her, he looked around. The moonlight reflected off the surface of the lake as if it were hitting a thousand shards of mirror. It made it difficult for Jack to see where she might be.

The water in front of him suddenly glowed as if someone had turned on a powerful underwater light. From the center of the beam Aisling appeared and reached out for him. Her lips found their way instinctively to his, her kiss leaving him weak and confused.

"Aisling, I…" he whispered, the taste of her lips still on his.

She placed a single finger on his lips, "Jack, darling," she mouthed, "you are now at the center of my universe. Here, I am one with all that is around me. Understand now why I cannot leave this place."

Jack could feel the warmth emanating from her naked body, engulfing him in a healing glow. The experience seemed to wrap him in a cocoon of pure restorative energy, freeing him from the pain of the poisons.

"Jack, mon amour," she continued, "I freely offer myself to you. To hold you, to love you, and to heal you."

Jack lovingly gathered her against his warm pulsing body. He looked upward toward the sky. "A full moon and a new beginning?"

Instinctively, her body arched toward him, offering her lips to his once more before, together, passion radiating from the very core of their being, they sank beneath the surface.

## END

# Member of a Book Club?

Contact the author at Edkinsbooks.com to find out how you can have the Author perform a reading at your next book club meeting.